ON THE BARE

Aaron sits on the edge of the bed and beckons me to his right side. And I realise what he has in mind. A hot flush covers my entire body and I clasp my hands beseechingly, like a silent movie heroine.

He lowers his voice. 'Come here, Delaney. Over my knee.'

My own knees threaten to buckle and I do as he says, turning my back to the open door and the two guards outside it, watching.

Aaron guides me over his lap and I stare ahead at the peeling paint on the wall at the back of the cell. A tiny ancient sink juts from the wall and the cell is so cramped I could reach out and touch it if I wanted.

I flinch when I feel his hand on my bottom. Just a pat, but it makes me jump. He gives each cheek a firm squeeze and I feel his hand lift away. I've never been spanked before in my life and I have no idea what to expect. I hold my breath.

With a resounding slap he brings his palm down on my right cheek. I arch my back with a yelp. He smacks my left cheek almost immediately and I writhe on his lap, clutching the edge of the bed. His hand imparts a wicked sting, covering each cheek completely.

ON THE BARE

Fiona Locke

This book is a work of fiction.
Always make sure you practise safe, sane and consensual sex.

Published by Nexus Enthusiast 2009

2 4 6 8 10 9 7 5 3 1

First published in Great Britain in 2009 by
Nexus Enthusiast
Virgin Books
Random House, 20 Vauxhall Bridge Road
London SW1V 2SA

www.virginbooks.com
www.rbooks.co.uk

Addresses for companies within The Random House Group Limited can be found at:
www.randomhouse.co.uk/offices.htm

The Random House Group Limited Reg. No. 954009

Distributed in the USA by Macmillan, 175 Fifth Avenue, New York, NY 10010, USA

A CIP catalogue record for this book is available from the British Library

ISBN 9780352345158

The Random House Group Limited supports The Forest Stewardship Council [FSC], the
leading international forest certification organisation. All our titles that are printed on
Greenpeace-approved FSC-certified paper carry the FSC logo.
Our paper procurement policy can be found at www.rbooks.co.uk/environment

Typeset by TW Typesetting, Plymouth, Devon
Printed in the UK by CPI Bookmarque, Croydon, CR0 4TD

nexus Symbols key

 Corporal Punishment

 Female Domination

 Institution

 Medical

 Period Setting

 Restraint/Bondage

 Rubber/Leather

 Spanking

 Transvestism

 Underwear

 Uniforms

For Chris

*Constant reader,
long-time friend*

CONTENTS

The Woodshed

'If you do that again, Angie . . .' Peter's threat hung in the air like a storm about to break.

'You'll what?' I was foolish enough to blurt out.

I saw his face darken and I looked down at my school shoes, instantly regretting my cheek.

'I'll put you over my knee and give your bare bottom a sound smacking,' he announced loudly.

I cringed at his words, turning scarlet and peering out from under my hair, wondering how many people were listening. The garden centre was bustling with activity and it was inconceivable that no one had heard. The Japanese man in the grey business suit must have. He'd watched me stamp through the puddle, looking startled by my behaviour. Yes, I was rather old to be acting so childishly, but in my school uniform I could easily pass for a sixth-former.

'Well, young lady?'

'I'm sorry, sir,' I babbled in a hasty placating whisper. 'I'll be good.'

Peter was completely unembarrassable and he had no qualms about making good on his threats, no matter where we were or how many people were around.

'See that you are,' he said. 'This is your final warning.'

I heaved a giant sigh of relief. It amazed me how often I felt the need to test him. Especially as I so often regretted it. But it was hard not to be a little bratty when he insisted on dragging me out in public dressed like a schoolgirl. What schoolgirl *wouldn't* be restless and fidgety at a garden centre?

1

We were there on such an unpleasant errand: Peter wanted a birch tree of his own so that we didn't have to go into the woods to cut switches whenever he needed a rod. I had tried unsuccessfully to convince him that it would be years and years before the trees were big enough for proper switches.

'Young trees are the best,' Peter had said coolly, 'but while they grow we'll continue to harvest the ones in the woods.'

My response to that was a sullen look and the first stamp of my feet in the puddles from last night's torrential rain.

We made our way towards the back of the enclosure where juvenile trees stood in neat rows, like orphans waiting to be adopted. As we reached the mini-orchard I suddenly noticed the Japanese businessman behind us. He stopped abruptly when I turned and he pretended to be engrossed in the care label of a rhododendron. What he was really doing was ogling me.

I grinned and tugged Peter's sleeve. 'Hey!' I whispered. 'That guy's stalking me!'

'Well, you do look rather fetching,' he said, giving my bottom a lecherous pinch that made me yelp. A few heads turned and I blushed, ducking into the rows of trees.

'Ah yes, here we are,' he said. '*Betula pendula*. Silver birch.'

I rolled my eyes, still sulking over the idea of home-grown disciplinary implements. Peter inspected each tree carefully, as if trying to decide which would yield the most effective switches.

I quickly grew bored and wandered away from the plants and the people onto the giant patio scattered with lawn furniture and garden gnomes. Beyond that were the sheds and children's playhouses, and with a childish sense of fun I skipped over to have a look. I'd always wanted a playhouse as a little girl – a place to hide and to hold secret meetings with my pets. Some of the tiny houses were amazingly elaborate and I felt a little stab of envy for all the fun I'd missed out on.

2

I crept inside one small wooden structure and peered out through the window. My stalker was loitering conspicuously by the sundials. He stood in profile to me, but I could see him casting sidelong glances my way.

Bloody perv, I thought.

It was then that I had my great idea. As I emerged from the playhouse he feigned interest in the nearest birdbath. Perfect. The entire area was wet and muddy and there was no one else around. I sidled past him nonchalantly, waiting for him to turn and follow my arse with his eyes. When he did I jumped as high as I could and came down with a terrific splash in the muddy water, soaking both of us.

I saw the whole thing in glorious slow motion. My legs tucked under me in midair, the flash of my white cotton panties, his eyes widening at the sight. Then a low protracted 'Noooooo!' from him, hands outstretched, as my shoes hit the puddle. Droplets shimmering in a *Matrix*-like freeze-frame all around us. Brilliant.

Time returned to normal and he stepped back, looking down at his suit in dismay. My white school socks – and my legs – were covered in muck and I laughed helplessly as my stalker plucked feebly at the little clumps of mud sticking to his trousers.

My laughter died in my throat as Peter's hand clapped down on my shoulder.

'Right,' he said. 'You were warned, young lady.'

Suddenly thrust back into the here and now, I chewed my lower lip and looked miserably down at my own muddy lower half.

'But – but –' I stammered.

'No buts, young lady. Now you will apologise to this gentleman for your childish behaviour. And then I'm going to take you into that woodshed over there and give you the spanking you deserve for being such a brat.'

My eyes widened in horror. They widened even more at the look of smug satisfaction on the 'gentleman's' face.

'But he was following me!' I wailed.

'That's as may be. But I'm certainly going to ask him to

3

witness your punishment.' Peter addressed him: 'If you wouldn't mind?'

'Not at all,' he said in perfect cultured English. 'It would be a pleasure.'

I cast a wretched, pleading look at Peter, though I knew it would do no good. He had spanked me once on a crowded Underground platform, oblivious to the astonishment of the waiting passengers; a private woodshed wasn't going to faze him. At least he hadn't threatened to birch me in the middle of the garden centre.

Peter took me by the hand and I dug my heels in, turning my sulky face up to his in a last desperate bid for mercy.

'Pouting won't get you anywhere but deeper in trouble, young lady. Do you want me to take my belt off?'

I gasped and shook my head frantically, my ears burning. The suit nodded approvingly. He probably thought Peter was my father.

'Are you going to apologise?' Peter asked.

I hung my head and mumbled, 'I'm sorry.'

Peter tutted. 'Did that sound sincere?' he asked his new friend.

'No, not very.'

'All right, I'm *very* sorry!'

My words fell into a heavy silence and I saw Peter shake his head. 'I'm afraid the apology may have to wait until she has something to be sorry *about*.'

He tilted my chin up so I had to face him. 'And you've only made it worse for yourself with your insolence.'

I had too much pride to beg, especially when punishment was inevitable. I couldn't take back what I had done and I suffered the same bout of second-guessing that I always did in such circumstances. If I could only hit the 'back' button and start over . . .

'Right,' Peter said. 'In you go. Let's get this over with.'

The woodshed smelled of fresh-cut pine. Though it was only about eight feet square, it felt like a cavern to me. There was ample room for the three of us.

'Stand here, Angie. Bend forward and put your hands on the wall.'

4

I knew that if I refused he could make it worse. Burning with shame, I obeyed. At least the position meant that I didn't have to look at our guest. He would surely want the view from behind.

I reached forward and pressed my sweaty palms against the rough-sawn wood, lowering my head.

'Bottom out,' Peter said. 'Arch your back.'

I did it without protest, presenting myself. I whimpered a little as Peter raised my navy-blue pleated skirt and tucked it into the waistband. Next I felt him smoothing the tail of my shirt up over my lower back. Now the businessman could have a proper look at the schoolgirl bottom he'd been ogling. I squeezed my eyes shut, mortified by the exposure.

'You were a very naughty girl, weren't you?' Peter asked.

I gave a little moan, resisting the urge to beg him just to get it over with. 'Yes, sir.'

'And what happens to naughty little girls?'

'They get punished.'

'How, Angie?'

'They get spanked.'

'Mm-hmm. And do they get spanked over their panties?'

I blushed to the roots of my hair, but I knew what I had to say. 'No, sir. On the bare.'

'On the bare,' Peter echoed, and I squirmed in embarrassed misery as he slowly peeled down my white cotton school knickers.

'A good sound smacking,' he said, 'to teach you a lesson.'

I held my breath and waited for the first smack. It wasn't gentle. It was terrifyingly loud in the confined space and I squealed with pain. I could feel the outline of his fingers burning across my left cheek, glowing as the blood rushed to the surface. I peered back over my shoulder to see the Japanese man nodding appreciatively.

Peter brought his hand down just as hard on my right cheek, eliciting a shriek from me. I danced in place, my hands hovering in the air behind me. I desperately wanted to clutch my bottom, to rub away the sting, but I didn't dare move too far out of position lest I make things worse. Peter was a master at demonstrating that, even at rock bottom, there was still room to fall.

'Angie . . .'

It was all the warning I needed. I resumed my position, sucking in my breath as I waited for him to start again.

Peter placed one hand in the small of my back and began to spank me in earnest. No matter how often he did it, it never ceased to embarrass me and it never ceased to hurt. And having an audience made it worse. I yelped and cried out with each swat, pressing my hands into the wall and trying to tune out the probing eyes. The familiar cadence was hard to take, giving me no time to register anything but the pain and the desire to make it stop. In moments like this I would do anything, promise anything, agree to anything.

'Please – no, stop! I'm sorry – honest! Oww! Please! I'll never – ouch! – I'll never do it again, I promise! Please . . .'

But Peter was never swayed by my pleas or protests.

He didn't neglect my thighs, either, and those well-aimed smacks made me beg even more frantically. I leaped and tried to kick, but my knickers were tangled around my ankles, preventing me raising my legs.

Finally, he stopped and I sagged against the wall, exhausted. But my relief was short-lived.

'That's for your childish behaviour,' Peter said. 'We still have to deal with your insolence.'

'But I'm sorry!' I wailed, truly and genuinely remorseful. My bottom was raw and aching with heat.

'You're always sorry, Angie. Just never sorry enough. At least not until you've been taught a firm lesson.'

My face burned as hotly as my bottom. The boards creaked beneath his feet as he moved around behind me, inspecting his work. He pinched the soft flesh of my right cheek and I hissed.

'Hmm. Yes, that does look a little tender. But I think a few cuts of a switch will make a lasting impression. As we're here to buy a birch tree I think it only fair to test their suitability.'

'Quite right,' our guest said with solemn approval.

I gasped in horror.

'I wonder if you'd mind keeping an eye on her while I step outside?' Peter said politely. 'A little cornertime is always good when a girl's due a well-deserved thrashing.'

Tears sprang to my eyes as I imagined the businessman's gleeful expression. The silence stretched to fill the woodshed and I waited for the hated command.

'In the corner,' Peter said at last. 'Hands on your head.'

I shuffled two feet to my left, the flimsy cotton panties like manacles around my ankles. My bottom was still on display, framed by my raised skirt. I laced my fingers on top of my head and touched my elbows to the walls either side of me. I was only too aware how the position arched my back, pushing my bottom up like an offering. Peter approached me and took his time arranging my school shirt carefully above my waist, exposing me fully and leaving nothing to the imagination.

'Do feel free to smack her if she misbehaves while I'm gone.'

There was a rough scrape as Peter opened the door and a thin bar of daylight rushed to embrace my feet. 'I shan't be long.'

'Take your time,' said my new keeper. 'I will watch her closely.'

The door closed, stealing my little beam of light and plunging me into confinement again. My skin prickled with hyper-awareness and my breathing grew shallow as I strained to hear the slightest shift of his weight on the floor. I froze in place, determined to deny him the slightest excuse to take Peter at his word. I expected him to edge closer, to talk to me, perhaps even take liberties. But he stayed where he was, his silence more unnerving than any amount of triumphant gloating would have been. I felt his eyes probing and I pressed my legs together in a futile attempt to hide myself from his gaze.

I squirmed as I imagined Peter outside, unhurriedly examining each little birch sapling, knowing that every minute was an eternity for me. It was made so much worse by the shame of being left here with the man I'd wronged. Beads of perspiration welled on my forehead and a droplet trickled down my face as I stood there in disgrace. The passage of time was excruciating, but the dread of knowing what would happen when Peter returned was even worse.

Back home I had the ticking grandfather clock to mark the crawling minutes while I waited for punishment. Here I couldn't make out even the hint of a wristwatch. My arms were beginning to ache from the position. I shifted nervously and my guardian cleared his throat.

'Keep still, little girl,' he said, each word a sharp little barb in my wounded pride.

As if mirroring my desolation, spatters of rain began to fall on my little wooden prison. Before long it was a proper downpour and I pictured the churchgoers scrambling in out of the rain. It brought Peter back as well, but that was little comfort. The rain only ensured that we would have total privacy.

'Was she good?' Peter asked.

After a cruel pause my jailer announced, 'A little restive, but she stayed where you put her.'

'Ah, very good.'

I didn't know who that comment was directed at, but I didn't care. I focused all my attention on the rain pounding down on the roof of the shed, praying it would last, praying it would stop. I had no idea which was the lesser of evils. There was no prospect that Peter would spare me if someone were to barge in. But the longer the three of us were trapped out here, the longer my sentence would be.

At last he said, 'You can come out now, Angie.'

I turned to face him, wincing at the pain in my shoulders as I lowered my arms. No use playing it up; it wouldn't earn me any sympathy.

Peter held up two switches – long and supple and stripped of their leaves. 'From two different saplings,' he explained. 'Perhaps one will be more effective than the other.'

To my dismay, he handed one of the switches to his new friend, who immediately swished it through the air and nodded appreciatively. I looked at the floor.

8

With a sigh Peter lifted my chin between his thumb and forefinger, forcing me to meet his eyes. 'Now. You know you were a naughty girl,' he said softly, 'and you know you deserved to be punished.'

I covered my face and Peter gently peeled my hands away.

'I am only going to give you six. And then this gentleman is going to give you six. You will count them and say "thank you, sir" after each one. When we have finished you will apologise to him for your childish antics. If we believe you're sincere, the matter will be forgiven. Now let's get this over with. Bend over and touch your toes for me.'

His tone was patronising but loving and it was always my undoing. It made me feel like a child, safe and guided. I could seek refuge in a place where all my misdeeds could be corrected with corporal punishment, the slate wiped clean. Nothing in my adult life was ever as certain and there was a strange comfort in the inevitability of his discipline.

I obeyed and Peter took up a position to my left, laying the switch against my bottom. He gave me one light tap before drawing back. I braced myself, pressing my fingertips against my shoes as he whipped the switch down sharply. A line of fire blazed across both cheeks, tearing an agonised cry from my throat.

My hands flew behind me to clutch my bottom and I panted for breath, struggling to regain my composure. Eventually the sting began to dissipate and I got control of myself.

'One. Thank you, sir.'

The second stroke fell as soon as I was back in position, wrenching the words from me. 'Two – oww! Thank you, sir.'

Number three was the hardest yet and I bit back a little scream, my knees wobbling unsteadily and my hands wavering for balance. But I got hold of myself and counted.

'Three. Thank you, sir.'

He didn't torture me by making me wait long between strokes and I did my best to make him proud of me. I locked my legs and breathed deeply as the pain of each burning stripe pulsed like fire throughout my skin.

'Four,' I gasped. 'Th-thank you, sir.'

Only two more, only two more, I chanted inside my head. Well, only two more from Peter. I still had another six to come from our guest.

The fifth stroke sliced into my bottom and I peered between my legs at the businessman as I counted. His face was impassive, betraying no sadistic delight in my suffering.

'Five. Thank you, sir.'

I closed my eyes and absorbed the sixth stroke with only a slight shudder.

'Six,' I said after a few moments. 'Thank you, sir.'

'Good girl,' Peter said kindly. 'Now show me how brave you can be for the last six.'

The men traded places without a word and I waited in the hollow silence, submissively accepting my fate. The businessman didn't address the target the way Peter had; he merely brought the switch down, striping both cheeks with flawless aim. Had he done this before?

I inhaled sharply as my bottom came alive with fire again. It was excruciating. But I accepted it, embraced it.

I tensed and relaxed, then counted. 'One. Thank you, sir.'

Again the switch found its mark with admirable precision. I released the breath I'd been holding and counted, letting the pain wash over me, in and around me. I had found the resonance of the pain and it flowed through me like pure energy, transporting me to a place of serenity. I felt the next stroke land and I counted it, but I was somewhere high above the pain now, floating in a zone where time had slowed down.

I felt as if I had stepped outside myself and I watched in blissful fascination as some other girl – not me – was whipped. She stood obediently touching her toes, her school skirt raised and her knickers around her knees, her white knee socks spattered with mud. The Japanese man sliced the length of birch into her bared bottom and she gasped with impossible pain. Or was it impossible pleasure? I couldn't tell.

In a dreamy voice she counted – four, five . . .

'Six. Thank you, sir.'

'*Very* good, Angie,' Peter said, his voice full of pride. 'You may get up now.'

I drifted slowly back to reality, still dazed as I rose unsteadily from my position. Peter embraced me fiercely and I blinked away tears as my arms limply tried to return the hug.

Then he held me at arm's length and his face grew serious again. 'Are you ready to apologise now?'

I nodded meekly.

Turning to the businessman, I bowed my head in a gesture of true humility, tears pricking my eyes. 'I'm very sorry, sir,' I said softly. 'I hope you feel I've paid for my behaviour.'

He couldn't suppress a smile as he wrapped his arms around me and told me I was forgiven.

'I think the rain has stopped,' Peter said brightly, 'so we should return to our selection. Tell me, Angie – which one of these was more effective?'

I blushed, gingerly pulling my knickers up over my scorched bottom. I smoothed my skirt down and gave him a pouty look.

'If I may repay your kindness,' said the businessman with a polite smile, 'take both the trees. With my compliments. Prune them regularly and I'm sure they'll flourish.'

At our surprised expressions he added, 'My supplier keeps me well stocked.'

11

The Good Old Days

'It's positively vile!'

Amelia wrinkled her nose in disgust. She lifted the pleated grey skirt with two fingers and dropped it onto the desk like a dead rat. 'I'm not wearing it.' She folded her arms across her chest, signalling an end to any further discussion.

The bookish woman behind the desk adjusted her glasses and gave a polite little cough. She lifted the phone and dialled a sequence of numbers while Amelia waited huffily.

'Mr Chandos? It's Miss North here. Sorry to trouble you, but I wonder if I could impose on you to come to my office? We have a . . .' She glanced up at Amelia, then back down at the desk. 'Situation. Yes, very good. Thank you.'

Miss North rang off and gestured expansively for Amelia to sit in one of the chairs opposite the desk. 'Mr Chandos is on his way. You may speak to him about your complaint.'

'Thank you,' Amelia said with excruciating politeness.

She sat down, feeling a minor triumph already at the extra attention. Yes, she'd signed a contract and yes, she'd agreed to sacrifice a little glamour for the sake of authenticity. But the uniform was a step too far. The housemates on *Big Brother* got to wear their own clothes; why couldn't the participants in this show wear their own school uniforms? Amelia was proud of the subtle alterations she'd made to hers, so that it set off her shapely

12

figure. But in the drab grey monstrosity Miss North had given her, she'd look like an evacuee from the Second World War.

Mr Chandos arrived and Amelia rose to greet him. He was younger than she'd been expecting – mid-forties, she guessed. She had imagined a crusty old buzzard of a headmaster, but the man in the crisp white shirt was darkly handsome.

'The young lady has a complaint about the uniform,' said Miss North in a patronising tone. 'She refuses to wear it.'

Amelia ignored her, giving Mr Chandos her sweetest smile. 'It's only that it's so unflattering for TV. I'm sure you understand.'

'Yes, I understand,' he said pleasantly. 'We're going to be recreating the school environment of the 1950s. Authentic uniforms are an essential part of the atmosphere.'

It was a tone he might have used to impart some dry historical fact – the date of a battle perhaps.

'Look, I realise what you're trying to do here and I'm being perfectly reasonable.'

'Miss Rutherford, it's quite straightforward.' His tone was sharper now. 'Either you wear the proper uniform of Queen Mary's College or you will not be a part of the show.'

Amelia's eyes flashed. She desperately wanted to be on TV, even on a silly reality show like *The Good Old Days*. The whole point was exposure and a shot at fame. But to imagine her friends seeing her in such a horrid uniform . . . no make-up . . . To say nothing of the film directors who might see the show . . .

'Oh, bother!' she said at last, her mouth set in a resentful pout. She snatched the hateful garments from the woman's desk and stalked off to find the dormitory.

Mr Chandos smiled knowingly.

The Good Old Days was the show everyone had been waiting for. A social experiment on the effectiveness of school discipline. Twenty pupils had agreed to spend six weeks in a recreated 1950s school, subject to 1950s discipline.

The theme had been explored before with modern students eating Spam fritters and languishing under the archaic 'chalk and talk' teaching regime. However, the authenticity had been severely compromised by the lack of corporal punishment – a famously prevalent feature of any such education in 'the good old days'. Critics had derided the concept of a post-war English school giving timeouts instead of canings for bad behaviour.

Mr Chandos intended to rectify that. His 1950s establishment would be authentic in every respect – especially the most vital one. And his guinea pigs knew exactly what they were getting into. They were all of legal age. They had signed consent forms and agreed to enter into the spirit of the thing. They would not be harmed or damaged – merely treated to the same punishment regime enjoyed by previous generations. They all seemed to think it was a small price to pay for being on TV.

Amelia stood glaring at her reflection. The shapeless grey blazer, the heavy woollen skirt, the itchy knee socks – all of it conspired to make her look fat. This was supposed to be her big break. Her big shot at fame. But the uniform!

The creature in the mirror looked like a nightmare version of herself. Her flaxen plaits were like wilted daffodils, and without make-up, the harsh fluorescent lights brought her every imperfection into sharp relief. The straw boater was an indignity, but the knickers were the ultimate humiliation. An atrocity in thick bottle-green cotton, they came up to her navel and pinched around the top of each thigh. She'd never even worn *shorts* that covered so much, let alone underwear. It was too awful!

She reached for her mobile phone before remembering that she'd handed it in along with all her other 'modern' items. For six weeks she would have access to nothing that wasn't available in the schools of the 1950s. She was already feeling the ache of withdrawal and it had only been twenty minutes.

14

'Hi! Cool uniforms, huh? I love the boater!'

Amelia stared glumly at the new arrival – a pale girl with mousy brown hair and glasses. The dreadful uniform suited her perfectly.

'I'm Lisa Jennings,' she chirped. 'You must be Amelia Rutherford. They said you were already up here. I'm so excited – are you? I mean, it'll be like going back in time!'

Amelia cringed as the girl prattled on.

'People say they had like, better teachers back then and that our parents got a better education than we're getting. I can't wait to see how different it all is.'

'I read the mission statement too,' Amelia snapped, still glowering at herself in the mirror.

Lisa positioned herself next to Amelia and gazed with childlike wonderment at their reflections. 'Hey, don't be sad,' she said. 'It's like an escape from the pressures of the modern world. No email, no Internet. Things were so much simpler back then.'

Did the girl always talk like that? Perhaps she'd been raised by motivational speakers – and not very good ones at that.

'I'll be fine,' Amelia said, deciding to put on a game face. 'Just wish I could text my boyfriend. I'll have to see if I can find out where they took our stuff and sneak in to get it.'

Lisa looked betrayed. 'But that's like, going against the whole spirit of the show. The idea is for us to experience life without all of that.'

Was she for real? 'Reality' TV wasn't about reality; it was about TV. No one would do it if there wasn't an audience. Keira Knightley might wear a corset in some period costume drama, but between takes she'd be drinking double lattes in her air-conditioned trailer with her iPod and all the comforts of the twenty-first century.

'The cameras are certainly authentic,' Amelia said, nodding towards the open doorway where a man stood filming them. She wiggled her fingers at the lens. 'Hi, Mum!'

Lisa ducked away shyly and headed off down the

corridor where Amelia could hear her infecting the new arrivals with her perkiness.

Things got off to a smooth enough start and the pupils quickly overcame their self-consciousness about the role play. After a couple of days of hamming it up and showing off to each other, they began to settle into the 1950s routine. They were roused at dawn each morning for breakfast, morning assembly, and then the most tedious lessons Amelia had ever endured. Lunch was barely edible. Games were a joke. And after a vile dinner they were expected to do prep for two hours before going to bed.

Amelia got on well enough with the other girls, most of whom weren't boarders at their own schools and were soon homesick. A couple of them were frightfully common and Amelia couldn't help but grimace at their regional accents, but she was still friendly towards them. The whole country was watching, after all.

Darcy Pickthorn, from Cheltenham Ladies' College, was made Head Girl, much to Amelia's chagrin; she had wanted the position for herself. She found a friend in Hedy Lyttelton-Cole, though, a boarder from Gordonstoun. They shared class notes and helped each other study.

The boys were generally a scruffy lot and the only one Amelia found appealing was Edward Gascoigne, whose movie-star looks almost made her forget his impenetrable Geordie accent.

In class they were segregated – boys on one side, girls on the other. And they had all been taken aback by the bizarre teaching style in this ancient regime. One day Mr Franklin had whacked an inattentive boy across the back of the skull with an exercise book. The entire class had frozen with shock. Such a thing would have meant a lawsuit back home; here it was just par for the course. Here they had to suffer the withering sarcasm of teachers who weren't obliged to entertain them and they had to memorise dates, parse sentences and use tables to figure out the square roots of ridiculously large numbers. The schoolbooks were a rude awakening too, filled with dense rows of text and few, if any, pictures.

16

There were also subjects they'd never encountered before. Mr Jones's announcement that they'd be studying measures and mensuration was met with much giggling.

'But sir,' Edward said with mock ignorance, 'surely it's only girls who do that.'

The childish joke continued throughout the lesson and Amelia couldn't resist inflicting it on Mr Lewis when she decided to take a break from history.

'Please may I go to the ladies', sir?' In a stage whisper she added, 'It's a Female Thing. I need to ... mensurate.'

Edward winked at her over the laughter and she imagined the wild speculation going on in the viewers' minds back in the real world. Actually, she kind of hoped her boyfriend wasn't watching.

Week Two found the pupils getting restless. The novelty had worn off and the lessons were becoming truly tiresome. And while the cameras had been a major distraction at first, now they hardly noticed them. Amelia often had to remind herself that this was a performance, a 24/7 screen test. Thousands of people were watching her at all times. The spectre of corporal punishment hung over them and they'd all been testing the waters to see how much they could get away with. A morbid curiosity simmered just beneath the surface. Who would be the first to push too far?

Although Amelia usually enjoyed English, swapping notes with Hedy was more fun than writing longhand compositions. They both agreed that Mr Campbell's obsession with *The Fall of the House of Usher* was slightly disturbing and they spent one lesson filling a page with gruesome speculation about the reasons behind it. However, Hedy's sketch of a dismembered schoolgirl was too much for Amelia and she blew their cover with an explosive burst of laughter.

Everyone spun to stare at them as Hedy tried desperately – and unsuccessfully – to hide the note. Amelia was still shaking with suppressed laughter as Mr Campbell read over their efforts, but she sobered up quickly when he set them lines.

I must pay attention in class. I must learn that, if I am naughty and disrespectful, I will be punished. Two hundred times. To be done that evening after prep and handed in the next day.

'And I shall check to make sure you get the paired commas right,' he added.

After the first dozen repetitions Amelia was beginning to regret their mischief. And when she finally finished the imposition late that night her hand was so cramped that she couldn't believe she'd ever been amused by Hedy's drawing in the first place.

'I'm going to complain to Matron tomorrow about Repetitive Stress Injury,' Amelia whimpered later in the dorm.

'No such thing,' came Lisa's cheerful voice from the far corner of the room. 'Not in the 50s.'

'Oh, shut up and go to sleep,' Hedy groaned. 'My hand hurts too, you know.'

Darcy compounded the humiliation by adding, 'And you don't want to get into any more trouble for talking after lights out.'

Power really went to some people's heads.

A few days later Amelia was feeling restless again. She'd had it with the horrible knickers. The skirt was thick enough that she didn't have to worry about an unsightly panty line, but even if no one could see, the ghastly things just made her *feel* hideous. Wearing sexy underwear made a woman feel sexy even when no one could see it, so the reverse must be true as well. There were no cameras in the loo, so she took them off and stuffed them into the bin. Of course, now there was nothing between her and the itchy wool skirt, but the trade-off was worth it. At least now the elastic wasn't biting into her thighs.

'What are you grinning about?' asked Darcy as they gathered their books in the dorm and prepared for the next class.

'Oh, nothing,' she said blithely, enjoying the sensation of cool air circulating beneath her skirt. Her little secret. In a way it was a pity no one knew about her rebellion; she was sure it would have been a hit with the audience.

Divide £2,318 16s. 9¼d. by 139.

Amelia stared in bewilderment at the problem before her. Not only was it long division, it was old money: pounds, shillings and pence. And she was expected to work that out by hand? With multiples of twelve and twenty where any sensible system used tens? And ninepence farthing! Two similarly monstrous problems had already been done on the blackboard with clumsy success. Amelia barely understood the amount, let alone the method.

Beside her Lisa was scribbling away dutifully, the little swot. So were some of the boys, who seemed to have a better understanding of numbers in general. To Amelia it might as well have been hieroglyphics.

She raised her hand with a petulant sigh, but didn't wait to be called on. 'Mr Jones, I don't understand why we can't use calculators for this.'

He gave her a condescending smile. 'You know we can't afford calculating machines here, Rutherford. They're far too expensive with all those wheels and cogs. So you need to learn how to work the answer out for yourself.'

She rolled her eyes. 'But it would only take five seconds with a calculator and this will take all day!'

His eyebrows climbed to his hairline as he eyed her with surprise. 'Don't answer me back, girl. And kindly show some respect for your elders and betters or you'll find out what happens to silly little girls who can't control themselves.'

Her face burned at his words and the heat deepened even more at the titters from the other pupils. She shot the nearest girl a filthy look and turned back to the hateful exercise, silently fuming. Even her bloody phone could work it out. It was so *stupid* that they had to do it the most cumbersome way imaginable. Bloody hell!

'I'm sorry, Rutherford, what was that?'

She looked up in surprise. Had she said it aloud?

'Did you say what I think you did, Rutherford? Because if so, I may have to send you to Matron to have your mouth washed out with soap. Carbolic soap. That will teach you to keep a civil tongue in your head.'

Amelia stared at him in disbelief, but had the sense to back off just a little. 'I'm sorry, sir,' she mumbled. 'It – erm, just slipped out. I'll be more careful, sir.'

'Yes, indeed, Rutherford. You certainly *will* be more careful. You will need to be. And to drive the point home, I think you would benefit from some corner-time to think about it. In the corner, hands on your head, nose against the wall.'

Her eyes bulged, but she made no move to obey.

'You heard me, Rutherford. In. The. Corner!' He pointed to the vacant corner to the left of the blackboard and Amelia had a sudden image of herself standing there in disgrace, all her 1950s classmates sniggering behind their hands at her. And that wasn't all. The cameramen at the back of the room, the ones who had all but blended into the walls, would be capturing it all on film for everyone – her friends, her boyfriend, her *real* teachers and classmates – to see. And laugh at.

No way.

'No fucking way,' she said with calculated defiance.

Mr Jones looked as scandalised as a genuine 1950s teacher would have been. Clearly he hadn't been expecting that. 'I beg your pardon!'

She made herself smile, the glacial smile of a Hollywood femme fatale. 'Oh, you don't have to beg, sir. Just ask nicely.'

The stunned silence that fell over the classroom was a satisfaction beyond anything Amelia had ever known. For that moment she was queen of the world. Unfortunately, a moment was precisely how long it lasted.

'This is disgraceful, Rutherford. Quite unprecedented behaviour. But if you won't take your punishment from me you can take it from the headmaster. I'm sure you know what that means.'

She did. The realisation hit her like an ice bath, but she swallowed her panic and looked at her fingernails as though unfazed. There was nothing for it now but to play to the crowd. 'Whatever,' she sighed.

Mr Jones strode to his desk and took out a sheet of paper. He calmly wrote out a note and folded it. Several pupils shifted uneasily in their seats. Amelia saw Hedy trying to catch her eye, but she didn't dare look. If she faced anyone they would see her coolness for what it was: false bravado. The only way she could save herself now was to maintain her dignity and go to her fate with aplomb. Or at least the illusion thereof.

For a moment she wished Edward would leap to his feet like Tom Sawyer and gallantly offer to take her place. Then she pushed the cowardly thought away and slid carefully out of her desk, smoothing her skirt down with forced nonchalance as she stood up. A fever-hot blush rose in her cheeks but she maintained her haughty demeanour as she snatched the note from Mr Jones and flounced out into the corridor.

As soon as she was away from the others she sagged against the wall and released a long shuddering breath. She was shaking all over, her heart pounding as she took in what had just happened, what she'd just done.

Stiff upper lip, she told herself, painfully aware of the cameras she wasn't meant to notice.

She wasn't afraid of the cane. Not really. Yes, she'd heard stories about it, but it couldn't possibly be as bad as all that when all the old comic strips and cartoons made such fun of it. Besides, the hideous skirt would offer plenty of protection. The knickers would have provided even more padding, but honestly – how bad could it be? She was far more concerned about the humiliation of everyone knowing what was going to happen. Every single person in Queen Mary's College and every viewer out there in the real world.

As she made her way to Mr Chandos's study she did her best to ignore the cameraman pacing her and trying to get close-ups of her face. She tried to imagine what the viewers would be seeing. The voyeuristic public would want to see her nervous, worried, fretting. Biting her nails and then pleading with the headmaster to let her off. Regretting her actions. Well, she wasn't going to give them that satisfaction.

21

Her stomach fluttered with dread, but she swallowed her panic and held her head up high. This was her Big Moment. She was playing a part and her role was that of martyr. She was the heroine in this little drama and the viewers would all side with her and think her terribly brave for facing such a cruel punishment.

She could see Mr Chandos through the little oblong window in the door of his study and he looked up at her tentative knock. His questioning look faded as understanding dawned, but he played the game. It was a performance, after all.

'Come in, Rutherford. What can I do for you?'

Amelia chewed her lip and looked at the floor, again forcing herself to tune out the cameraman who took up a position behind the headmaster's desk. Amelia clutched the little note behind her back, where her fingers toyed with it nervously.

'Well? Don't just stand there, girl.'

She showed him the note and mumbled, 'Mr Jones told me to bring you this, sir.'

Mr Chandos held out his hand for it and she stumbled a little as she stepped forward. She hated the way her hand trembled as she passed it to him and her fingers nervously plucked at her skirt as he unfolded the slip of paper.

'Hands at your sides, girl,' he said sharply. 'Stop fidgeting.'

She obeyed, withering under his stern gaze until he finally turned his attention to the note.

'"Grossly offensive language of a sexually explicit nature".' He looked up, eyebrows raised. 'Is this true, Rutherford?'

'Sir, I –'

'Is it true?'

She shifted her feet. 'Yes, sir.'

He pushed back his chair and stood up, his height making her feel small and weak as he circled her.

'I can only imagine, Rutherford, what possessed you to say what you did. We pride ourselves on turning out *ladies* from this school, not foul-mouthed guttersnipes. And when we do encounter debased and vulgar behaviour, we take the strongest possible action to eradicate it. And to punish the offender. Do you understand me, Rutherford?'

There was no way out. Amelia looked down at the floor. 'Yes, sir,' she whispered.

'Very well, Rutherford. You are about to have the distinction of being the first pupil at Queen Mary's College to be caned. Are you proud of yourself?'

She shook her head miserably, unable to think of an appropriate response.

'Cat got your tongue, Rutherford? I asked you a question. Are you proud of yourself?'

Amelia couldn't bring herself to look at him. She felt her cheeks burning and she just managed to mutter, 'No, sir.'

'Right. Let's get this over with, shall we? Take off your blazer.'

Amelia swallowed hard as her fingers fumbled with the buttons. She was shaking so violently that she began to fear she'd never get the thing off.

'Oh, do get on with it, girl,' he barked.

His annoyance only made her clumsier, but at last she managed to struggle out of the blazer. She held it limply until Mr Chandos nodded at the chair against the wall. She folded it and set it down carefully as though laying flowers on a grave.

As she stood waiting, her head well down, she heard a cupboard open and close. Her stomach churned and for a moment she feared she might be sick. Her heart thundered in her chest and she finally dragged her gaze up to meet the headmaster's.

He flexed the cane in his hands, bending it so far into a C-shape that she cringed, expecting it to snap in two. The fact that it didn't break only made her more nervous and she clenched her bottom cheeks, unable to imagine how the whippy length of rattan would feel.

'Six of the best, Rutherford. What we call a short, sharp shock.'

Amelia's face burned as she glanced uncertainly over at the camera. Its cold glass eye was a spyhole through which millions of people were about to witness her punishment.

'Lift your skirt and bend over the desk,' he said, all business.

She froze. 'What?' she blurted.

Mr Chandos furrowed his brow, as though he hadn't quite heard her. He repeated his instruction, this time more firmly.

Lift her *skirt*? But she wasn't wearing . . . Frantically her mind searched for a solution. Should she say something? Pull him aside and confess her little rebellion out of earshot of the cameras? Surely they wouldn't show her bare bottom on TV.

'I'm waiting,' came the headmaster's voice. There was no hint of sympathy in his tone and she knew that it would only magnify her humiliation if she tried to get out of it. Oh, for the courage just to hoist her skirt brazenly!

The three feet to his desk seemed like miles, but she made her unsteady legs carry her there. She gathered the heavy grey wool in her hands, peeling it slowly up to reveal her long legs.

The sudden noise of the door opening made her start and she dropped the skirt and spun around. To her horror, a second cameraman entered and closed the door behind himself without a word. Mr Chandos didn't speak, but it made sense that they'd want two cameras for this pivotal moment. It was the whole idea behind the show, after all.

'Carry on, Rutherford,' Mr Chandos said.

With a miserable little whimper she faced the desk and reached behind her again. She bent forward and lifted her skirt, unveiling her legs with slow and painful reluctance. The wool felt unbelievably heavy, like the massive curtains in front of a stage. She hesitated for a second, then pressed on, raising the material all the way over her bottom and dropping her elbows down onto the desk where she was grateful of its support.

In the icy silence that followed she imagined herself as though in a dream, both participant and observer. Behind her the cameraman made a flustered little noise and she had a clear vision of the moment from his perspective, could see perfectly the slight camera-wobble as she exposed the peach of her bottom, the soft round cheeks indecently bare beneath her chaste school skirt.

For a moment there was no response, and Amelia realised that Mr Chandos was facing away from her, pacing around behind the desk to reach her left side. Then his footsteps stopped abruptly and Amelia imagined she heard a quick intake of breath. His voice, when it came, was shocked.

'And just *what* does this shameful exhibition mean, girl?'

She lowered her head, blushing furiously. What could she possibly say?

The headmaster thought for a moment. 'Very well, Rutherford. Since you seem determined to make this worse for yourself . . .'

He slashed the cane through the air, making her jump.

'Your knickers would have given you some small protection from the cane. But now it will be on your bare bottom, and I shall make sure that every stroke counts.'

Mr Chandos took some time arranging her and making sure that her bottom was presented at the perfect angle for his cane – and the camera. He also made sure that her head was lifted so that her face was in full view.

There was no escape from either indignity. The camera behind her would show the world her bare bottom while the other would capture every wince, every yelp of pain and even – God forbid – her tears. She couldn't allow herself to show any pain or embarrassment and she made a promise to herself to be stoic. She was not going to disgrace herself further by making a fuss on television. A new game had begun, one where her only chance of survival was taking what he gave her with pluck. The whole world would be watching. It was both terrifying and exhilarating. She closed her eyes as she stretched out across the polished wood, taking hold of the edge of the desk.

Mr Chandos stood behind her and beyond her line of sight. She felt him lay the cane across her bottom. The implement tapped once and she flinched, every muscle in her body taut and tensed.

'You will count for me, Rutherford.'

'Yes, sir,' came her whisper-thin reply.

Time slowed to a crawl and she heard the first stroke cleave the air like a faraway jet. The cane landed evenly across both cheeks with a fearful crack. A moment later the nerve endings began to process what had been done and came to life to produce a line of fire where the cane had struck. Her eyes flew open as the pain began to build – burning, freezing, itching, stinging and aching all at once.

Amelia gasped, gripping the desk, waiting for the sensation to fade. Instead it only seemed to intensify with each passing second. She pressed her forehead into the wood. She would not yelp. She would not cry.

Be brave, be brave, she told herself, feeling anything but.

She waited for the next stroke, panting and bracing herself for the impact and she grew more anxious when it didn't come. Finally Mr Chandos prompted her.

'Rutherford. You're to count, remember? Or do you want the next stroke to be number one?'

'I'm sorry, sir,' she blurted. 'One, sir!'

Almost immediately, the second stroke landed. This one was a little lower and a lot harder. She let go of the desk, nearly jumping up, as the pain bloomed. But then she stopped herself, realising what that would display to the camera in front of her. She forced herself back down, but she couldn't help wriggling as the burn swarmed across her cheeks. It was a long time before the sting began to fade to a tolerable blur. She could clearly feel the two distinct lines and she imagined they looked like the searing marks on a steak from the grill. Whatever they looked like, she knew the camera behind her was recording it all. Everyone would see her bare bottom, caned and striped.

'Two, sir,' she whimpered, preparing herself for the third stroke. Her whole body vibrated with tension as she resumed her death grip on the edge of the desk. She stared straight ahead at the books on the shelves behind the desk. The camera was there too, just off to the right, and she tried not to think about what it was seeing.

Mr Chandos delivered the third stroke and Amelia arched her back, struggling to keep in position. This time

26

she couldn't hold back a small strangled cry and she immediately bit her lip so as not to give it full voice. She writhed, her hips rolling in what she knew must be an obscene display. She didn't care. The pain had all her attention.

'Three, sir.'

The next stroke forced a louder cry from her and she kicked her leg up behind her, twisting her foot in the air as she waited for the fearsome sting to dwindle. Her eyes began to prickle with tears and she squeezed them shut in misery and pain as she lowered her foot. No one must see. She curled and flexed her toes over and over inside her shoes, trying to focus on anything but her bottom and the terrible pain blossoming there. She had to admit it: the cane was formidable. The threat of even a single stroke from it would be enough to make her shudder in future.

'Four, sir,' she managed at last.

She'd come this far. She could do this. She *would* do this. Bracing herself, she waited for the next stroke.

Number five fell. Astonishing. Amelia clenched her teeth, grinding them together painfully, making her jaw ache.

She counted through her teeth. 'Five, sir.'

Only one more, she told herself. A bizarre calm had begun to settle over her. She locked her knees to keep herself from moving out of position. She wasn't about to ruin it now.

The final stroke was, predictably, the hardest of all and she bit back the strangled little sob that rose in her throat. She'd lost all her dignity earlier. This was her only chance to get it back. She had to show the headmaster – and the viewers – what she was made of. She desperately wanted to make them all proud of her.

As the fire in her bottom coalesced into a terrible pulsating burn she heard Mr Chandos's voice, as though from miles away.

'You may stand, Rutherford.'

She pushed herself up, swaying on shaky legs. She faced him, no longer self-conscious about what the camera might

27

see. Nothing mattered but her sense of triumph. It was over and she had taken six strokes of the cane. That was something none of her friends could claim, either here or back home. It was something to be proud of.

When Amelia returned to the modern world she was overwhelmed by the publicity. The caning had been dramatic and controversial, making front page news in all the major papers. Everyone knew her name. Her face was everywhere and so was her bottom. She was a heroine, a martyr, a conquering hero. Whether the show had proved any point or not was irrelevant; Amelia was a celebrity.

As she worked through the mountain of correspondence waiting for her she found an email from a film director whose name made her squeal. Her heart soared as she read his words.

Dear Ms Rutherford,

First let me express my admiration. You took that caning with real pluck. I often lament that punishment scenes in movies are so unrealistic. I've even considered hiring stunt performers to give some authenticity to onscreen punishments. Oh, but how much better it would be if the actors had your courage and conviction! Plenty of them do their own stunts, but how many would be willing to take what you did for the sake of a film?

I am currently working on a new project. It's a Victorian melodrama about a young woman who escapes her cruel circumstances and disguises herself as a boy with the intention of running away to sea. However, a kind gentleman takes her in and offers to educate her instead. She's a spirited girl (rather like you, in fact!) and she soon gets herself into trouble. The gentleman decides that he must birch her. There are several such episodes in the story and I just hate the thought of such a crucial element looking fake. Therefore I wonder if you would consider . . .

Amelia didn't need to read any further. She was going to be a star.

The Fourth Index

Scargrieve stood silent, its jagged roofline gouging the moonlit sky, its boarded windows like the eyes of a sleeping giant. Simon helped me out of the stolen punt and we crept stealthily up the riverbank towards the Victorian house. The wooden fence had rotted through and we slipped easily into the overgrown garden. I shone my torch across the jungle of weeds, scanning the back of the house until I located the back door beneath a gothic arch. Planks of wood had been nailed across it and signs announced in strident capitals, DANGER! KEEP OUT! and PRIVATE PROPERTY – NO TRESPASSING!

Simon examined the archway, looking for loose boards, while I tried to find another way in. Playing my torch along the exterior, I saw a pair of sash windows set low in the wall, presumably leading into a drawing room or a library. They weren't barricaded as thoroughly as the door and would be easier to get into. I chose a window and set to work on the boards with a hammer, trying to balance the torch under my arm.

Simon grabbed at the hammer. 'Here, let me do that.'

'I know what I'm doing,' I said impatiently, digging the claws under one of the boards and prying it up. 'Just hold the torch for me.'

The nails pulled free with a squeal and we froze, looking around warily. I waited a few seconds and then went to work on the other side of the plank. Simon flinched as the wood splintered noisily.

'Someone's going to hear us,' he hissed.

'Will you stop worrying? Don't be such an old lady.'

In truth, I was just as nervous, but Simon was so on edge I was afraid he would jeopardise the whole operation. His hands could barely even hold the torch still.

The window lifted easily, its catch rusted through. That was a relief, as I didn't fancy having to break it and crawl across broken glass to get in. Feeling like a proper tomb raider, I began prying up another board to widen the opening. I freed one side, but I couldn't wedge the hammer under the other half. Gritting my teeth with the effort, I slid my hands underneath the board it to pull it away from the window, ignoring the muffled protests behind me.

'Kate, I really think –'

'Oww, fuck!' I glared at the blood streaked across the back of my left hand. Simon shone his torch at the window. A contorted nail jutted from the edge of the window frame, my blood glistening on its rusty point. It had carved a vicious furrow along the length of my hand and just beyond the wrist.

'This is crazy,' he said. 'You're going to get yourself killed.'

Wincing with pain, I wiped my hand on my jeans and picked up the hammer again. I felt a touch of pride at the thought that I'd have a scar to show for my adventure.

'That needs a tetanus shot, Kate.'

'I'm not leaving here until I get what I came for.'

He shook his head with frustrated defeat. 'Why do you always have to be so bloody-minded?'

Simon had been against the whole idea from the start and I had to work fast now to get inside before he changed his mind and left me there. I'd needed him to 'borrow' the punt from the Cherwell Boathouse and I needed him to get me back when I was done. The Cher was notoriously muddy upstream from the Boathouse and I was afraid I'd lose the pole if I tried it alone.

Reluctantly, Simon helped me remove the second board and I dusted my hands. 'Good enough. I can fit through that.'

He looked fretfully out across the garden and then back at the window. He opened his mouth to say something, but I cut him off.

'It's not the British Museum, for God's sake. We won't get arrested.'

'It's not that, it's just . . .'

'What?'

He looked away and suddenly I understood why he'd been so jumpy all along. 'Don't tell me you're afraid of ghosts!'

He shot me a sullen look.

I'd never believed any of the stories about Scargrieve. The sightings. The noises.

Well, I wasn't looking for ghosts. I was after something far more substantial. Something I'd only read about, but which I was certain existed and was still there in the boarded-up house.

'It's a little creepy,' I admitted, 'and Health and Safety wouldn't approve of us going in there. But come on – it's not haunted.'

He still looked unconvinced.

'Look, you don't even have to go in. Just stay here and stand guard. Make sure no one steals the punt.'

He shifted his feet nervously before finally muttering something about my stubbornness. I kissed his cheek and clambered through the window.

Late in the nineteenth century, an eccentric gentleman named Henry Spencer Ashbee had compiled a three-volume bibliography of all the pornographic literature of the time. With tongue-in-cheek scholarship he called his works the *Index Librorum Prohibitorum*, the *Centuria Librorum Absconditorum* and the *Catena Librorum Tacendorum* and published them under the name of Pisanus Fraxi – an anagram of his other pseudonyms Fraxinus and Apis, the Ash and the bee. Ashbee was a compulsive collector, with interests ranging from erotic ephemera to Cervantes. He was also commonly believed to be 'Walter', the author of the infamous 11-volume sexual memoir, *My Secret Life*.

Ashbee's circle included many Victorian luminaries, including the explorer Richard Burton, the poet Algernon Charles Swinburne and the politician Richard Monckton Milnes. But of his many correspondents, William Henry Fox interested me the most. Under the pseudonym Verity, Fox submitted phony letters to the newspapers extolling the virtues of strict governesses and convent schools where corporal punishment was de rigueur. This was a popular game amongst Ashbee's circle of flagellant friends, all well-known rebels against the stifling Victorian social mores.

I was certain Fox was also the author of the anonymous classic *Curiosities of Flagellation*. Like 'Walter', Fox had a penchant for servants and other working-class girls and he chronicled his exploits with obsessive glee. A true 'lover of the rod', he described in copious detail the birchings he administered to his maids at the slightest provocation. I'd referenced it heavily in my thesis, *The Wages of Sin: Prostitution and Perversity in Victorian England*.

Fox lived in North Oxford, in the house known as Scargrieve, which had been built by his father Samuel with money from his steel-framed umbrella business. Fox never married and he left Scargrieve to a cousin, who in turn bequeathed it to his only daughter, Maria Radcliffe. After her sweetheart was killed in the Great War, Maria remained a spinster and lived out the rest of her days in the house. It had lain empty ever since.

The urban legends sprang up immediately: Maria's restless spirit roamed the halls at night, calling her lover to return from battle. Fox himself prowled the empty house, cursing those who disturbed his rest. There were reports of noises in the night and muffled cries of pain – the stuff of ghost stories since time began.

My work on Fox's biography had unearthed a previously unknown package of letters between Fox and Ashbee. As I pored over the letters I became fascinated by their relationship. On more than one occasion they had shared a prostitute and compared notes afterwards on her performance. And while there was a bragging locker-room tone to their discussions, there was also something oddly scholarly about it. I read the two men's correspondence with amusement, wondering what their female companions would have made of their meticulous accounts.

One day I came across a cryptic reference in one of Ashbee's letters to 'the fourth index'. He was wondering what to call it. Ashbee's life had been well chronicled by historians and writers like Steven Marcus and Ian Gibson. So where was this fourth index and why had no one ever mentioned it?

'Your *Codex* is quite safe,' Fox wrote some months later, adding the peculiar detail, 'Nell's drawers keep it warm.'

A subsequent letter from Ashbee – actually the last before he died – made no mention of this at all. I was left scratching my head. Then something clicked. I hurriedly paged back through Fox's book to a half-remembered episode with a parlour maid, Nell, whom he had caught with one of the footmen. After birching the girl, he'd taken her to bed. Then he'd sent her away, keeping her drawers as a souvenir. Nell was too flustered to ask for them back.

I recalled a letter to Ashbee where Fox had described 'checking' her the next day, ostensibly to see how she was healing. The sight of her welted bottom had inflamed his passion and he'd given her 'a good frigging' by his desk with a finger. He'd then told her that she should go bare from then on in case she needed to be disciplined again. To Ashbee he added the prurient detail that he kept her 'unmentionables' in his desk – in a secret compartment.

My heart was racing. As far as I knew, none of the furniture in Scargrieve had been touched since Maria Radcliffe's death in 1999. Distant relatives were still squabbling in court to be recognised as her heir. If Ashbee had in fact written a fourth index and entrusted it to his friend, it was probably still there. And I was the only one who knew it.

I found myself in a library filled with the musty reek of damp and rotting books. A threadbare Persian rug covered

33

the floor and every surface was coated with dust. Cobwebs swayed above me as I swung my torch upwards to reveal the cornice.

I found the desk at once, squatting beside a large window on the side wall. Broken glass littered the floor beneath the window and threads of moonlight filtered in through gaps in the boards.

It was a simple roll-top desk, with its key in the latch. I rolled it open, releasing a cloud of dust that made me cough. Was it really going to be this easy? Hardly worthy of Lara Croft, but I was still excited at the adventure.

I sifted through the papers on the surface of the desk. All modern, mundane stuff relating to Maria Radcliffe. I searched the drawers, feeling for hidden compartments. Nothing. I groped underneath it and along the underside of the roll-top. Still nothing. Secret compartments weren't rare. Nor were they especially difficult to find if you knew one was there. But there was nothing. Crestfallen, I finally had to admit that I'd drawn a blank.

'Damn!' I thumped the desk hard with my fist.

I heard movement outside and then Simon's worried voice. 'Kate? You OK?'

His torch beam found me through the window and I blinked, shielding my eyes from the glare.

'Yeah, I'm fine. It's not here.'

He couldn't keep the relief out of his voice. 'Oh. I'm sorry. Well, come on, let's get out of here before –'

'It must be somewhere else in the house,' I mused aloud. 'He wouldn't keep something like that in the library.'

My eyes wandered to the door as I tried to imagine the house as it had been in the late 1800s. Where would a Victorian gentleman keep something personal and private?

'I'm going upstairs,' I said suddenly, heading for the door.

Behind me I heard Simon's nerves unravelling as he called after me as loudly as he dared, both furious and frightened.

The door led me into a large oak-panelled entrance hall flanked by austere mediaeval-style carved chairs and an ecclesiastical settle. I couldn't believe the house hadn't been looted of its antiques. The damp would claim them soon if someone didn't rescue them.

The floor tiles were laid in the elaborate geometric pattern typical of the period. They had probably been lovely in their day, but now they were cracked and caked with grime. The front door stood opposite me – a vast gothic behemoth beneath a pseudo-Tudor arch. Above me a frayed wire dangled from the decaying ceiling rose where a chandelier had once hung.

A scuttling sound made me jump and I whirled to see the retreating tail of a rat scurrying into a corner. I shuddered and pulled my coat a little tighter, feeling suddenly vulnerable. My feeble torch beam was no match for the great hall and I felt the darkness pressing in on me. Unnerved, I took a few cautious steps further in, listening intently. All I heard was my own pounding heart.

I sensed a looming shape to my left and my torch revealed a curving staircase with gilded wrought-iron balusters. I didn't like the idea of going up there, but if I left the house now there would be no coming back. Simon certainly wouldn't help me again. I reminded myself how important this discovery was. I would keep my find secret until I'd written a book about it. By then no one would care how I'd got hold of the manuscript.

Many of the brass stair rods were missing and the runner was damp and spongy underfoot. I made a face at the squishing sounds as I went up, keeping to the centre so as not to brush against the hanging strips of mildewed wallpaper. On the landing was an imposing stained-glass window. Several panes had been broken in the process of boarding it up.

Shards of glass crunched underfoot as I headed up the second flight of the stairs. A parade of dusty and neglected portraits marched along the wall to the top. Frock-coated gentlemen and dour ladies sat in their frames in starchy Victorian disapproval. I half expected their cold eyes to follow me as I continued up the stairs, but the paintings were as dead as their subjects.

To my delight, I found Fox himself near the top. He was quite striking. His eyes seemed more alive than those of his neighbours as he scrutinised me from the confines of his tarnished frame, sizing me up. His black morning suit emphasised his jet-black hair and beard. His imposing demeanour and obvious refinement put me in mind of Professor Moriarty. Given his predilections, I wasn't surprised he had an air of the sinister about him.

A hallway branched from the top of the stairs. I followed my instincts and took the right turning, arriving at a panelled door. I turned the handle slowly and it swung open without even a creak, admitting me to what was clearly the master bedroom.

My torch beam unveiled a black iron bedstead with so many cobwebs woven through the swirls of ironwork that it looked as though they were holding the bed together. The rest of the furniture was just as stark and masculine. There was a hulking wardrobe against the far wall with a small dressing-table and a simple chair beside it. But there was no desk.

A sudden heavy thud made me gasp and I quickly switched the torch off. I tried to calm my breathing as I strained to discern the source of the noise. Another rat? I didn't like to imagine the size it would have to be to make a sound like that. Then I heard the unmistakable noise of a door banging shut downstairs. Panting with real fear, I edged towards the wall, suddenly feeling exposed in the centre of the room.

Cold sweat plastered my clothing to me and I waited for what seemed like an hour in the dark silence before the realisation set in. Simon. I switched the torch back on, angrier with myself for getting spooked than with him for scaring me.

'Very funny,' I called through the open bedroom door-way.

Returning to my quest, I searched for a door to a connecting room. My torch quickly discovered it, on the wall adjacent to the door I'd just come through. A cheval mirror stood incongruously before it, reflecting the dusty room back at me. I laid my torch down on the bed and dragged the mirror away. The effort reawakened the pain in my injured hand and I frowned as I saw it was bleeding again.

I glanced around hurriedly for something to bandage it with. In the wardrobe I found a pile of crisply folded, moth-eaten linen that probably hadn't been used in a century. Not exactly hygienic, but better than nothing. I flapped open one of the sheets and tore a strip off it to wrap around my hand, grimacing. I wadded the sheet into a ball and stuffed it back into the wardrobe.

Something caught my eye as I did. A maid's cap. I couldn't resist setting the little scrap of yellowing lace on my head and grinning at my reflection. Further exploration revealed a long black Victorian maid's dress and white lace pinafore, both showing signs of wear from their days in service to Mr Fox. I wanted to investigate further, but that could wait until I'd found my treasure. I was in no hurry now that I knew Simon was in the house playing games.

I returned to the door, but to my dismay, I found that it was locked. There was no keyhole and I suddenly understood that it wasn't a door at all; it was a fake. Odd. I stepped back to look at the wall with its pair of doors and noticed something equally odd about the panelling beside the false one. A pair of thin parallel lines ran down the flocked wallpaper from behind a nondescript framed landscape, disappearing into the skirting board. At first I thought they were simply clumsy joins in the paper, but they were too wide for that. I realised that together they were the width of a small door.

I knelt down and pulled at the skirting board. It came away neatly to reveal a handle set into the wall, like that of a dumbwaiter. Now I was really beginning to feel like Lara Croft!

'Eureka,' I whispered, pulling the handle upward. The door groaned on its rusty hinges as it rose. Beyond it was a study. William Henry Fox's private study.

There was an extravagantly carved mahogany writing desk against the far wall. At its feet sat teetering stacks of mouldy books, like stalagmites growing from the floor. I smirked as I recognised some of the titles, including some that scholars had believed lost when the vandals at the British Library burned Ashbee's collection.

It was a formidable piece of furniture, imperiously tall and ornate. The tilt-top folded down to display a set of pigeonholes and small drawers. Too small to conceal what I was after. I closed the top again and searched lower.

There was a built-in bookshelf just beneath where the writing surface folded down and I felt around behind the carved scroll that formed the lip of the opening. It shifted easily and I held my breath as I pulled open the secret drawer. I stared at the white fabric on top before daring to take it out. It was a pair of Victorian pantalets. Nell's drawers. Flushed with excitement, I gently removed the ream of papers they concealed. Across the top page, in Ashbee's meticulous copperplate, was written *Codex Librorum Suppressorum*. I released the breath I'd been holding and restrained the urge to kiss the manuscript.

I was about to replace the pantalets when I suddenly thought of Simon. First too scared to come in, then happy to thump on the walls and slam doors to scare *me*. *I'll show you a ghost*, I thought wickedly.

I hurried back to the bedroom and, after concealing the study once more, I stripped off my clothes. I stepped into the pantalets and drew them on. They came down to the knees and fastened with a drawstring around the waist. A front seam was the only semblance of modesty; the crotch and rear were completely open. No wonder they called them 'unmentionables'!

Next I slipped into the dress and tied the pinafore on over it. Dust motes spun in the beam of the torch and my movements threw creepy shadows on the walls as I costumed myself. Finally, I pinned the cap into my hair and admired myself in the cheval glass. I couldn't wait to see Simon's terrified face when I confronted him like the vengeful spirit in a Japanese horror film.

But I was going to treat myself to something else first. I sat down on Fox's bed and opened the manuscript. As I leafed through it I was thrilled to see handwritten notes in fountain pen, curious little notations made by Ashbee – or Fox. My discovery. *Mine*. I felt positively buoyant.

But as I skimmed an excerpt from *The Merry Order of St Bridget*, I became aware of the unpleasant chill. A minute ago I had been comfortable; now my teeth were chattering. How had the room suddenly become so bitterly cold? A convulsive shudder racked my body and I looked at my bandaged hand with concern. Had Simon been right about tetanus? I didn't even know what the symptoms were.

My breath plumed in front of me and all at once I felt a crawling sensation in the pit of my stomach. There was nothing wrong with me; it was the room. The temperature had plummeted in seconds. And there was something else. The bedroom door, which I'd left open, was closed. My torch flickered like a guttering candle flame and went out. I stifled a scream and flicked the switch back and forth, on and off. It was dead. I shrank back onto the bed as slow, measured footsteps grew steadily louder in the corridor. Someone knew I was here.

The footsteps stopped outside the door and my chest began to ache with the hammering of my heart. I could hardly breathe. The shadows felt alive as I cowered in the dark, waiting. I was too scared to move, but I couldn't just sit here all night in terror. 'Simon? Is that you?' I called hoarsely. My throat felt full of dust and I barely recognised my voice.

The door flew open with a bang and I cried out. A man was standing there. William Henry Fox.

'Nell!' he said sharply. 'What do you think you are doing?'

I stared in disbelief at him, my eyes taking in the immaculate black suit and starched white collar. This was no insubstantial ghost; this was a man, solid and real. He held a brass candelabrum which illuminated the room and made the shadows dance around us, as though the furniture had come to life. His eyes gleamed with a dark vibrancy.

He strode to the bed and snatched the manuscript away. 'This is not for the eyes of servants,' he said severely. 'But more to the point – what do you think you're doing in my room, lounging on my bed?'

I glanced down at myself, still in Nell's parlour maid uniform, stunned beyond words.

Mr Fox glared at me. 'Well, girl? Cat got your tongue?'

'I . . .'

'And who's this "Simon" you called out to? Hmm? Another of your admirers, I expect.' He set the candelabrum down on the dressing-table with a thump and laid the manuscript beside it before turning to glare at me. 'On your feet, girl!'

I rose slowly, completely at a loss for anything to say.

'It seems you didn't learn your lesson last time,' he said, heading for the wardrobe and flinging it open. 'But we'll cure you of your nosy ways.'

He paused when he saw the balled-up sheet I'd stuffed inside and he turned slowly to me, holding up the ragged end where I'd torn it. 'What is the meaning of *this*?'

At last he'd asked something I could answer. I felt connected to a filament of reality as I showed him my left hand. Blood had seeped through the makeshift dressing and I hoped he would take pity on me.

'I see,' he said, nodding. 'You destroy my fine linens to dress scratches you sustained breaking into my private rooms. Well, I know how to deal with you, Nell. You know I do.'

He took something from the wardrobe and swished it through the air. I knew immediately what it was. I'd read his book.

'Please, I don't –'

'You know the position, Nell,' he said, calmer now that he was about to indulge in his favourite pastime.

Nell may have known the position, but I didn't. I stared blankly at him, still too astonished to believe what was happening.

He took my hesitation for dumb insolence and seized me by the arm, hauling me away from the bed. He fetched a low padded foot-stool from beside the wardrobe and placed it in the centre of the room. He tapped it with the bundle of thin whippy switches and I suddenly wondered who had cut them and bound them with twine. And when.

As though under a spell, I moved towards the stool. I looked up at him fearfully and he tapped the rod impatiently against his leg. 'Kneel. Hands on the floor,' he instructed. 'Bottom well up.'

Someone else's voice meekly said, 'Yes, sir' and I felt my body obeying his command. But there was no one else in the room. Unable to resist, I rested my knees on the stool and bent down to place my palms flat on the dusty wooden floorboards. The position raised my bottom high in the air and I felt the chill air of the room against the stretched skin of my bottom and thighs.

'A birching must always be given on the bare,' he said loftily, 'so we'll have this up.'

And just like that, he raised my skirt.

'What's this?' he asked, sounding amused. 'I thought I had these safely tucked away, along with that manuscript. My, but you are a disobedient little thing, aren't you? Well, we'll soon put you right.'

He peeled the drawers apart, baring my cheeks, as I whimpered softly.

'Two dozen,' he pronounced.

I felt the rasp of the twigs against my bare flesh. Fox pressed the rod against my bottom, forcing the individual switches to spread out and cover it fully. Frightened by the realisation of how much area the birch would cover, I slowly filled my lungs with air in an effort to prepare myself.

The rod tapped once, held its position, and then struck.

I heard the swish of the birch cutting the air and then there was a burst of fiery pain, as though I'd been stung by fifty bees at once. I'd never even been spanked as a child and I had no idea how much it could hurt. I cried out and struggled awkwardly up onto my knees, clutching my bottom.

'Hands down, girl,' he growled. 'A birching is meant to hurt.'

41

His words brooked no disobedience and I forced myself to resume the position. My hands had left two perfect prints in the dust and I fitted my palms into them again. The second stroke fell as soon as I did. Again I leapt up and grabbed my bottom, wailing in pain.

'Nell,' he warned.

It was absolutely the worst pain I'd ever felt in my life. How was I ever supposed to endure two dozen strokes? Again I felt myself eased into place, presenting myself to him.

Stroke three caught my legs and I yelped, writhing over the stool and trying to stay still.

When he told me to get back into position again, I saw that my handprints had vanished. I looked to my right to see that the iron bedstead was no longer covered in cobwebs. The flocked red wallpaper looked like velvet, showing not a trace of decay. Even my uniform – what I could see of it – was immaculate.

'Back in position,' he repeated firmly.

I surrendered myself to another series of strokes, one right after another. With each stroke, pieces of the rod broke off and flew into the corners of the room. Close to tears, I watched as tiny buds and twigs landed beneath me on the polished floorboards.

'How many was that, Nell?'

The response came easily. 'Ten, sir.'

He delivered the next two in rapid succession and I began to cry. I still had a dozen to go.

The next three strokes came fast and hard, as though the first dozen had only been a warm-up. My voice was growing more ragged and tortured with every cry. Fox's voice finally reached me through a haze of pain and I realised he was repeating something he'd already said.

'How many, Nell?'

Startled, I realised I had lost count. 'I don't know, sir,' I choked out.

'Dear me,' he said. 'Should I start again?' He paused long enough to savour my horrified silence before softly telling me it was twenty.

I gritted my teeth and locked every joint in my body to stay in position as he laid on the last four strokes. I cried out with each one and I actually heard the birch twigs snapping as they struck.

I could hardly believe it was finally over. I was shaking with sobs and gasping for breath. I couldn't remember ever crying so hard in my life. Fox stood aloof, watching, as I got shakily to my feet. Through tear-blurred eyes, I saw what remained of the birch – lying scattered over the floor.

Eventually my tears subsided and I began to come back to myself. I felt oddly weightless. Light-headed but not unpleasantly so. I remembered a description Fox had written of Nell clinging to him after she had been birched. He spoke glowingly of how she always seemed more settled after a punishment. And more affectionate.

The pain had been terrible and I had truly hated every second of the birching. But now that it was over I drew strange comfort from the warm glow in my bottom. I reached behind and could feel the thin raised wheals, the tiny bee-sting knots where the buds had landed. I had even forgotten the pain in my hand.

'Kate!'

My eyes snapped open and I looked up to see Simon standing in the doorway, shining his torch onto me. He was panting and out of breath.

'What happened? Are you all right?'

I looked around in confusion, as though waking from a dream. Fox was gone. I was curled on the dust-choked bed, my arms wrapped round the torn and yellowing sheet, clinging to it.

'I'm fine,' I said slowly.

'It sounded like you were in pain. I heard you crying out.' He frowned. 'What are you wearing?'

I still had Nell's uniform on, once more aged and covered in dust. Under the skirt I could feel the cool air through the parting in Nell's drawers. How could I possibly explain what had just happened?

'Oh, I thought it would be fun to surprise you,' I said awkwardly, forcing a smile.

Simon looked utterly baffled. 'Right. Well, you've done that. Can we go now?' he pleaded.

I sat up and immediately yelped with pain. 'My hand,' I lied quickly, answering Simon's concerned look. Whatever had just happened, my bottom was proof of it. But proof no one was ever going to see – not even Simon.

'Did you find it?'

I looked around for the manuscript, but it was gone.

'No,' I said sadly. 'I didn't find anything.'

As I gathered up my clothes and followed Simon out the door I noticed the candelabrum still burning on the dressing-table. I smiled to myself as I blew the flames out one by one.

I would return to Scargrieve – alone. I felt sure Mr Fox would eventually trust me with the manuscript. When he felt I'd paid for it.

A Suitable Match

Cambridge, England, 1865

I was bored. Another dinner, another suitor. Why was my
uncle trying so hard to marry me off? I hadn't even met
this Captain Hawksley. Back home in Atlanta I'd had my
pick of southern gentlemen, but Englishmen were so dull
and unimaginative.

There was a timid knock at the door and Polly poked
her head inside. Her white cap sat askew on her head and
I grimaced at the streaks of soot on her pinafore. Her
slovenliness only soured my mood further.

'Well, don't just stand there letting in the chill,' I
snapped. 'Do you expect me to dress myself?'

'Sorry, Miss Angelina!' The waifish girl scurried to my
side and helped me into my corset. I wrapped my arms
round the bedpost while she tightened the laces. It was
obvious she'd never helped a lady dress before and I soon
lost patience with her clumsiness.

'Tighter,' I hissed. 'Pull tighter!'

I exhaled, emptying my body of the last breath of air
and winced as she tightened the laces, drawing the
whalebones in to constrict my frame. Only after much
incompetent fumbling did she finally manage to tie the
laces. Next came the voluminous petticoats, which Polly
helped me step into. Then she pinned them in place over
my frilly white bloomers: a French indulgence my uncle
wouldn't have permitted, but he wasn't likely to *see* them.

Polly gasped as she stabbed herself with the pin. Hopeless. 'Which frock will you be wanting, miss?'

'The green,' I said, inspecting my waistline in the mirror, admiring the impeccable posture enforced by the corset. I honestly didn't care what our dinner companion thought. I found military men pompous and tiresome and I expected the captain would be no exception. No doubt he would boast of his exploits all night, one bombastic tirade after another, while I grew bored and restless. But to spurn a suitor properly, a lady must look her best.

Polly raised the rustling gown above my head and I swam through the layers of emerald green silk until the garment moulded itself to my curves. The maid had difficulty fastening it in back and I lost patience as she groped behind me like a blind beggar.

'Wretched girl! Do those clumsy hands of yours know what they're doing?'

'I'm sorry, miss,' she said, lowering her head.

'Have you any experience at all of being a ladies' maid?'

'A little, miss.'

I didn't believe her, but she finally managed the task. Dressed at last, I admired the southern belle in the mirror. My flaxen curls were pulled back from my face and adorned with matching green ribbons, setting off the deep contrasting brown of my eyes. The gown emphasised the porcelain swell of my bust and I smiled.

'Uncle won't be pleased with me showing so much décolletage,' I confided to the maid. 'But I don't care.'

'Ain't that what a nice dress is supposed to do, miss?' Polly asked shyly.

'Oh, I had much nicer dresses before that beastly war. You should have seen me!' I sighed. Then I grew annoyed with her for reminding me of all I had lost. I had been to all the finest balls and parties, worn the richest gowns and jewels. And now here I was in this damp gloomy country, bored silly by my uncle James and his parade of tedious suitors.

I held up the emerald necklace my uncle had given me. It matched the gown perfectly, but I didn't care for the earrings, which made my face look too long. I tried a smaller necklace of semi-precious stones, but I didn't like the idea of wearing inferior jewels.

At a loss, I turned to Polly. 'Which do you think looks best?'

She gazed at the jewels, mesmerised. 'Them big ones is awful nice, miss.'

I couldn't help but grin. Yes, 'them big ones' would do for Captain Hawksley. He should know what he wasn't getting. I fastened them on, not wanting to let the maid handle them.

'You look very pretty, miss,' she said softly.

I confess her little awestruck voice did brighten my mood somewhat. 'What time does our guest arrive, Polly?'

'Sir James ordered sherry in the library for half six, miss.'

It was nearly that now, which gave me at least half an hour before I needed to make an appearance. I wouldn't dream of being on time. I sat down so Polly could lace my shoes.

'What's the gossip below stairs about this Captain Hawksley?' I asked.

The girl hesitated, then shrugged. The pause told me she'd heard a thing or two. Servants' gossip was notoriously exaggerated, but still often valuable.

'Polly?'

She blushed and fidgeted with the edge of her pinafore. 'Well, miss, they say he... that he ...'

'Out with it, girl!'

Polly looked up at me, then back down at the floor. 'That he – rides his fillies hard.'

I blinked. 'What's that supposed to mean?'

She shrugged sullenly. 'Don't know, miss. Just what they say.'

It was likely some crude reference to his courtship methods. He was a cavalry officer, after all. It wasn't hard to figure out and I didn't really care to hear such vulgarity.

Before I could tell her to forget it there was a knock at the door. This time it was the cook, Mrs Carson.

47

'Begging your pardon, miss, but we've run out of sherry and I was wondering if we could offer Madeira instead.'

Why were they bothering me with such trivial matters? I sighed with exasperation. 'Has my uncle gone missing?'

Mrs Carson had no answer for that, so I told her that Madeira would be acceptable. I didn't care one way or another.

'Very good, miss,' she said. 'And I wonder ... could Polly help me in the kitchen now?'

My shoes were laced and I didn't need the girl any more, so I dismissed her with a wave of my hand.

Polly dropped a little curtsey and left. I decided to take a turn round the grounds before presenting myself.

'Ah, Angelina,' Uncle James said, smiling. 'Come in. Captain Hawksley, may I introduce my niece, Angelina Duke?'

The captain was younger than I'd been expecting. Most of the gentlemen my uncle introduced me to were old enough to be my father. I was also surprised he wore a plain black tailcoat – impeccably tailored – instead of his uniform. Most soldiers seemed to think that the very sight of a uniform would make a lady swoon from excitement. I thought the practice simply vulgar. But the captain cut a dashing figure and I confess I found him not entirely unappealing.

I closed my fan and extended one gloved hand to the stranger.

'Enchanté,' he said, kissing my hand in an affectedly old-fashioned manner. Oh, he was a sly one.

'Charmed,' I said, inclining my head and offering only the most minimal of curtseys. I loathed curtseying.

'Would you care for some Madeira?'

'Yes, please, Uncle,' I said, flouncing past the captain in an impertinent rustle. My skirts brushed against him and he was obliged to take a polite step back, though I sensed it was more for my uncle's sake than for mine.

The conversation was predictably dull and I soon grew weary of it.

'Shooting and hunting,' I said with a dramatic sigh. 'The Crimean War. Is that all you *gentlemen* can talk about?'

The captain apologised with a great show of gallantry and began to tell me of London, appalling me with stories of the dreadful smells and smoke there. I had no wish to visit such a vile place and I explained that Atlanta had been far more civilised. Before the dreadful Yankees had burnt it, that was. Here I spied an opportunity and gave a little sniffle.

He offered me his handkerchief at once and I took it, dabbing at my eyes.

'I am very sorry to have disturbed you with such talk, miss,' he said, giving a little bow.

I hid my grin of victory.

Conversation soon turned towards my uncle's new maid and I didn't hesitate to voice my frustration.

'Honestly, Uncle, she's hopeless! I don't wonder her previous employer no longer wanted her, but how on earth *you* came to hire her –'

'She had no previous employer, Angelina. Mr Squyres sent her from the reformatory.'

I stared at him, aghast. A criminal serving in my uncle's house! Could he not get proper servants?

He and the captain shared a strange smile. I didn't care for the vulpine look that passed between them, so I decided to let the matter lie. Soon after, Polly knocked at the door and announced that dinner was served. I was relieved that my uncle didn't insist on a formal procession, so I didn't have to surrender my arm to the captain.

As soon as we were seated my uncle furrowed his brow at the place settings. Polly filled our wine glasses from a decanter and set plates of asparagus before us.

'From the right, if you please, Polly,' my uncle said with a pinched smile.

'Yes, sir.'

When we were alone, my uncle looked down at the table. 'The place settings are rather . . . creative, don't you think?'

The captain agreed and I rolled my eyes.

'What do you expect, Uncle?' I asked. 'She's not even a proper maid.'

'Oh, but such girls can be taught,' said the captain.

I didn't appreciate being contradicted, so I ignored him and ate my asparagus.

When it was time for the soup, Polly displeased my uncle by slopping soup onto the lip of his bowl. Sir James and the captain discussed 'civic duty' and charity and the chance she was being given, but I was simply weary of her incompetence.

When she came to clear the soup bowls Sir James addressed her. 'Who set the table, Polly?'

'I did, sir.'

'Were you never taught how to arrange the cutlery?'

She didn't have a satisfactory answer for that. How on earth was the wretched girl expected to know anything about it? Surely all she knew was a life of crime and wickedness. While he kindly explained to her that the places were to be set outside in, I noticed that one of the tines of my fork was tarnished. I waited until she was almost to the door before calling her back.

'Oh, girl? Do you think I might have a cleaner fork?'

She scurried to my side and took the fork from me with a worried expression. 'Certainly, miss,' she said with a curtsey before scampering out.

I took a sip of my wine and noticed the captain smiling at me.

It was a few minutes before Polly arrived with another fork and I inspected it, slightly disappointed to find it immaculate.

She refilled our wine glasses, then served the lamb and potatoes. And parsnips. I loathed parsnips. I snapped my fan open to show my displeasure.

'I'm not eating that,' I informed her curtly. 'You can take that plate straight back to the kitchen and fetch me a clean one. With no parsnips. And tell Mrs Carson that in the future she needn't bother cooking them for me.'

Perhaps a little humiliation would help her learn. It was unlikely she'd forget my preferences next time.

Polly looked worriedly at my uncle, then dropped a little curtsey. 'I'm sorry, miss.'

Sir James and the captain continued to discuss the merits of his method of 'reformation' while Polly bustled around us. I didn't doubt she would be nibbling off the plates in the kitchen and probably stealing wine from the cellar as well. Not to mention the silver. My uncle's 'charity' was sheer folly.

I became more interested in the conversation when the men began to discuss discipline. The birch was used liberally in the reformatory, they said, so Polly would have no reason to suppose herself above such measures simply because she was a maid now. My uncle supposed his charity would provide her with an extra incentive and that in the end she would prove more reliable – and more loyal – than maids in the finest country estates. Maids, he added, who were *not* subject to such chastisement.

I was intrigued. Naturally, no one had ever raised a hand to me, but I found myself fascinated by the prospect of seeing the maid under discipline. The captain made no secret of his interest either. He really was quite handsome, I decided.

Several minutes had passed without Polly arriving to refill our wine glasses and I felt myself growing warm at the thought of getting the girl into trouble. I lifted my empty glass to my lips and then affected a blush, as though surprised to find myself suddenly with nothing to drink.

Frowning, Sir James pushed his chair back and strode to the far end of the table to get the decanter and refill our glasses. He left his own empty, however. He rang the bell and within seconds Polly was at his side.

'Yes, sir?'

'I have served wine to my guests,' he said in a simmering voice. 'I do not care to serve wine to *myself*.'

The girl looked forlornly at his empty glass and grabbed the decanter with unsteady hands, just managing to pour the wine without spilling it.

'Will there be anything else, sir?'

'Yes. Go and fetch my riding crop from the hall.'

Polly whispered, 'Yes, sir' and couldn't leave the room fast enough.

I giggled and covered my mouth with my hand. The evening had finally taken an interesting turn.

'I'm terribly sorry, Captain,' my uncle said. 'I must apologise for the deplorable service.'

Captain Hawksley shook his head. 'It's quite all right, sir,' he said. 'Your hospitality is certainly not at fault. And I must say I'm interested to see how your little experiment turns out.'

'Well, it is high time for a practical demonstration.'

'Indeed.'

The nervous maid arrived and stood to attention in front of the table. She clutched the riding crop in her hands, which I could see were shaking.

Sir James pushed back his chair and got slowly to his feet. He held out his hand and Polly relinquished the crop to him, seeming both relieved to be rid of it and reluctant to progress to the obvious next stage.

My uncle sliced the crop through the air, making a fearsome sound.

The maid looked pointedly at the floor.

'Right, Polly. Let's get this over with, girl.' He tapped the table with the end of the crop. Immediately she stretched out along it, clutching the edges for support. It did look like a position she was familiar with.

'Raise your skirt. And unfasten your drawers.'

She gasped and glanced up at the captain, but it was only a moment's hesitation. With a resigned expression, she obeyed.

The captain stood to one side, watching. My uncle wasted no time. He brought the crop down sharply across her bare bottom, making her wince. I stood up and rushed behind her to get a view of her bottom as the second stroke landed. It did look terribly painful, but I had little sympathy. It was no more than she was accustomed to. Certainly no more than she should expect, given her lowly station.

'She's remarkably stoic,' the captain observed.

Polly did her best to be brave as the riding crop bit into her cheeks twice more. I was struck by the sight of the four livid wheals the leather tip had raised on her fair skin and

52

I wished for it to go on until her entire posterior was scarlet. The whole event was over far too quickly.

When my uncle allowed her up, I studied her face. Her cheeks were flushed and her eyes shone with tears. Nonetheless, she looked oddly relaxed to me. The captain praised her stoicism again and I could have sworn I saw her smile with something like pride. It was most peculiar.

'You may adjust your clothing,' my uncle said, and the girl hurriedly obeyed.

As Polly adjusted her dress, my uncle gave her a warning glance and told her to fetch the dessert. She left the room, wiping her eyes on the edge of her pinafore.

'A fascinating exercise, sir,' the captain remarked, raising his glass. 'And what did you think, Miss Angelina?'

I felt a little flushed and fanned myself, replaying the spectacle again in my mind as I returned to my seat.

'As you say, sir – fascinating. But we'll have to see whether her performance improves. I have my doubts.' Then, as he raised his water glass to his lips I added, 'Of course, I suppose there are those who might proclaim the benefits of such an exercise merely for a peek at a girl's naked bottom.'

'Angelina,' my uncle said warningly.

'Oh? And what will you do, Uncle – ask our guest to thrash me for my indiscretion?' If he didn't want me to simper and flirt, he shouldn't inflict suitors on me. To his credit, the captain hadn't batted an eye.

Polly appeared very soon to refill the wine glasses, this time before they were empty. It seemed she'd learnt something after all.

'Tell me, Polly,' I said. 'Was it awfully painful?'

A rueful expression flickered across her features. 'Painful enough, miss.'

'Well, don't feel too bad. My uncle does drink a lot. It's a wonder anyone can keep up.'

'Angelina,' my uncle said under his breath. 'That will be quite enough.'

I winked conspiratorially at the captain, but he didn't seem amused.

Polly served the crème brulée and when she had gone Captain Hawksley turned to my uncle. 'I wonder, sir, if I might take your niece up on her offer.'

I blinked. Offer?

My uncle nodded slowly, looking at me sternly. 'Yes, I think that might be salutary.'

Suddenly, I understood. 'You will do no such thing!'

But before I knew it, the captain had come round to my side of the table to help me up from my seat. I backed away, glaring at him. He moved to take my arm and my eyes flashed.

'Take your hands off me!' I hissed.

But he reached for my arm again and I slapped his face.

'You, sir, are no gentleman!'

A look of calm cold fury shone in his eyes and I knew at once my situation was hopeless. He and my uncle each took me by one arm and hauled me across the end of the table where Polly had been whipped. The girl was in the kitchen now, but I was sure she could hear everything. More than that, I was sure she was *listening*.

I shrieked at the effrontery as they raised my skirts and my petticoats, exposing my drawers.

'Why, Miss Angelina,' said the captain with exaggerated surprise. 'I didn't realise you'd been to Paris.'

'The devil take your tongue, sir! How dare you!' I turned to my uncle with a pleading look.

But he only shook his head and offered the crop to Captain Hawksley. 'I think she should get the same as the maid,' he said.

'Very good, sir.'

'I will never forgive you for this, Uncle!' I cried, tears springing to my eyes.

'Or perhaps double?'

I gasped. Eight strokes! But Sir James wasn't finished.

'I also think she should count,' he said, studying my face.

The humiliation was not to be borne!

But the villain agreed. 'Yes, that's a splendid idea. Miss Angelina? Be so good as to take down your drawers.'

My cold silence only prompted him to offer to take them down himself. I obeyed hurriedly, trembling with embarrassment and fury.

'Say "Thank you, Captain" after each one, please.'

Before I could protest again, I heard the now-familiar slicing sound and my bottom came alive with agony. I howled at the pain, the indignity and the unfairness of it all, gasping for breath. The room was silent but for my outraged panting. I drummed my feet on the floor and glared up at my uncle, determined to hate him till the day I died.

He stared impassively at me and addressed Captain Hawksley. 'Perhaps you didn't make your point strongly enough. It seems only to have provoked another tantrum.'

'Pity,' said the captain, and he immediately brought the crop down even harder.

The shocking pain tore the very breath from my throat. I froze, staring down the length of the table at the candle flames. They grew blurry as tears of hot shame filled my eyes.

The captain's voice startled me out of my misery.

'I trust she felt that one. If not I'll have to make the next one even harder.'

'Two,' I said at once. Then I gritted my teeth to steel myself for the rest. 'Thank you, Captain.'

'No, Miss Angelina,' he said with mock sympathy. 'It was not even one, since you did not count it correctly. This, perhaps, will be one.'

Again the leather cracked down across my helpless bottom. I writhed like a wounded animal over the table, wishing I had the stoicism of a martyr. But I didn't. I didn't even have the brave resignation of a reformatory girl, accustomed to such treatment and expecting no better.

- I lowered my head to the cool wood and whimpered, 'One, thank you, Captain.'

Another stroke. Another pitiable yelp and I counted. My tight-laced corset wouldn't allow me to fill my lungs completely and I panted shallowly, afraid that I would faint. But if I did at least they might realise what brutes they had been. To treat a lady so!

'Ahh! Two, thank you, Captain.'

On and on it went. I had never known eight of anything to last so long. I kicked and struggled, but my uncle held me firmly. And the captain was merciless, whipping me as though I were a horse. Rides his fillies hard indeed!

I was determined not to give him the satisfaction of another sound from me and I hissed through my teeth as another stroke slashed into my bottom.

'Six,' I growled, drawing strength from the injustice. 'Thank you, Captain.'

I heard the scoundrel laugh and the seventh stroke was harder. I bit back a wild cry and remembered Polly's composure. If she could do it, so could I. I kept my wits about me as I counted.

The crop sliced through the air once more and this time I did cry out, cursing myself silently. But my voice was steady as I spoke the hateful words for the final time. 'Eight, thank you, Captain.'

'You may return to your place, Angelina,' said my uncle. 'And finish your dessert.'

I stood forlornly at the end of the table, helpless to replace my underthings. I couldn't bend to reach them.

'I think perhaps the young lady needs her maid,' the captain said, his tone exaggeratedly sympathetic.

I grimaced at him and nodded helplessly to my uncle.

He rang the bell and Polly appeared meekly at the door.

'Polly, please help Miss Angelina,' he said, as though it were the most natural thing in the world for me to be standing in the dining room with my Parisian scanties around my ankles and my ill-treated bottom on display.

I burned with shame as I knew she could see the stripes painted on my skin. But her hands were cool and gentle as she helped me adjust my drawers and smooth down my petticoats. And I was astonished when she offered me a brave little smile. It vexed me. Had I been brought down to her level or had she been raised to mine?

I returned to my place and tried to avoid the men's eyes. I seated myself gingerly, for my bottom was dreadfully sore. Still, I wouldn't give them the pleasure of seeing me wince with the pain. I scowled at my dessert plate and pushed it away pointedly.

'Sir,' the captain said coolly, 'if Miss Angelina is going to sulk, perhaps she should be sent to her room while we discuss her marriage portion.'

I tried hard not to react, though my face fairly blazed with fury. Never would I consent to such a match – never!

But my uncle nodded. 'Very well. Angelina, you may retire. Go to bed and think about your behaviour tonight.'

Both humiliated and relieved, I pushed my chair back and got to my feet. Affecting a conciliatory tone I asked, 'May I take Polly with me? I can't undress without her help.'

'That does look awful sore, miss,' the maid said with genuine sympathy.

I was still surprised at her kindness and I replayed the entire evening in my mind as she unlaced my corset and helped me into my nightgown. I had all but engineered her own whipping. Why did she not hate me? Instead she helped me into my bed with sisterly affection. I winced as I crawled beneath the blankets.

'How ever do you stand it, Polly?'

She shrugged. 'It clears the air, miss. Means I can get on with things without worrying any more. And really, truth be told, miss – when it's over it actually feels rather warm and pleasant.'

'But the shame!'

'It's not so bad really, miss. I mean, there's worse things. Like being hungry and cold and not having nowhere to sleep.'

'There are indeed worse things,' I said bitterly. 'Like Captain Hawksley.'

The maid pursed her lips, a peculiar expression which I marked at once.

'What, Polly?'

She took a breath and looked me right in the eye. 'If you don't mind me saying so, miss, I think perhaps it ain't such a bad match.'

I opened my mouth to curse the villain's name, but stopped myself.

'He's a handsome one,' she continued quickly. 'Young too. Not like them old gentlemen what we had round here last month. And ... he does seem able to ... well, I ain't exactly sure how to say it, miss.'

I finished her thought. 'Handle me.'

Polly blushed and looked away.

I was silent for a long time, considering. My bottom hurt terribly and the indignity had been awful. But now that it was over I did feel calmer. And Polly was right; the sensation now wasn't altogether unpleasant.

'Well, good night, miss,' she said, turning to go.

'Good night, Polly.'

But as she closed the door I called her back. She was at my side in an instant.

'Yes, miss?'

'If my uncle does insist on this marriage,' I said, choosing my words carefully, 'I'll need a ladies' maid. One who ... understands.'

'Certainly, miss!'

Polly beamed and kissed me impulsively on the cheek, a familiarity that might have enraged me before tonight. Now it made me smile.

Old-Fashioned Solutions

Erica stared up at the building, checking the address. Pebbledash post-war houses bracketed the nondescript brick façade, as though vouching for the normality of whatever went on inside. She'd walked past it twice before locating the tiny brass number 17 on the wall, partly obscured by ivy. She glanced at the business card again, worrying it between her fingers.

Modern problems, old-fashioned solutions

Ranks of butter-yellow tulips stood to attention either side of the path leading to the windowless door. Not exactly inviting, but somehow – enticing? Was that the word?

Behaviour modification

Conscience clearing

Below that was an address. No phone number, no website. No clue to what the business was.

A few days ago she'd been flipping desultorily through a rack of business cards at the supermarket. Taking two cards that promised to help consolidate her debts, she'd blinked as the words 'old-fashioned' and 'behaviour' jumped out at her from another card. The cryptic phrases gave her a funny feeling inside. And Erica knew instinctively that this place offered exactly what she needed.

She made her way up the path and stood nervously before the door. There was no bell and the idea of knocking filled her with unease. It seemed too self-assured, too decisive, when she was anything but. Indeed, what was she supposed to say when someone answered?

All her life Erica had been quiet and unassuming. Still single at thirty-five, she had never done anything that could be called adventurous. She lived with four golden retrievers in the seaside cottage where she'd grown up and she made a tidy living designing wedding cakes. But she had one serious vice: eBay.

She spent countless hours online, searching for obscure treasures – antiques, old photographs, vintage clothing. The ease of Internet shopping had been her downfall, catering as it did to impulsive and often reckless behaviour. She'd even found one of the dogs on eBay.

It wasn't just the money she spent, though. Online auctions brought out an aggressive streak in Erica. As soon as she found something she wanted, she considered it hers. She was outraged and affronted if someone dared to bid against her. The anonymity gave her courage she didn't have in the real world. She was a proper keyboard-warrior when she felt wronged, telling off sellers for items that had been poorly packaged or weren't exactly as they'd been described.

Now she stood hesitating on the threshold of a place she thought could help her. She needed more than debt consolidation and financial advice; she needed an incentive to change.

Taking a deep breath, she lifted her hand and rested the knuckles against the door. All she had to do was knock. Surely the people inside would take it from there. Before she could deliberate any longer she rapped the door quickly, a jolt of fear coursing through her as she listened to the hollow echo. She had established her presence, made a statement by her very willingness to come here and investigate.

Several seconds passed as she strained to hear any noise from within. And when she heard the sound of footsteps descending stairs she tensed like an animal ready to flee. The footsteps grew louder as they neared the door and Erica heard the metallic clunk of a lock being undone. She swallowed hard, feeling her face flush with nervous anticipation.

The door swung open to reveal a petite blonde of about twenty, wearing an old-fashioned maid's uniform. She gazed passively at Erica, but didn't speak.

Uncertain what to say, Erica stammered out a greeting. 'Um, hello. My name's Erica Turner. I don't know if I've got the right place, but I think this is your card?' She thrust the scrap of paper at the maid, who peered at it silently, then looked back up at Erica.

'Come in.'

The girl stood aside to let Erica pass. Then she closed and locked the door. Instantly Erica feared the worst. What if this was all a setup by some psychopathic killer to lure victims to his home? Would they find her body the next morning?

'Have a seat. Mr Haversham will be with you shortly.' The maid lowered her head demurely before hurrying back upstairs.

A row of hard wooden chairs stood against the wall and Erica sat warily, glancing at her surroundings. On the wall opposite was a framed Victorian drawing of a portly man in an academic gown brandishing some kind of broom. And on the adjoining wall she saw a pair of illustrations of an old schoolroom, its oak beams and panelling carved with hundreds of sets of initials. Peculiar. But then, it probably wasn't any odder than the eclectic stuff she crammed her own house with.

She listened to the steady ticking of the grandfather clock at the end of the austere hall while she waited, growing more and more uncertain. She hadn't brought anything to read and time slowed down without distraction. She couldn't help but think of the two auctions ending today – one for an antique gramophone in perfect working order (so the seller claimed) and the other for a seventeenth-century map of Cornwall.

From somewhere in the house a cat meowed and Erica thought of her dogs waiting for her back at home. She glanced at the clock, wondering how long the meeting here would take. She'd received an order for a wedding cake that morning from a very fussy university student who wanted every flower known to man. It would be easy enough to find a book on exotic flowers online; learning to sculpt them in icing would be trickier. But perhaps . . .

The cat yowled again, this time sounding oddly human. As she listened, Erica heard a swishing sound and then another cry. It was no cat.

Both puzzled and intrigued, she rose to her feet and crept to the base of the stairs, listening. Another swish, another yelp. Erica jumped, wrapping her arms around herself, startled by the heat she suddenly felt between her legs. A sharp, precise heat. It was the same response she'd experienced during certain scenes in films or books. The same response as when she'd first found the card. A strange erotic frisson. Old-fashioned solutions.

Embarrassed, she pressed her legs together and listened as there were three more pairs of sounds. Then silence. She waited, heart racing.

It wasn't long before the little maid appeared again, hurrying halfway down the stairs and stopping. 'Miss Turner? You can come up now.' The girl's face was flushed and her voice was subdued as she beckoned with one pale arm, like a ghost in an M R James story.

Was that a sniffle Erica had heard? And had the girl wiped her eyes as she turned to lead the way? Erica's knees trembled as she ascended the stairs and she felt as though she were stepping into a different world. A world where things were simpler and actions earned very real consequences.

The maid stood to one side at the top of the stairs, her head down. Strands of blonde hair had come loose from her cap and her eyes were distinctly red. Erica opened her mouth to say something, but closed it again when she could think of nothing appropriate to say.

'It's the last door on the left,' the maid said softly.

'Thank you,' Erica whispered. She made her way down a narrow corridor lined with more framed drawings. Late afternoon shadows hid the images from her, but she was too nervous to pay them much attention.

She stopped before the door and looked back the way

she had come. The maid was gone. Erica gathered her courage again and knocked.

A deep male voice from within said 'Come in.'

Erica took a deep breath and entered. The room was sparsely furnished and lined with bookshelves. Two straight-backed wooden chairs stood opposite a large oak desk. There was something clerical in its austerity, something innately authoritarian in the design. Like the building's exterior; everything here served a purpose. It wasn't meant to be pretty.

A man in his late fifties rose from the desk and extended his hand. 'Ah, Miss Turner. I'm Mr Haversham.'

Erica stepped forward, feeling like a schoolgirl running into her headmaster out of school hours. 'Yes,' she said, flustered. 'I mean, yes I am.' She shook his hand limply and was about to add 'nice to meet you', but she stopped herself. If she started babbling banal pleasantries she'd never shut up.

'Please sit,' he said, smiling with his voice if not his face. It was a nice face – serious and even somewhat brooding, but with soft grey eyes that reassured her. He looked like someone she could confide in. More than that – he looked like someone who could solve her problems.

She manoeuvred herself into one of the chairs, grateful not to have to stand on her wobbly legs any longer. 'Thank you.'

Mr Haversham resumed his seat and steepled his fingers beneath his chin, regarding her solemnly. 'Tell me what brings you here today.'

She produced the card again, hoping it would answer for her. But Mr Haversham didn't respond.

Erica laughed nervously. 'I suppose I have a problem. And I thought maybe you could help me.'

'You *suppose* you have a problem. *Maybe*. Well, Miss Turner? Do you have a problem or not?'

Abashed, Erica twisted the card in her hands and looked down at the floor. 'Yes,' she murmured, then added with more conviction, 'I have a problem.'

He raised his eyebrows expectantly and she soldiered on.

'I think I have a compulsion, Mr Haversham. No, I *know* I do. For buying things. Online. Both my credit cards are maxed out, but I can't stop. I was looking for help with debts when I found your card.'

'So your problem is one of impulse control.'

'Yes. But . . .'

She hesitated, toying with the art deco pendant she'd won last weekend. She'd had a mighty row with the seller over how much it was reasonable to charge for shipping from the States for such a small item. eBay had deleted her negative feedback and cautioned her to try and resolve future disputes without resorting to abuse.

'I can sometimes be a little unpleasant online,' she finally said, shamed by the admission, softened though it was.

'I see. You say things in email that you'd never say in person, is that it?'

'I know it's pathetic, but –'

'And at present it would seem that your actions carry no consequences, is that right?'

'Yes.'

'Very well, then. If you are sincere in your desire to change and if you agree to obey my instructions, I will help you.'

Erica's heart fluttered as she nodded agreement.

'I didn't hear you, Miss Turner.' His tone was more commanding now, his gaze sterner.

She swallowed. 'Yes. I'll do whatever you say.' Even as she agreed, she recalled the sounds she had heard before. The maid's teary face.

Mr Haversham opened a desk drawer and took out a form. 'Sign here, please.' He tapped the end of a line of type with his pen and passed both to Erica. She glanced at the wording, but it was as vague as the business card. And nowhere was there any mention of the cost.

'I'm confused,' she said. 'How much do I owe you?'

He smiled. 'Oh, we don't charge for our services. You repay us simply by responding to our methods.'

Methods. Her stomach clenched. Methods like she'd overheard?

'It's quite safe, I assure you, Miss Turner.'

If she didn't have to pay anything, surely there was nothing to lose. Besides, she trusted Mr Haversham. He seemed to have total confidence that he could help her. She did want help. And if that help involved a little discomfort . . . Well, perhaps it wasn't so different from a visit to the dentist.

Before her anxiety could influence her decision, she scrawled her name at the bottom of the form and handed it back. He tucked it into a file and recapped his pen neatly.

'Stand up.'

Erica got shakily to her feet, her clammy fingers still clutching the little card as though it were the only thing tying her to reality. He took it from her gently and placed it on the corner of the desk.

'From this moment on you will address me as "sir". Is that clear?'

Blushing, Erica lowered her head. 'Yes, sir,' she said softly.

Mr Haversham removed his jacket and arranged it neatly on the back of his chair. He came around the front of the desk and began rolling up his right sleeve with businesslike efficiency.

'You lack discipline, Miss Turner, because you have no incentive to control your impulses. The credit card company isn't going to call you to account; they're happy to let you run up more than you can pay because you wind up paying them more in the end. Correct?'

'Yes,' she admitted.

'Yes what?'

She blushed deeply, her scalp tingling. 'Yes, sir.'

'Your online aggression is merely another example of your lack of control. You'd never behave that way face to face but in email there are no consequences. What you need is someone to account to for your bad behaviour. Someone who will address your lapses in judgment and provide you with a deterrent. In short, what you need is punishment.'

Erica's pulse quickened and her face felt hot and feverish. She had to look away. Her eyes drifted to a picture on the wall – an image she remembered from a visit to the Museum of Eton Life years ago: the birching block.

Mr Haversham seated himself in the chair Erica had just vacated. He eyed her severely. 'For some clients, one punishment is enough. In your case, however, I anticipate many such meetings. Now you're going to place yourself over my knee for a sound spanking.' He patted his thigh.

Erica felt limp on hearing the words. She stood frozen, staring at his lap. She couldn't do it, couldn't surrender her dignity like this. She closed her eyes and imagined him yanking her across his knee like a naughty child. But when she dared to look at his face again she saw that he had no intention of making it easy for her. He simply waited for her to comply.

His patient expression rendered her incapable of dis-obedience. With a soft moan she leaned forward and lowered herself awkwardly into position, placing her hands on the floor in front of her. She didn't question what she was doing; she merely obeyed. Both terrified and exhilarated, she lay draped across a stranger's lap, awaiting a childish punishment. She whimpered as he lifted her skirt. The cool air caressed her bare legs and she suddenly regretted the flirty silk knickers she'd worn. A minor extravagance, they retailed for £200. She'd got them for a quarter that. Would they still seem like a bargain when this was over?

Mr Haversham didn't linger over the fancy apricot silk. He slipped his fingers into the waistband and peeled them down to her knees without ceremony.

Erica gasped with shame and apprehension. What had she let herself in for? She'd seen the way the maid had behaved, heard the birching. What was *her* crime?

Her musing ended with the first sharp swat to her naked bottom. The rosy heat swelled and she wriggled over his knees. Another swat followed quickly to the other cheek and she uttered a little squeak of pain, determined not to humiliate herself further by making a howling spectacle of herself.

But the smacks grew harder and harder, gradually covering the whole of her bottom with a stinging warmth and she couldn't keep quiet any more. In no time she was yelping properly.

Mr Haversham paused and Erica squeezed her eyes tightly shut. The silence reinforced her indignity, reminding her that she lay willingly across this man's lap, paying the price for her lack of discipline. It was an admission of failure. She had failed to act like a grown-up, so she was reduced to being treated like a child. No, worse: she had reduced *herself* to this.

She moaned plaintively – anything to fill the hideous silence. Anything to distract her from the reality of her situation. Anything to take away the responsibility for the position she was in now.

'I've barely started,' Mr Haversham said. 'You've a long way to go before this has any effect.'

He resumed the spanking, peppering her bottom with even harder smacks that made her kick and struggle. She howled as the intensity increased, twisting and writhing as though she could escape. Without breaking his rhythm, he clamped her in place around the waist, pinning her down. Again and again his unrelenting palm met the soft and burning flesh of her bottom.

'Oh, it hurts!' she cried. 'Please, I can't take it!'

'Of course it hurts,' he said coolly, as though he'd said it a hundred times before. 'Make no mistake: you're being *punished*. And I intend to make a thorough job of it. You won't learn a thing otherwise.'

Erica cried out, wild pitiful sounds that earned her no sympathy from this implacable man. Any erotic frisson she'd felt before was long gone. She would never come back, never submit to this again! The pain was monstrous. She hated herself for giving him the pleasure of seeing how much it hurt her, but she'd show him. As soon as she got home she would find something exotic on eBay to soothe away the pain and humiliation.

Even as she entertained the petulant thought she knew she was only reinforcing his position. Online she would have called him a brute and a bully, cursed him for the degradation he'd inflicted on her. Except she couldn't hide behind her computer here. And he *hadn't* forced her; she'd come here on her own and asked for his help. She'd agreed to this. She had no one to blame but herself.

She did need help. She did need someone to address her wrongs. She did need consequences for her actions. It was a hard, cold truth to face, but as her resentful stubbornness crumbled, so did her composure. Her eyes burned and soon her face was streaming with cathartic tears.

Mr Haversham ignored her strangled sobs, delivering several more hard slaps to her burning cheeks before finally stopping. She lay crying over his lap for a long time, too ashamed to get up, not wanting to meet his eyes.

'There, there,' said Mr Haversham. 'It's all over now.'

He stroked her back as she wept and when her tears at last subsided, he helped her to her feet. She stumbled unsteadily, as though drunk.

He pressed a tissue into her hands. 'Brave girl,' he said with something like affection.

Without thinking, she mumbled 'Thank you, sir' as she mopped the tears from her face and blew her nose. When she had calmed herself she reached down to touch the flaming skin of her bottom, wincing at the pain.

She twisted round to look. Her cheeks were bright red and speckled with tiny purple bruises. She wondered if the maid had similar bruises. The silk knickers were cool against her warm flesh and she smoothed her skirt down over her throbbing bottom.

'Well, Miss Turner,' said Mr Haversham, resuming his businesslike demeanour. 'I think that was most effective.'

Erica blushed and nodded her head. 'Yes, sir. I've learned my lesson.'

'You realise that a second visit will be more severe. Next time it will be a birching.'

She felt the soft warm flash between her legs again. She plucked the business card off the desk, tucking it into her bag. She felt weightless. As though her feet didn't quite reach the floor. 'Can I ask you a question, sir?'

'Certainly.'

'The maid. Is she a client too?'

The corners of his eyes crinkled, hinting at a smile, as he opened the door for her. 'Good day, Miss Turner. I hope I won't be seeing you again for a while.'

CONGRATULATIONS! The item is yours!

Erica beamed with delight, then followed the link to PayPal. She hesitated only momentarily before clicking the button that would remove £357.82 from her account, putting her considerably in the red. But she couldn't live without the three-tail Lochgelly tawse. It was a bargain too. The three-tailed ones were rare, and often sold for much more than that.

As Erica printed out the receipt, her eyes flicked to the business card propped against her computer.

Modern problems, old-fashioned solutions

She wondered if the utility of her latest extravagance would placate Mr Haversham. Perhaps this time he wouldn't birch her after all.

The Decoy

I have the coolest job in the world. It consists solely of getting chased by paparazzi and deranged fans. I get to ride in limos and blow kisses from the balconies of fancy hotels. Queen for a day. And all because I look like . . . well, I can't really tell you. But you know her. You've heard her songs, seen her music videos. She's a megastar. And – lucky me – I could be her twin.

Her handlers spotted me at a club one night (mistook me for her, as a matter of fact) and offered me the job on the spot. All I had to do was pretend to be her, to lure the press and public away while she made her escape. Me – in oversized sunglasses, hurrying past with a tiny wave at the adoring masses. It's the easiest money I've ever made. And that includes the fiver my cousin Dave gave me when I was ten to watch me pee.

You know those 'What were they thinking?' pics you see in the gossip rags? The ones of celebrities in bulky tracksuits and mismatched socks, with snide captions like 'Laundry Day'? The fashion Nazis take everything so seriously. Well, it's not just a disguise; it's a piss-take. Some stars enjoy the charade. They're like urban guerrillas, camouflaged in drab discount clothes no one would ever expect them to wear. That way they can move undetected amongst the masses.

Except some people are too blinded by their own brilliance to laugh at themselves. You see, I get to wear the fancy stuff while Boss Lady wears the crocheted jumpers and clumpy boots. And oh, does she hate it!

I'll be honest: she's not exactly Little Miss Sunshine. I don't hang out with her or anything. I'm not even part of her entourage; I'm just an employee. And our encounters tend to be, shall we say, a bit frosty. She resents me in a big way.

But hey, I'm not complaining. It's money for nothing. Though I swear if I have to endure another one of Miss Snot's sulks because some fashionista hinted at an eating disorder ...

I'm not on call 24/7 and she does get snapped plenty herself. You've seen the screaming headlines about how she was a size 8 last week and suddenly now she's a size 10? That's because the paparazzi can't tell us apart. I'm sure as hell not eating leaves and berries just to make *her* look good; I like my curves.

I was listening at the door one night as she harangued Alex – that's her manager – about why I seemed intent on humiliating her. When they photograph *me*, they accuse *her* of putting on weight. When they shoot *her*, she's anorexic. It's actually pretty funny.

I was just stifling a laugh when I caught the phrase 'her fat arse' and nearly broke down the door.

Then I got hold of myself. No, Kelly, be nice to the poor little prima donna. You have no idea how hard it is to be her. The pressure of being admired and desired all the time, the pressure to be perfect. Everything open to exposure and ridicule. If every one of her personal demons manifested itself, you could populate a small country.

I'm a year younger (and I have better hair), but I'm more grown up than she is. I guess the fame and glory insulates you from reality, makes you forget what it's like to be human. Hell, having seen what the tabloids do to her love life, I wouldn't want to be in her overpriced shoes. Well, except when it's to make those glamorous little scampers between hotels and limos.

Things, however, were about to change. Big time. It may have been her money that paid my salary and kept me well fed and clothed, but I didn't sign on for her abuse. Without me running interference for her, she'd have had to face the explosions of flash cameras every single time she set foot outside. Even when she didn't feel like it. Let's face it – she's just another overrated performer with a smidgen of talent and an ego the size of space. (And about as much between the ears.) I was sick of feeling unappreciated.

So I stole her boyfriend.

You know him too. He's the not-quite-cutest one in an equally famous boy band whose songs are like bubblegum on steroids. He's also the only one in the band with any brains. He and Miss Shit-Don't-Stink had just had a massive row because she'd actually suggested hiring his band as a support act for her. I know – can you believe the cheek of the girl?

He stormed into the hotel bar and sat fuming in a corner, drinking pint after pint to anaesthetise his bruised ego. I watched until he had cooled off a bit before going over to say hi.

'Hey, Will.'

'Kelly,' he drawled, waving at the nearest chair. 'Sit down. I'll buy you a drink.'

I ordered a Kir Royal. No use skimping when a pop star's paying.

Boy-toy stared glumly at the tabletop, then examined his fingernails for several minutes while I waited for him to say something.

'Bitch,' he muttered at last.

I hid my catty grin behind my glass.

'I guess you know about the fight,' he said, turning his earnest puppy-dog eyes to me. 'The support act thing?'

'Yeah. I know. She's not exactly renowned for her humble spirit.'

He snorted in agreement and drained the rest of his pint before signalling to the bartender. He stirred his finger in the air over our empty glasses and gave me an unsubtle appraising glance.

I affected a feline stretch and shifted my chair a little closer to his. Boys are so easy.

By the time we'd finished another two rounds, my feet were in his lap and he was giving me dirt a reporter would have sold his soul for. Her collagen injections. Her rehab last year. (Even I hadn't known about that!) The tantrum she'd thrown at the studio during her *Cosmo* cover shoot because she didn't like what the make-up artist had done with her hair.

'The photographer actually called her a spoilt brat,' Will laughed, relishing the memory, 'and said if she was his daughter he'd put her over his knee and warm her overpaid little bottom.'

I wept with laughter at the image of the little diva, her legs kicking madly as the photographer's hand came down again and again on her scrawny little arse.

Will was stroking my insteps with casual affection, his long guitar-player nails strumming the straps of my sandals in time to the Bowie song playing in the bar. A wistful expression crossed his face and I waited for the I-coulda-been-a-serious-musician speech. Instead, he unlaced my sandals and caressed my bare feet, his insinuating fingers making me gasp with pleasure. I writhed under his touch, feeling the unmistakable hardness of his own arousal beneath my thighs.

He looked at me with an expression of frank longing, his shaggy black hair falling over one eye. A little pulse of heat flared between my legs and I closed my eyes to encourage him. His hands crept up the length of my calf, hesitating at the hem of my tight denim skirt. I bit my lip as he worked his hand up under the skirt, along my inner thigh and, finally, to the hot moist place at the top.

His knuckles slid over the gusset of my knickers and I gave a little cry of surprise. Encouraged, his skilled hand cupped my sex, exerting gentle pressure in just the right place. *Too* gentle. With real hunger I thrust myself against his hand, grinding my crotch into the stimulation.

His left hand made its way up under my T-shirt and pushed my flimsy bra up and out of the way. He tweaked my nipples roughly, making me whimper with both pain and pleasure. I spread my legs as wide as I could on his lap, darting one quick glance at our surroundings. We were alone.

I bit my lip as his fingers slipped inside my knickers, finding their way to the slippery crease and stroking my clit with agonising precision. All the while he continued to play with my nipples, squeezing, stroking, pinching. I clutched the seat of my chair, arching my body up to meet his touch. It had been months; it didn't take long.

Electric spasms flashed through my nerves as I writhed shamelessly against him, throwing my head back with a silent scream as the climax overtook me.

I lay sprawled, panting like a well-used whore, my body vibrating and hungry for more.

You have to give those stealth photographers credit; Will and I never saw or heard a thing. But there we were on the front page the next morning. Two pop celebrities overcome with lust in a hotel bar.

The diva went postal, knocking over a wire rack of newspapers at a street kiosk and injuring a little girl who was waiting for an autograph. More headlines.

'That's not me!' she'd screamed on seeing the photos of Will and her hated decoy. The paparazzi gleefully snapped away at what they'd describe as a full-on psychotic fugue the next day. Spectacular.

I roll my eyes at the sound of breaking glass, the familiar whine of her drama-queen voice as she plays the martyr. Alex trying to calm her down. Will banished from her life. Come on, it's not like she's never cheated on *him* before.

I can't help but laugh. Always practical, Alex tries to convince her that a break-up would be very bad for publicity right now, given her front page freak-out and the injured fan. Even the payoff to the girl's parents couldn't remove the stain. She's the talk of the town – in the worst possible way. Alex tells her it's time to be a big girl and repair the damage. He reminds her about the photo spread she and Will are scheduled to do for *Rolling Stone* in two weeks, publicity for the film they're shooting at Christmas.

'I don't care!' the diva wails. 'I never want to see him again!'

There's a weighty pause before Alex says, 'Then let Kelly play the girlfriend in public until you get over it.'

I nearly choke. I can just imagine the icy glare she must be giving him as she seethes at this suggestion. And I can hear her thoughts as though she's speaking them aloud. If she appears in public with Will she'll never be able to pretend to be the starry-eyed lover. Yet how can she possibly let *me* be photographed on his arm? Which one of us does she hate more?

Another bout of sobbing, but nothing else coherent. I go back to my room. Will is still in bed, lolling in the sweaty tangle of sheets. We've been learning a lot about each other since our indiscretion in the bar. He's a far more adventurous lover than anyone would guess from the cheesy music his band puts out. And who'd ever have guessed he was into such kinky stuff?

An hour later Alex phones, interrupting us. While I try to focus on what he's saying, Will teases my legs apart with a riding crop. I arch my back with a little gasp as he taps my clit with the leather tip.

The news is like early Christmas. The prima donna is going to a glamorous Swiss retreat for two weeks. To 'recuperate'. While she's away, Will and I have to repair her image.

'Repair her image,' I repeat for Will, covering the mouthpiece to hide my laughter. He grins.

To Alex I say, 'Of course we will.'

This is my chance – *our* chance – to pay her back good and proper. And I can tell from the way Will thumbs my clit like the safety of a gun that he's thinking the exact same thing.

In public we're the beautiful couple, oversexed and unable to keep our hands off each other. The press eat it up, shooting us with merry abandon everywhere we go and framing us with gleeful headlines. NYMPHOMANIAC! they cry, ever eager to rip the diva to shreds.

In private we're a far more interesting story – the one no one gets to read. We laugh about how 'good for me' the press think he is, as he handcuffs me to the bed and slowly unbuckles his belt. I hiss with pain as he tugs ruthlessly on the chain connecting my nipple clamps. And I scream with pleasure as his tireless cock fills me again and again and again.

We're both aware of a distinct chill coming from the direction of Switzerland.

'Look!' I grab Will's hand, dragging him towards the display window of a designer boutique. Insectoid mannequins pose for us in unlikely contortions, draped in overpriced clothes.

'No,' Will says firmly, steering me away.

'But I want the pink skirt,' I whine.

He pulls me into a fierce kiss, as though trying to distract me from my need for retail therapy.

I smile sappily when he pulls away, pretending not to notice the photographer with the telephoto lens in the taxi up ahead. OFF DUTY, the sign says.

Will and I stroll on, past a handful of other pricey shops.

'Shoes!' I shriek suddenly, charging another window. This one features a display of those witchy pointy-toed jobs everyone's wearing these days.

Will holds me back. 'No,' he says even more firmly. His bedroom voice.

'I *have* to have those!' I insist with all the conviction of a dictator declaring war.

'You have enough shoes.'

'There's no such thing as enough shoes!' I stamp my foot for emphasis. The ones of hers I'm wearing now cost more than my sister's wedding.

He says something about kids in Cambodian sweatshops and I simply wail that I don't care. 'I want those shoooes!'

'That guy at *Cosmo* was right,' Will says darkly, loudly. 'You're nothing but a spoilt brat.'

My eyes flash as I whirl to confront him, hands on hips. 'How dare you!'

I swear I can hear cameras clicking from every corner of the street – from behind parked cars and lampposts and newspapers.

'A spoilt little brat who desperately needs taking down a peg.' He looks me up and down, considering. 'I think a good hard spanking would do you a world of good.'

I gape at him, my skin prickling with wild exhilaration. Several people have stopped to stare at us. Most know who we are too, though they wouldn't dream of approaching us to ask for autographs just now.

Will takes a step towards me and I glare at him. 'If you so much as fucking *touch* me . . .'

'And such language,' he scolds. 'Would you like your mouth washed out with soap as well?'

In one fluid movement he seizes my wrist and drags me to the off-duty taxi. He leans back against the bonnet and hauls me across his lap.

'What you deserve – and what you're going to get – is a hard bare-bottom spanking.'

I howl with outrage as he yanks up my skirt. My right hand flails impotently behind me, as though trying to preserve my modesty. He catches it easily, pinning it in the small of my back. My tarty little red thong offers me no protection as he brings his hand down on my cheeks with a ringing slap.

I cry out wildly, kicking my feet as a second slap connects with my other cheek. One expensive shoe goes flying and out of the corner of my eye I see someone grab it. Celebrity souvenir.

'This is long overdue,' Will says sternly, increasing the tempo as he rains heavy smacks down onto my defenceless bottom.

A crowd has gathered and – surprise, surprise – not a single person tries to stop him. My face blazes with embarrassment at the appreciative murmur from an elderly lady somewhere behind me.

'About time, too,' another lady chimes in. 'That little girl needed stitches, you know.'

A man with a Yorkshire accent declares, 'Aye, it's all that money. Goes to their heads, it does. Makes 'em think they're better than t' rest of us.'

'Always thought her songs were crap anyway.'

'Not so glamorous now, is she?'

Their approval almost makes me forget the pain. But Will lays it on smartly and I kick my feet in desperation, yelping pitifully as he paints my bottom with scorching handprints.

I can't disagree with a single word they're saying and the humiliation is almost worse than the pain. I'm dying to tell them it's not really me, that I'm not really *her*.

Will has a heavy hand and normally I enjoy being over his knee. But today isn't about pleasure; today is about payback. I'm willing to suffer any amount of shame or pain for my revenge.

'Please – please – please,' I babble, writhing under the merciless barrage of smacks. I can almost see my flesh turning from ivory to pink to bright red.

'No,' he says curtly, his fingers curling into the crease below my cheeks as he aims lower. 'I'm not going to stop until you're sorry for being such an insufferable little madam.'

I squirm at his authoritarian tone, my sex moistening in spite of the pain.

'OK, I'm sorry!'

Will ignores my insincere apology, his palm striking me even harder and eliciting wilder cries and yelps. The other shoe goes flying. On my right I see a teenager filming us with his mobile phone. We'll be on YouTube within the hour.

I squeal in delirious pain and humiliation as Will spanks me for the delectation of the whole world. Literally. It's agony – far beyond the naughty pleasure he usually gives me. But I'm doing my job and so is he. Repairing her image, just like we said. The tabloids will forgive her all her sins by the time Will's finished with me. Though I have a hard time imagining she'll be remotely grateful.

It's an eternity before I finally surrender and begin to cry. Now my pleas are genuine and no one could mistake the true contrition in my voice.

'I'm really sorry,' I blubber, 'really – I mean it, I swear!'

Will rests his hand on my flaming backside, giving each cheek a cruel squeeze. 'Are you going to be a good girl?'

'Yes,' I sniffle.

'Have you learnt your lesson?'

'Yes.'

'Going to behave yourself from now on? No more tantrums? No more bad behaviour?'

His words are making me melt and I hope my shameless arousal isn't obvious to anyone else. 'No,' I promise meekly. 'Please . . .'

'The next time you act like a spoilt little girl, you'll be treated like a spoilt little girl. I don't care if we're on stage performing for the Queen. I will turn you over my knee then and there and smack your naughty little bottom until you can't sit down. Do you understand?'

The colour of my face must match the colour of my bottom. 'Yes,' I moan.

He lets me up and I throw my arms around him, my back hitching with huge dramatic sobs as I apologise for being such a bitch. I press myself against his erection, clutching my burning posterior as the crowd begins to shuffle away. The show's over. For them anyway. Will and I are just getting started.

Didn't I say I had the coolest job in the world?

Six of the Best

'Yes *what?*'

We all have our trigger words and hot buttons. Our little turn-ons. I think for me the seed was planted at the age of sixteen by Mr Sheridan, my eleventh grade English teacher. He was the only Brit in my Boston high school and he was accustomed to more discipline than American students are used to. He had the most exacting standards and was merciless with his grades. Everyone hated him.

He was old-fashioned and out of place. But he was also young and devastatingly cute. It was his first year of teaching in the States. We all thought he'd have to learn to lighten up to survive, but he never showed any sign of wavering.

He delighted in telling us about the superior disciplinary regime in English schools of the past. Uniforms and six of the best. A good dose of the cane, he claimed, would cure us all of our incorrigible behaviour. As if.

They used the paddle in American schools, but Mr Sheridan would never have deigned to touch it. Instead he tortured us with diabolical assignments in detention, like copying out entire pages of the OED or writing interminable lines.

I am the quintessential product of the American school system. I never had to wear a uniform. I had no clue how to tie a tie. With the exception of Mr Sheridan, I never called my teachers 'sir' or 'miss'. The very idea would have been archaic and offensive. I wore whatever I wanted, usually something carefully devised to shock, alienate and offend parents and teachers alike. I was used to doing my own thing, making my own rules and pretty much running the show.

But one day Mr Sheridan kept me after class, just the two of us, to accuse me of handing in work that was 'beneath my abilities'. Beneath my priorities, maybe; I had more important things going on in my teenage life. I told him so.

He shook his head and called me a spoiled ex-colonial. His favourite term. Well, I just couldn't keep my big mouth shut. Americans hate formality. We hate titles and class consciousness and etiquette and all the pretension that has made English culture the butt of so many jokes. We don't like being told what to do. Hence the American Revolution. I told him that too. Then I told him where he could stick his split infinitives.

It was my first real act of teen rebellion and it felt so good I didn't want the moment to end. I was terrified and I knew I'd regret it, but for those few exhilarating seconds I was the leader of my own little revolution. It felt *so* good.

Mr Sheridan was unperturbed, and my elation didn't last long. I remember the dressing-down that followed like it was yesterday.

'You have a good deal to learn about respect, young lady,' he said in his clipped British accent. 'And your attitude needs smartening up.'

I lifted my chin, trying not to let my fear show.

He narrowed his eyes, meeting my stubborn glare. And when he spoke his voice was low and chillingly calm. 'What you deserve, Jenny, is a caning. Six parallel lines. Right where you sit. It would be a lesson you'd never forget.'

His words conjured up images in my mind, memories of films I'd seen and stories I'd read. Images of strict English schoolmasters brandishing swishy canes and terrified schoolboys touching their toes. Was that how it really was? Were English girls subjected to the same treatment?

I just stood there, blinking. My courage had evaporated.

81

He looked so serious, so resolute, that when he turned and opened his desk drawer I flinched, expecting him to take out the cane. No doubt that was exactly what he wanted me to think because the corners of his mouth turned up slightly.

But all he took out was a form and he sat down at the desk to fill it out. Detention every afternoon for a week. I groaned.

He handed me the slip of paper and his expression was unreadable. 'I have high standards for you,' he said. 'And I expect you to live up to your potential.'

'Uh-huh,' I mumbled, still a little startled. 'I mean yes.'

'Yes *what*?'

'Yes, sir.'

My first revolutionary act. And over so soon.

I spent my week of detention writing lines: *I will learn to apply myself and live up to my potential. I will not submit work that is beneath my abilities.* Five hundred times. And each time I paused to shake the cramps out of my hand I stole a glance at Mr Sheridan. I couldn't get his words out of my head. *Six parallel lines. Right where you sit.* And I couldn't keep from wondering . . .

Five years later, a strange twist of fate led me across the Atlantic, to take the third year of my literature degree at the University of Durham. It was like something straight out of the period novels I loved. The dark majestic cathedral was breathtaking. Ominously beautiful, with the kind of ancient formality you never find in the States. But the university had a musty intimidating air that made me feel like an impostor. A slacker among the scholars. I didn't quite fit in.

Oh, I was diligent at first, but it wasn't long before my old habits began to return. I was bored. Restless. Craving adventure. Besides, once the initial charm wore off, I was finding England cold and dismal. It got dark obscenely early and it never seemed to stop raining.

My love life was just as dismal and after one particularly catastrophic date, I just couldn't face doing any work. So

I skipped my first tutorial in Victorian literature, only to discover afterwards that the tutor had assigned an essay. It was the next week before I found out about it. That meant I had to go see him with some excuse for not being there. I wasn't looking forward to that, but I noted with a chuckle that his name was Sheridan as I read the timetable to find his office room number.

It was early and the halls were deserted, making my footsteps echo unpleasantly. It was as though the university itself was scolding me for my indolence.

When I reached his office I knocked and a voice told me to enter. After I closed the door behind me, I turned back to face him and froze. It was my old tormentor!

The years had distinguished him. He sat behind the desk, a darkly handsome older man with a somewhat gloomy countenance, like Jeremy Irons. He was also wearing glasses, something I've always found appealing.

I must have been gaping because he raised his eyebrows and asked me if something was wrong.

'Oh,' I began, not sure what to say. I stood there stupidly for a small eternity, but he made no attempt to help me. When the awkwardness became too much I finally blurted out, 'Do you remember me?'

He just peered at me over the rims of his glasses, inscrutable. 'Should I?'

I giggled like the nervous schoolgirl I'd reverted to. Of course he wouldn't remember me. He had only aged a few years; I had grown up.

'It's Jenny,' I said with a flirtatious smile.

But whatever he'd been doing since I last saw him hadn't shaken his imperturbable nature. I had thought to embarrass him and make him feel uncomfortable for forgetting someone he ought to know.

My smile faded. 'Jenny Adams?'

Still no reaction.

Then he glanced down at a sheet of paper on his vast expanse of a desk. 'Ah, yes,' he said at last, apparently finding my name there. 'You were absent from your first tutorial.'

He hadn't placed me at all.

'I assume you've come to ask me for an extension on the essay, but if you can't be bothered to come to tutorials, I'm afraid I don't grant extensions. Now, if you'll excuse me . . .'

I stood there, stunned. Here I was, taking the trouble to come to him so I could do what he'd told me I should do all those years ago – apply myself. Hell, he'd made me promise five hundred times that I would – in writing. I was offended.

'No,' I said.

He looked up. 'I beg your pardon?'

'No, I won't excuse you.' I crossed my arms over my chest, appalled at his arrogance. 'I may be a spoiled ex-colonial, but I'm not the only one whose attitude needs "smartening up".'

There was a flicker of curiosity, then of recognition. He peered at me as though through a microscope. At last he smiled.

'Little Jenny Adams,' he said, leaning back in his chair. 'Yes, I remember you now.'

He laughed and got up, shaking off his Professor Snape persona. To my surprise, he hugged me instead of shaking my hand and a little thrill ran through my limbs as I recalled all the times I'd heard his voice inside my head and fantasised about even more intimate contact with him.

The years had been kind to him and I instantly felt my body responding the way it always did to attractive guys. I wanted him: I was lonely, bored, depressed, frustrated and starved for attention. England wasn't the paradise I'd envisioned. University was harder than I'd expected. And the solitude I thought would be freedom was merely isolation. Here was my fantasy come to life. It was not an opportunity I would let slip away.

I held him as tightly as I dared, not wanting to be too subtle. The English boys I'd dated were so different from Americans. They were slow to warm up and I had been frustrated more than once by their inability to pick up my hints. Then again, maybe they were just being 'gentleman-ly'. Brits could be so charmingly clueless.

But Mr Sheridan wasn't clueless. He had no trouble reading my body language, as he returned my tighter embrace.

I closed my eyes and pictured him pushing me down on his desk, reaching under my skirt and ripping my panties away. Pinning me down with one arm while he wrestled himself free of his trousers and penetrated me, rough and nasty, telling me what a dirty little girl I was. I melted under the image.

I had never actually seduced a teacher before, though I'd certainly fantasised about it. Here was the classic scenario right in front of me. The cheesiest cliché. *Please, Professor, I'll do absolutely* anything *for that A!* I giggled again, relishing my teen memories.

'About this essay,' I purred, classic coquette. I pressed my pelvis into his, rotating my hips ever so gently.

He pushed me out at arm's length. 'You *are* incorrigible,' he said, but he was laughing.

'You had your chance to fix that,' I reminded him. 'Now it's too late.'

A serious look crossed his features. 'Oh?'

'Perhaps we can work something out,' I said.

There was a gleam in his eyes, sinister and sexy all at once. 'Perhaps we can.'

I was ready to strip off then and there. I had never wanted a man so much.

But instead he calmly looked at his watch. 'Come back tonight,' he said, shocking me into silence. 'At seven.'

I must have looked stung or spurned because he gave me a reassuring pat on the backside.

'Now, now, none of that, my girl.' His tone was affectionately patronising. 'You suggested "working something out" and that's exactly what we're going to do. But you're not going to get out of doing your assignment, you know.'

I closed my eyes and his words took me right back. It was the old Mr Sheridan speaking to me now, the English disciplinarian who had so terrorised us at school. I felt my crotch begin to pulse, practically screaming for him to touch me.

'Do you remember what my detentions were like?'

Did I ever. 'Yes.'

'Yes *what*?'

I thought I would wet my panties. It had been five years since I last said that word and this was the man I last said it to. It came back to me like a forgotten foreign tongue, making my legs feel like rubber. 'Yes, sir.'

'I told you once that you were squandering your potential, that an English school would get more effort from you than you gave in America.'

I remembered that tone well. I used to imagine him kidnapping me and spiriting me away to England, imprisoning me in some gloomy manor and giving me private lessons like Eliza Doolittle.

'I still think you would benefit from some traditional English discipline. If you accept it, you will be allowed to submit your essay. But you're free to decline. The choice is yours.'

My face was scarlet and I couldn't look him in the eye. I stared at the floor, squeezing my legs together. I could never resist a challenge, but this was beyond any I'd ever been given. He was going to cane me. I knew it. After all the years of wondering and fantasising, it was actually going to happen. And my pride wouldn't let me back out. I'd show this Brit what American girls were made of.

I raised my head and it took everything I had to keep my voice steady. 'I'll be here.'

The smile that spread across his face was slow and deliberate. Like the almost sensual way a snake has of coiling around its prey. 'Good. Then let me tell you what will happen. We will structure this as the punishment detention you deserved all those years ago. I'm sure you can find something suitable to wear as a school uniform. And I think the orthodox "six of the best" should make a salutary impression on you.'

This wasn't going to be easy. I'd thought all I had to do was come on to him and he'd fall prey to my feminine charms. He'd screw me and I'd get my way. But no, this promised to transcend my adolescent fantasies. I dropped my gaze to the floor, but he wasn't finished.

86

'Then you will have one hour to write your essay. You will remember that work produced in detention periods is judged by much higher standards than ordinary homework, and it will not be easy to satisfy me.'

How many times had he spoken to me like that in the past? In high school it seemed fitting; now it was surreal. It was also presumptuous, inappropriate and unbearably erotic. I silently prayed he would just throw me down on the desk and ravish me.

He was looking at me expectantly and I managed to squeak out another 'Yes, sir.'

'Good. I shall see you at seven, then.'

It took me an hour to decide what to wear, but I was happy with the final product. It was the closest thing I could find to a school uniform – short green tartan skirt and white midriff blouse. The blouse had a wide splayed collar and those sassy French-style cuffs that turn back. I unbuttoned it enough to show a hint of cleavage. I winked at the saucy tart in the mirror and set off.

Of course I had no problem getting a taxi, but the traffic wasn't so obliging. I was fifteen minutes late and it wasn't my fault, but I knew that would make no difference to the implacable Mr Sheridan.

The cathedral bells were ringing out a peal as I raced through the cobblestone streets to Hallgarth House. They seemed to be delighting in my lateness. I could easily think the change-ringers were in on the game with Mr Sheridan – wanting to see me dig myself an even deeper hole. But that was silly. Paranoid. I had no one to blame but myself. After all, he'd said it himself; this was a pattern with me.

I knocked and he made me wait, then looked up as I came in. 'Ah. Adams,' he said with a thin smile. 'Nice of you to turn up.'

I was startled to be addressed by my last name. Was that what they called you at school in this country? I offered him a sheepish apology, surprised by the teenage tremble in my voice.

'Your tardiness will be addressed in due course,' he said, looking me up and down. 'After you dress.'

'Huh? But you said –'

'I said you were to report to me in school uniform.'

'Yeah, and I worked hard to find something uniform-like.'

Again that sinister smile. 'Yes, but in my school you wear a *uniform*, not provocative adult clothes that are "uniform-like".'

Silly me. 'But I don't have –'

'I do.'

I was starting to catch on.

Warmth was spreading through my limbs. I was stepping straight into a fantasy, into another world. I opened my mouth to say something, but nothing came out.

'Now, young lady. I realise you were accustomed to a different way of life in Boston. American girls tend to be spoiled, taking for granted the privileges that English girls are expected to earn. I also know that you have never been required to wear a school uniform before, but I am not prepared to be lax on that account.'

I was mesmerised by his little speech.

He reached down behind the desk and retrieved a shopping bag. 'You may change next door, in Mr Wilson's office. You have ten minutes.'

Was he serious? I knew Wilson. A bookish man who taught Romantic poetry. What if he came back and found me there? But unless I wanted to forfeit this little game, I knew I had to do it.

I took the bag from Mr Sheridan and left his office in a daze.

Once next door I emptied the bag and grimaced at the uniform. It was hideous! I'd expected a cute tartan skirt at least. This one was plain navy blue with starchy pleats. There was a simple white shirt and blue striped tie. White cotton knee socks. White cotton panties. And a navy blue blazer with a large patch on the left breast pocket. It said something in Latin. I never took Latin.

This was not frivolous. This was the Real Thing.

I managed everything easily but the tie. I knew what it was supposed to look like, but I couldn't figure out how to do it. And after four attempts I saw that I only had one minute left. My fingers trembled as I undid it and tried again. It still wasn't right, but it would have to do. Besides, I was terrified that Mr Wilson would appear at any moment. That idea was mortifying, but it was also hot as hell.

I looked at the schoolgirl in the mirror. The uniform was a unique sort of bondage. I felt restricted and uncomfortable. It stripped me of my sexual power. All my assets were under tight control and I couldn't use them to get my way. The vulnerability was overwhelming.

I had never been so turned on in my life.

Mr Sheridan stood right in front of me, assessing my uniform.

He didn't have to tell me he expected me to stand straight and still, but I just couldn't. The bells had no doubt stopped ringing long ago, but only now did I notice the heavy silence. It hung in the air like the early dark and I shuddered in the cloying absence of sound. I shifted my feet and smoothed down my skirt with my hands.

'Do you think *this*,' he asked, lifting my tie with disdain, 'is adequate?'

'I tried, sir. Really. But I've never worn a tie before and –'

'Disgraceful.'

With that, he untied my tie and did it up properly himself, pulling it snug beneath my collar. He also fastened the top button, which I had deliberately left undone. I felt like a child being dressed for school. It was intensely humbling.

'Right, young lady. Let's get on with this, shall we?' With that, he strode to the closet behind his desk and took out the dreaded cane.

I was surprised. It looked pretty harmless – just a thin whippy length of polished rattan about three feet long, with a crooked handle. After all the build-up, I couldn't believe this was it.

Then he sliced it through the air and the sound alone told me what it was capable of. I paled and took a step back.

My heart was pounding in my ears and a delicious thrill of fear raced through me as I realised I was truly at the point of no return. The roller coaster's big plunge.

He flexed the cane in his hands. 'Discipline,' he began, his voice low and measured, 'is essential to education. And I am a firm believer in the efficacy of corporal punishment.'

I flushed and wrapped my arms around myself, eyeing the cane with dread.

'Hands at your sides, Adams,' he said sharply.

I obeyed.

But then he laid the cane on the desk and took a straight-backed chair from behind it. He set it in front of me and sat down.

'Before I cane you, I shall address your tardiness. As I recall, you were often late to my classes in Boston. And after all these years, you haven't changed. But now I can deal with the matter. Remove your blazer and hang it up.'

My feet were glued to the floor, but Mr Sheridan eyed me sternly until I finally forced myself to move. There was a coat hook on the back of the door and the blazer just covered the little window, a perfect curtain.

'Now come here.'

At last I stood beside him, fidgeting and trembling.

'Tardiness,' he said, 'shows a childish disregard for rules. As such it warrants a childish punishment. A spanking.' He patted his lap. 'Over my knee.'

I thought I would faint. My legs were incapable of holding me up and I felt like a limp rag as I stretched myself across his lap.

'Naughty girls must be punished,' he said, placing his left hand in the small of my back to hold me in place. 'And nothing teaches a girl a lesson better than a good sound spanking. Skirt up. Knickers down. Right on her bare bottom.'

I hadn't known it was possible to blush so deeply. The throbbing between my legs was nothing short of agony. My body was screaming for release. I pressed my hands against the floor as he lifted my pleated skirt and tucked my shirttail high up over my back. Then his fingers were in the waistband of my white cotton school knickers and he took his time pulling them down to expose my bottom. He rested his hand on my back and I shivered with fear and delight.

He scolded me in a soft voice and I felt like a little girl again. My face was so flushed I felt feverish and my ears burned with each word. I had no idea embarrassment could be so exquisite. He cupped my cheeks as he spoke and I thought I would drown in the anticipation. His touch held both authority and affection. Claiming and caressing.

Then his hand fell, sharp and purposeful, and the sting made me gasp. I couldn't believe this was actually happening. It was intoxicating.

I jumped each time I felt his heavy palm, trying not to yelp, but unable to help it. He lectured me the whole time, emphasising each trigger word with a well-placed smack. Bad girl. Naughty. Punishment. It was excruciatingly erotic and I could feel myself writhing shamelessly in spite of myself.

It was no play-spanking, either. He laid it on with a will and my cries and whimpers were genuine. I could feel my flesh reddening under his palm and the pain only intensified the hot throbbing girlish longing.

Mr Sheridan paused and rested his hand on my bottom, stroking the tender flesh. Teasing me. My body was willing him to plunge his hand between my legs and end the torture, but that wasn't part of his plan. Not yet.

After a short pause he began again, spanking me even harder. Now the stinging smacks made me kick and struggle and when I couldn't take any more I reached behind to deflect his hand. He simply caught my wrist and pinned it in the small of my back, not breaking his rhythm for an instant.

'No, young lady,' he chided. 'This is long overdue and you're going to take what's coming to you.'

With a shudder I reminded myself that I still had the caning to look forward to. I knew he'd stop if I really insisted. But those two deadly sins, pride and lust, wouldn't allow me to consider it. I resolved to see it through to the reward at the end.

His hand rose and fell tirelessly, smacking me again and again, harder and harder. I wriggled and squirmed, but couldn't escape the stinging smacks. I couldn't keep silent and I was yelping loudly. What if someone heard? Mr Sheridan didn't seem worried. I pictured Mr Wilson returning to his office, cocking his head at the sounds coming from next door. Perhaps he was used to this? Mr Sheridan's very lack of concern was exciting and I sank even further into submission.

Finally, sensing my surrender, he stopped. He had to help me to my feet. I was panting and my face was almost as flushed as my backside. I desperately wanted to rub the stinging flesh, but I still had too much pride to make such a display of myself. My knickers were down around my ankles and I knew better than to replace them. This was only a warm-up, after all. The worst was yet to come.

'Now then, Adams.' He was all business. 'I know that you have considerable ability and are capable of good work. But you need a little incentive. And a lot of discipline.'

He retrieved the cane from his desk and the sense of dread I felt as he cleaved the empty air with it took me right back to the schoolroom in Boston. I gasped and took a step back. I had to bite my lower lip to keep my traitorous tongue from pleading with him to spare me.

He turned the chair around and tapped the back of it with the end of the cane. 'Over the chair,' he directed. 'Raise your skirt.'

It was as though the chair had invisible tendrils that reached out and pulled me to it. I bent down over the high back of it, mortified at the way it raised my bottom up so invitingly. I lifted my skirt up over my back as he had done. It was awful to have to do it myself and I lowered my head, putting my hands on the seat of the chair. It was warm from where he'd been sitting.

Mr Sheridan was behind me and he seemed in no hurry.

He adjusted my shirttail, smoothing it over my skirt to hold it in place. He ran a hand over my sore backside.

I shivered and let out a little moan.

'You will learn to apply yourself in my class. I put a great deal of work into teaching you, and I will tolerate nothing less than your best effort in return. Don't you think that is fair?'

With that he tapped the cane against my backside. I flinched and tensed my bottom in anticipation. This was it. After five years, I was finally going to be caned.

'I think I'd better ask you that again, Adams. Do you think it is fair?'

I'd thought it was a rhetorical question. 'Yes, sir,' I mumbled, drowning in the delicious misery of the moment. I had never felt so completely controlled by a man before. I didn't want it to end.

'Six strokes,' he said. 'You will count them aloud for me. Say "Thank you, sir" after each one.'

My God.

I felt the cane touch my bottom gently, then glide down over it and up again. It tapped, announcing exactly where it would strike, then rose. I felt rather than saw his arm lift behind me. Then there was the unmistakable *swoosh-thwack!* as it met my tender bottom at last.

For a moment I felt nothing. But a split second later the pain began to bloom in a thin stripe that burned so intensely it felt like ice. It swelled and swelled until it became unendurable and I cried out and leapt up, clutching my backside to soothe away the astonishing sting.

'Back in position, girl,' said Mr Sheridan impassively. 'Next time you do that, it will earn you an extra stroke.'

I stared at him for a moment, horrified. Then I obeyed, gritting my teeth as I waited. The silence was stifling and I suddenly remembered.

'One,' I said, my voice a moan of shame. 'Thank you, sir.'

'Very good.'

Tapping again, and then the same *swoosh-thwack!* The second stroke was even harder, but I forced myself to stay

93

down. The white-hot sting eclipsed all other thoughts and I yelped and squirmed over the chair.

I had to take a deep breath before I could count. 'Two. Thank you, s-sir.' Oh, this was torture!

The third stroke fell precisely between the first two. His aim was unerring. And again the sensation was unbelievable. I cried out and gripped the edge of the chair to keep my hands in place. If I had been drunk on the intimate erotic power of the spanking, the cane had sobered me completely.

'Three,' I made myself say, loathing the tremor in my voice and the humiliation of the words. 'Thank you, sir.'

I gritted my teeth and braced myself for the fourth stroke, which literally took my breath away. I nearly screamed as it seared another parallel stripe across my burning cheeks. I locked my knees and rose on my toes so I could lower my forehead to the seat of the chair. Breathing fast and shallow, I told myself I had only two more to go. Just two.

Just?

I resumed the position and counted dutifully. I was already learning that Mr Sheridan was not a man to be trifled with. Oh, yes, this would have made an impression on me as a teenager.

The fifth stroke brought tears to my eyes and I could barely keep from grabbing my poor backside. But the terror of even one extra stroke was enough to keep me in place. The revolutionary in me wanted to rebel, but the price was just too high. I bounced up and down on my heels, trying to overcome the agony. But the fire burned even deeper.

I heard my voice counting and it sounded like someone far away.

He delivered the sixth stroke, right in the crease between my bottom and my thighs. And I couldn't help it – my hands left the seat of the chair and before I knew it I was dancing in place, clutching my poor punished backside and pleading for mercy. This time he got his display.

He shook his head sadly. 'Back in position, Adams,' he said. 'And you were doing so well.'

My precious dignity was gone. 'Oh, no, please, sir,' I babbled. 'Please, I can't take any more!'

Mr Sheridan merely looked at me, indifferent to my suffering.

I had come so far. I had already taken six of the best. I had invested too much in this little powerplay to back out now.

With great reluctance and dread, I bent back over the chair. He took his time readjusting my skirt and shirttail before laying the cane against my bottom again, tapping it against the burning flesh.

'Come on, girl,' he said. 'It's nearly over. Make me proud.'

The words of encouragement were unexpected and they made me lift my head. I took hold of the chair seat and stared straight ahead.

At last he gave me the final stroke. It was harder than any of the original six, but I refused to cry out. I crossed my legs, bending at the knees, relishing the heady blend of pleasure and pain as I reconnected with the insistent warmth between my thighs.

'Six,' I panted at last. 'Thank you, sir.'

His hand cupped my aching backside, just near the pantyline, where the worst stroke had fallen. The air around me resonated with electricity. I waited.

Then, moving like a dream spider, his hand crept closer inside. I arched slightly, inviting him with my silence. Another fraction of an inch. My skin prickled. I was trembling. Then I felt his touch. His fingertips grazed the silky dampness and I gasped.

I felt like a rippling reflection of myself and I needed the chair for support.

His voice was a distant echo, but there was another unmistakable sound: his zipper. He gently parted my thighs and I relaxed in his grip as he took hold of me from behind.

'You see, even the most rebellious girls will surrender in the end,' he murmured.

Oh, yes.

I went limp as he entered me, my head hanging down to the seat of the chair. I could see my knickers pooled on the floor beside my left foot. I shuddered with each thrust and I uttered soft little squeaks and whimpers as his pelvis slapped against the punished skin of my bottom.

Mr Sheridan entwined a hand in my hair and pulled me up until my back was parallel with the floor. I could just make out our silhouette reflected in the steel filing cabinet against the wall. A dark blur behind a white one. I tried to visualise us. The schoolmaster and his errant schoolgirl, her tie properly knotted, her knickers discarded, her bottom on fire. This was a painful lesson, but one I could see myself learning again. And again.

He pounded into me over and over until the pleasure overtook the pain and he clutched me tightly as he came. But my teacher wasn't going to leave me unsatisfied. He drew his hands down the front of my body, spreading my legs and my sex with skilled fingers.

'Have you learned your lesson, naughty girl?'

My body was ready to explode. 'Oh, yes,' I breathed, oblivious to everything but the storm of passion in my tingling flesh.

'Yes *what*?'

He touched my clit and I gasped. That was all it took. The wave broke over me and I surrendered to the pulsing throbbing orgasm as he held me up. Without his support I would have slipped to the floor.

When the euphoria at last began to fade he turned me around. I stood before him in a daze, my eyes unfocused and dreamy.

He was smiling.

'You see, you *can* learn to apply yourself.' He patted my bottom and I winced, drawing a hissing breath through my teeth.

Too embarrassed to meet his eyes, I could do nothing but stand there and squirm.

His eyes glinted. 'I think the American girl is finally learning that she can't get her way in an English school.'

I had to admit defeat there. I couldn't argue with the

effectiveness of his methods. 'You know, you're the only man in the world I've ever called "sir".' I shook my head, still marvelling that he had humbled me so completely.

'How typically American,' he said, amused but not surprised.

'I know, I know, I'm a spoiled ex-colonial.' And I couldn't resist adding, 'But we did defeat you and escape your stifling rule, if you recall.'

'Ah, that,' he said with a grin. 'That was just a tantrum by a rebellious daughter colony. But she knows where to turn for guidance when she's overstepped the mark. And there are still times when her excesses need to be curbed.'

I blushed and looked down at the floor, savouring the thought.

'Right,' he said. 'Now about that essay . . .'

Damsel in Distress

'Hold on now, miss. I've got you.'

Charlie whimpered, tightening her arms around the big man's neck as he lifted her effortlessly from the hiking trail. She'd torn the knees of her jeans in the fall and she watched blood flecks blossom like tiny flowers on her rescuer's shirt where her scraped knees rested against his chest. She pressed closer to his warm bulk and closed her eyes against the comforting rhythm of his pace.

'Not far now,' he assured her, panting.

She liked his Old West drawl and she felt secure as a child in the cradle of his arms as he carried her down the trail and back to the car park. The perfect ending to her twenty-first birthday.

'It's the red Mercedes,' she said, nodding towards the gleaming convertible sitting in the shade of a tour bus.

He set her gently on her feet and she hobbled to the door to unlock the car. Slowly she manoeuvred herself into the driver's seat, favouring her right leg.

'Are you sure you want to drive?' he asked doubtfully. 'Maybe you should have someone look at that ankle.'

'No, it's OK, I'm all right.'

'They probably have first aid stuff at the Visitor Centre. It'd be no trouble to take you over there.'

'That's very sweet, but I'll be fine now. My hotel isn't far.' She fixed him with an intense gaze, her green eyes sparkling. 'You saved my life.'

The big man turned bashful, looking at the ground and

grinning faintly. 'It's nothing,' he said. 'Easy enough for me with a little thing like you.'

Charlie returned his grin, pressing her legs together against a flash of warmth as she gave him a last appraising look. His well muscled arms gleamed with sweat from the effort of pulling her back up onto the path and carrying her for half a mile. Even her slight weight had winded him and she felt a little guilty for the trouble she'd put him to.

As she pulled out onto the highway she abandoned her pretence of injury, flooring the accelerator to get back to the hotel room so she could relive the moment in private.

Charlie liked to be rescued. She had been carried down from mountains after countless hiking, skiing and climbing accidents – some of them genuine. She'd been pulled from a few rivers too. Once she had even gone into a burning building purely so she could be slung over a fireman's shoulder and carried to safety.

She thrived on the feeling of helplessness, enhanced by the competence of her rescuers. Whether she was actually hurt or not, she would play her role, wincing and groaning as appropriate, while her saviour gathered her in his arms and delivered her from danger. Occasionally he would scold her, admonishing her careless behaviour. Blushing and squirming, Charlie would bat her eyes and promise to be good, though more often than not she was already plotting her next adventure.

It wasn't an exact science and sometimes she got more than she bargained for. She'd spent a tedious month in hospital with a broken ankle after falling harder than she'd intended on a ski slope in Verbier. Nineteen at the time, she'd sworn to herself then that she was done with her antics, that it wasn't worth six weeks of boredom and pain, even if Daddy had found her the best private hospital in Switzerland.

But less than a year later, she was feeling the urge again. She tested the waters with a few minor stumbles before regaining her courage with an unexpected – and totally genuine – boating accident in Australia. Three rugged Aussies rescued her from the undertow and then, in an ostentatious display of machismo, they took turns carrying her from the boat, to the dock, all the way to her hotel on the waterfront. Of course their gallantry wasn't entirely selfless. They were showing off to each other as much as to her. Honestly, how many men would grumble too much about saving a petite blonde teenager from drowning and carrying her tanned bikini-clad body a few hundred yards?

Charlie was buzzing for weeks afterwards. Her three rescuers could have done anything to her and she would have been powerless to stop them. There was nothing in the world to compete with that feeling and she knew there was no curing her of the need for it. Nor could she see any reason to deprive herself. Serious injuries were no fun at all, but she could still indulge her rescue addiction in moderation. She couldn't enjoy being carried to safety when she was delirious with pain. But sprains, strains, scrapes, cuts and bruises – these she could handle.

Now as she lay curled in bed, she replayed the latest episode in her mind. She'd encountered the big American on the way up the path to the canyon overlook. And she knew his type – old-fashioned and chivalrous. Inherently a little sexist, but in just the right way. Men like that could never refuse a lady in need.

Timing her 'accidents' could sometimes be tricky, but this one had been easy. She'd followed him down the dusty trail on the way back from the lip of the canyon. She chose her moment, waiting until he was only a few feet ahead of her before slipping on the gravel and tumbling over the edge of the slope. She cried out in alarm, clutching at a shrub and scrabbling for purchase with her boots. In her mind she hung suspended over a deep ravine, where a dislodged stone bounced hundreds of yards down the side of the crevasse, disappearing into the gaping abyss. The reality was less exciting: if she lost her grip she would only slide a few feet down the scree into the bushes. Still, she could sustain some nasty scratches.

The American reassured her with his voice as he knelt beside the path and reached down for her. He hauled her back up with an easy one-armed yank and Charlie clutched him fearfully, gratefully. Then she took a step and crumpled to the ground. 'My ankle!' she cried. His duty was clear.

She smiled at the memory of her deceit, embellishing the little drama in her mind. In her fantasy he fought his way through a nest of rattlesnakes to save her, carrying her through the cacti and scrub to the cool safety of a cave. There he tore strips from his shirt to bind her wounds, displaying his bronzed torso as he staunched her bleeding. His physical superiority was both arousing and intimidating and she submitted to his ministrations like a trusting child. So he caught her off guard when he suddenly withdrew a length of rope from his rucksack and deftly tied her wrists together over her head.

'What are you –?' she couldn't finish the question. She knew the answer. The bulge in his trousers left her in no doubt.

His eyes had turned hard and flinty. 'There's no one around for miles,' he told her evenly as he slowly began unbuttoning her shirt.

She struggled feebly, but she was no match for his strength. And her injuries inhibited her further.

Like a predator lingering over a fresh catch, he took his time unwrapping her. He unfastened her jeans and slowly pulled them down over her legs as she pleaded with him to let her go. With a cruel smile he traced the outline of her cotton panties, finally slipping a finger into the waistband and peeling them down to her knees.

He stood over her as he unbuckled his belt, snaking it through the loops of his trousers and doubling it. He laid the doubled leather strap aside – a threat, a warning. Cowed, Charlie melted into the cold stone of the cave floor as the big man straddled her and held her down, using her in heartless exquisite ways.

The swell of ecstasy flooded Charlie's mind and tore her from the fantasy. She arched her back painfully, crying out as she surrendered to the spasms of pleasure.

Afterwards she lay flushed and panting on the bed, satisfied but embarrassed. As always, she felt guilty for exploiting her rescuer's compassion and then defiling it further by recasting him as a villain in her fantasy. Of course, none of her chivalrous knights would ever know the roles they played in her private thoughts afterwards, but the guilt lingered nonetheless. The feeling was sometimes mitigated if she'd suffered actual injuries for her efforts, but this time she only had a scraped knee to show for it.

'Sorry, cowboy,' she murmured later, rinsing off the dust and dried blood in the shower.

Later that night, as she picked at her room service food, she felt strangely unfulfilled. Usually she indulged her hobby and treated herself to something obscenely chocolatey after dinner, but tonight she had little appetite. The thrill had passed so quickly. It had been fun, certainly, but not exhilarating. Nothing like the three Australians. That was the benchmark. She yearned for an experience that would top it and she wasn't going to find it stumbling around on hiking trails. It was time to up the ante.

'So, is this your first time?'

'No, I've been rafting before,' Charlie lied.

'Well, the river's pretty wild after all the rain this summer,' the guide said. 'Lots of Class III rapids and a couple of Class IV. Hope you're up to it.'

Was he trying to scare her? Put her off? Fat chance. Lots of rapids meant lots of opportunities to fall in. A good swimmer, Charlie was exceptionally skilled at falling out of boats, flailing in panicky desperation and gulping mouthfuls of water in between cries for help. She'd joined a lifesaver course one summer in California, playing pretend drowning victim to lifeguards and rescue divers, but it hadn't been the same. They all knew it wasn't for real, which spoiled the 'hero' aspect for her. Still, it had helped her to hone her special skills.

'Sounds exciting,' she said, looking him over, assessing his potential.

The whitewater guides tended to be fit university students – guys her own age who spent the summers earning tourist dollars to pay for school. Paddling was hard work and they had the bodies to show for it. Josh was no exception. A proper river rat, he had the baked skin and surfer hair of someone who lived for and on the river. He smiled as he took her money and told her where to go for the safety talk.

There were seven of them in all, including Charlie and the guide. They put in and paddled downstream and within minutes they reached the first set of rapids. Josh shouted commands and his crew responded, steering the raft so as to time the drops for maximum effect. Water splashed up over the sides of the boat, soaking them.

As they approached the first set of serious rapids, Charlie slipped her feet out of the foot-pockets and prepared for the big moment.

'Forward! Forward!' Josh called over the roar of water. Charlie leaned out as far as she could, digging her paddle into the churning water as they went over the drop. The force knocked her out of the raft and the swirling waves pulled her under. She popped up instantly like a cork and looked around for the raft. The current swept her along before she could find it and she struggled to maintain the position she'd been taught: on her back, feet pointed up, facing downstream.

She went over another small rapid before she heard the others calling her name. The river was calmer here, but the current was still strong and she played her part, shouting for help and waving her arms as though lost at sea.

The raft was only fifty yards away and she could easily wait until it drew near to climb back in. But there was no fun in that. She splashed and kicked, looking around frantically.

'Something's got my foot!' she cried, thrashing in the water like a shark attack victim.

Seeing her distress, Josh executed a graceful dive into the river and swam for her. He reached her in seconds and grabbed her life vest, hauling her back to the raft while she clung to him, thanking him effusively and trying not to grin. She ate two slices of German chocolate cake that night.

But in the days that followed she found the experience wanting, as she so often did lately. It had been exciting, but she'd felt silly acting so scared when she wasn't actually in any danger. The life vest had returned her to the surface at once and calmer water waited beyond almost every set of rapids. Still, she was on to something. It had been a successful first attempt, but she needed to go further.

Charlie went to a different rafting company for her next outing. But after flirting with the well-built Latino guy in the shop, she wound up with a female guide instead in a raft full of schoolkids. Charlie sulked throughout the ride, grumbling as the kids shrieked at every minor swell and surge and their harried teacher tried to keep them in line.

Fortunately, the group was too incompetent to follow the guide's instructions and they managed to wrap the raft, stranding it on a cluster of rocks. Charlie pretended to be disappointed as the guide explained that there was no way to free the raft. It was pinned there by the force of the current, like a wet newspaper plastered against a signpost.

The kids made faces and looked bored while the guide radioed for help and Charlie made a mental note to avoid this particular outfit in future. At least she would be spared the rest of the trip with them.

She perked up a little at the arrival of the rescue services, but it was more a conditioned response. She was no longer in the mood and she couldn't contrive a last-minute disaster anyway. The two men in khaki shorts quickly strung a rope from the stranded raft to the riverbank and helped the kids clamber across one by one. It was a precarious operation. One girl lost her Hogwarts baseball cap and screamed as it flashed out of sight beneath the water. It surfaced some way downstream, but there was no way to reach it. Charlie smiled as an idea came to her.

'High side! High side!'

The guide and the other four crew jumped to the forward side of the raft and Charlie jumped to the back. It was just enough to upset the balance. Instead of bouncing off the obstacle, the boat reared up in the water. For a dizzying moment it hovered, threatening to capsize, before the oncoming water broke over the trailing edge and sucked it down against the rock. Wrapped.

The guide muttered a curse and Charlie apologised, looking fearful and wide-eyed at the churning water surrounding them.

'I'm really sorry. I just got scared when I thought we were going to hit the rocks.'

It was a good wrap. Since the aborted run with the school group, Charlie had discovered a real talent for sabotaging rafting trips. She'd done it up and down the river all summer, with each of several different rafting companies. The guys from the rescue service were always so gentle and considerate. With infinite patience they would coax her to the shore with praise for every halting step, as though she were an invalid learning to walk again. Best of all were the times when she could strand the boat in intense rapids. Then her scared little girl act was more believable.

'No, no, I can't, the current's too fast!' she would whimper, cowering on the rocks like a stranded kitten. Eventually one of the rescuers would have to climb across to her and give her a piggyback ride to the shore. She was hooked. The more she did it the more she needed it.

This time she'd outdone herself. The water was violently hazardous. A maelstrom roared just beneath where the raft was pinned. The gnarled roots of a drowned tree seemed to be clawing their way out of the froth like skeletal hands. Going over that drop in the raft would have been risky, but falling in without the raft's protection could be fatal. Especially since her only protection was the life vest. Some paddlers wore wetsuits or even jeans to protect against scrapes, but Charlie only ever wore her most revealing swimwear. Or, like today, a tight white T-shirt and hot-pants.

She huddled in the trapped raft, refusing to move as the others were guided safely to the riverbank by two men from the rescue services. First the young Swedish couple, whose pale skin had suffered terribly in the sun despite their numerous applications of sunscreen. Still, they looked distraught to be ending the adventure prematurely.

Next across was the geology professor, who had bored Charlie silly by pointing out every geological feature along the run. When she'd asked him sweetly if there would be a test, he had looked wounded and gone silent until they reached the next weathered sandstone outcropping he could exclaim over. He wasn't finding much of geological interest now as he made his way tentatively across the slippery rocks, clinging to the rope for dear life.

Charlie watched in fascination as a tangle of debris made its way downriver, swept along by the ferocious current. An uprooted tree tumbled through the waves before hitting a cluster of rocks. The wood splintered with a sickening crack and the remnants flowed like matchsticks past the raft.

The guide, Tyler, gestured for Charlie to go next. But she stayed where she was, shaking her head frantically.

'I can't, I can't!'

He rolled his eyes. Without another attempt to encourage her he climbed out of the raft and headed for the bank, negotiating the rope with skill. Charlie was a little taken aback at the desertion. Shouldn't the captain go down with the ship? Then again, the rescue services boys were there to save them. And besides, his lack of chivalry only gave her more ammunition. Not that she needed to pretend; the hungry turbulence already had her second-guessing this particular adventure.

That left Charlie and the last passenger, a man around forty with the brooding manner of a Hollywood tough guy. He hadn't said anything throughout the trip and while the others had chatted after stopping for lunch along the bank an hour before, he'd gone off by himself into the woods.

Now he locked eyes with Charlie and she couldn't discern the meaning of his black-eyed stare. Was he simply pissed off at her for messing up the run?

'Please,' she said, trying to sound conciliatory, 'you go first. I'm too scared. I'll wait for the rangers to help me.'

He stared at her for several seconds, his eyes inscrutable. Then he shouldered his bag and made his way along the rope to join the others. On the bank, the Swedish girl was texting someone on her phone while her husband slathered more sunscreen on his legs. Tyler and the professor stood staring at the ground, looking bored and frustrated, while the black-eyed stranger watched Charlie closely.

The two rangers beckoned to her, coaxing and encouraging. 'Come on, we'll help you. We won't let you fall in.'

They were both athletic outdoor types, fit and capable. The younger of the two looked about thirty, with short spiky bleached hair. The older one looked disconcertingly like her father. He moved to the very edge of the bank and, smiling, held his arms out as though inviting Charlie to jump the thirty-foot stretch and be caught. His attempt at encouragement felt like a parody and Charlie wasn't going to let him off the hook.

'I can't swim,' she called across the roar of water, as though confessing a shameful secret.

The men exchanged a glance and then the younger one began making his way along the rope to her. He moved cautiously, watching closely where he put his feet and keeping a firm grip on the rope. He stopped halfway across and called to her.

'What's your name?'

'Charlie.'

'Pleased to meet you, Charlie,' he said cheerily. 'I'm Scott. But I have to warn you: you can't stay there all day. The cell phone reception sucks and the pizza delivery guy will never find you.'

She liked him immediately. His breezy confidence was reassuring and she imagined he could talk the most despondent suicide in from a ledge. But, frightened though she was, she was determined to get what she'd come for. He would have to rescue her.

She made a half-hearted thrust at the rope to show willing before pulling back and covering her face with a little moan. 'I can't!' It was becoming her mantra.

107

Scott wasn't daunted. He offered her a sympathetic smile as she peered through her fingers at him. 'It's OK. Stay there. I'll come to you.'

She could barely contain her excitement as he covered the rest of the distance. Then, just as she was leaning out to reach for him, a freak wave struck the raft, causing the front end to lift. Only a fraction, but it was enough to make Charlie lose her balance. Her arms pinwheeled and she tumbled into the whitewater, just as Scott grabbed her hand.

She screamed with real fear, terrified that he'd lose his grip on her. Her bare legs thrashed in the water as the current tried to drag her down.

'I've got you,' he said firmly, but somehow he didn't seem quite as self-assured now.

All she could think of was the tree trunk shattering against the jagged rocks; the debris rising like spears from the water to impale her; the many ways this could all go horribly wrong. Tears sprang to her eyes and she felt herself mouthing prayers she hadn't resorted to in years. All pretence abandoned, she was at the mercy of very real fear and in very real danger.

'Don't let go,' she sobbed, clinging to his hand with both of hers. If he was struggling to maintain his own balance, she didn't notice. She was too frightened to think of anything but the fury of the water and the treacherous death that awaited her if she lost her grip.

'Charlie, listen to me,' he said, his voice calm and measured. Back in control. 'I'm going to pull you up and I want you to grab the rope. Can you do that for me?'

At first she shook her head, terrified.

'Yes you can,' he said with reassuring authority. 'I won't let you fall.'

Charlie steeled herself and followed his instructions, allowing him to haul her up onto the rocks so she could take hold of the rope with both hands. The current had swallowed her flip-flops, but they wouldn't have given her much protection anyway. Scott entwined one arm in the rope and grabbed Charlie's life vest with his free hand, pulling her across step by step until at last they reached the riverbank.

When her feet touched stable ground she clung to her hero in an ecstasy of gratitude. He had saved her. Really and truly saved her! Her heart was pounding with adrenalin. This was it. The pinnacle. Not even the Australian adventure could beat this. And tonight she would –

'Don't I know you?'

Charlie blinked in confusion and looked up. It wasn't her rescuer who had spoken. The black-eyed stranger was watching her, his eyes narrowed. There was something cynical in his tone, something suggesting that he'd known all along.

And all at once she remembered him. He'd been with her on a rafting trip back in June. She'd only fallen in that time, but suddenly she remembered his knowing expression as she flailed in the water and the guide hauled her back into the raft. Quickly she turned away, burying her face in Scott's chest.

The stranger laughed, a sharp ugly sound. 'Yeah, I thought so.'

'Holy shit. It's her,' Tyler said, realisation dawning. 'Serial Wrapper.'

Charlie looked nervously up at Scott. His kind face was now frowning. 'Are you sure?' he asked the guide.

'Yeah, I've heard the descriptions and it must be her. This little girl's been a serious nuisance all summer – wrapping boats in every company on the river, then crying wolf when the rescue team arrives. I bet you're an excellent swimmer.' He addressed this last comment to Charlie, who nodded sheepishly.

The mood on the riverbank was like a gathering storm. Tyler cursed and stalked a few paces away. The Swedes were muttering angrily to each other and the tough guy crossed his arms in satisfaction. Even the mild-mannered professor looked ready to blow his cool. As Charlie stood there, soaking wet from the escapade and with water puddling at her feet, she began to fear they might lynch her.

'Look,' she said, 'it's just a bit of harmless fun. I'll go now and you'll never see me again.'

'Not so fast,' Scott said. All his good-natured cheer had evaporated and he caught her by the wrist. 'You didn't just put yourself in danger; you put all of us in danger *with* you. For "a bit of fun".'

She squirmed a little at the lecture in spite of herself as the others murmured approval at his words.

'I know, I know, and I –'

'No, I don't think you *do* know. I risked my life for you.'

She hung her head. 'I'm really *really* sorry,' she mumbled. Perhaps if she could make herself cry they would see how sorry . . .

The stranger snorted with derision, as though reading her mind. 'She's not a bit sorry,' he said, adding after a weighty pause, 'but we can do something about that.'

Charlie looked up, alarmed. And her eyes widened as he set his bag down on the grass and withdrew something from it. Something about two feet long and wooden with a wide flat bit on one end. It was a miniature version of the rafting paddles they'd been using; she'd seen them for sale in the gift shop. For one crazy moment Charlie thought he was going to order her to paddle the raft down to the takeout with it. But when he smacked it sharply against his palm she was left in no doubt about his intentions.

'You've given us all such a memorable summer I think it's only fair we give you something in return. Something to remember *us* by – every time you try to sit down.'

She backed away warily. 'Look, I –'

'I think that's an excellent idea,' said Scott, tightening his grip on her arm. 'I've never seen such reckless behaviour in my life.'

'And flagrant disregard for safety,' his partner added.

'But there's no harm done!' Charlie protested.

Scott looked aghast. 'No harm? Did you fail to notice all the jagged rocks and tree limbs in the water? Either you or I could have come to a very messy end. Or any of these people here.' He gestured with his arm and from the corner of her eye Charlie saw them all nodding.

'Oh, she noticed all right,' Tyler said angrily. 'She just thought it would be exciting. Didn't you, Charlie?'

If this kept up much longer she wouldn't have to *make* herself cry. She was already feeling guilty enough. She'd had no idea just how dangerous the whole fiasco was going to turn out to be.

The stranger regarded her coldly, underscoring with his icy stare the wrong she had done everyone. 'Take off your life vest.'

When she hesitated Tyler said, 'It's the property of the rafting company. Hand it over.'

Her fingers fluttered nervously at the buckles and she only managed to unclip herself after several attempts. She slid out of the vest and passed it to the guide before realising that her flimsy white shirt was soaked through and torn in places. Her nipples stood out in sharp relief. Blushing deeply, she covered herself as much as she could with her free hand. In desperation she sought the face of the professor. He was the only one she thought might take pity on her. But his expression was as unforgiving as the rest.

The brooding stranger was rolling up his right sleeve and Charlie tensed, ready to run. But Scott tightened his grip on her arm. He shot her a warning glance and she looked at the ground in despair. There was no way out and she knew it. What was worse – she knew she deserved it.

The stranger smacked the paddle against his hand again. 'I suspect no one's ever taken you in hand or you wouldn't be so desperate for attention. Well, you're about to get it.' He nodded at Scott. 'If you wouldn't mind holding her . . .'

'Certainly. And I know just the position.'

Charlie squealed in surprise as Scott brusquely turned away from her, grabbed her by the arms and hoisted her up on his broad back. He settled her into position with her legs dangling on either side of him. Earlier his grip had felt so strong and capable, so secure. Now it made her feel trapped and displayed.

'Very pretty,' the stranger said, patting the generous expanse of cheek revealed by her hotpants. 'But these will have to come down.'

111

'No!' she cried in dismay.

'It's no use protesting now, girl. They hardly cover you anyway. But that's the whole point, right? Showing off. But a naughty little girl who's about to have her bottom paddled doesn't get to keep her cute little shorts on.'

His words made her writhe with embarrassment and a hot flush stained her cheeks.

He hooked his fingers in the waistband and dragged the clingy cotton shorts down, baring her bottom. 'Well, well,' he said, chuckling darkly. 'No panties. How thoughtful of you, my dear.'

Charlie's face burned as she hung there, helpless, her lower half completely exposed and vulnerable. Scott planted his feet wide apart and bent forward at the waist, raising her bottom up provocatively. Charlie whimpered and pinned her thighs together in a vain attempt to limit the view.

'I don't know what you're complaining about,' the stranger told her scornfully. 'I don't see any tan lines, so it's not as if you're shy about flaunting yourself.'

That was true; she was proud of her body. But that was when she was in control of what she was showing. Nude sunbathing was a far cry from the public shame of being held half-naked on a man's back.

'Now then,' the stranger continued, 'you've endangered all our lives for "a bit of fun" –'

' "Harmless" fun,' the professor corrected.

'Oh yes, quite right. It was "harmless" fun, wasn't it? Well, you're going to learn your lesson today, young lady. And I intend to make sure it's one you don't forget. This bottom of yours is going to be soundly paddled until it's red and sore and you're a very sorry little girl indeed.'

His words shamed and belittled her and she blushed so fiercely her ears burned. She lowered her head with a plaintive moan, burying her face in Scott's short spiky hair.

The cool wood of the paddle rested against her bottom and she squeezed her eyes shut in expectation of the pain. Water droplets crawled down her back and over her bottom, tickling her and making her wriggle. The paddle

112

tapped gently. Once. Twice. Each time she clenched her cheeks, quivering with awful anticipation, fearing it, dreading it, but at the same time wishing he'd get it over with.

She waited, helpless to do anything else, until at last she sensed he was about to start. She held her breath, gritting her teeth. A second later the paddle met her defenceless cheeks with a resounding crack that startled the birds and sent them flapping into the sky.

The pain was astonishing. She howled, forgetting her determination to keep her legs together as the sting blazed across her backside.

When she felt the paddle tap her in readiness for another stroke, she froze in horror. No way could she take another swat! She opened her mouth to protest, but before she could utter a sound, the wood smacked against her tender flesh again. She found her voice at once.

'Owww! Oh please, please, it hurts!'

'A spanking is meant to hurt,' the stranger said, tapping her cheeks with the implement again. 'And it's nothing compared to the injuries you might have caused with your antics.'

The paddle cracked down again and this time her legs scissored wildly as she strove to contain the deep burning pain.

'My, you are making a fuss. Haven't you ever been spanked before?'

'No, never,' she whimpered.

'I'm not surprised. Might have done you a world of good.' He brought the smooth wood down across her cheeks again, eliciting another anguished cry.

'I'm sorry! I'm really sorry, I mean it!'

'It's a bit late for "sorry", young lady.' There was no sympathy in his voice.

'She's only sorry she got caught,' said the man who looked like her father.

The full weight of her disgrace was too much to bear. And she knew it was true. She moaned, a low wretched animal sound. Water continued to trickle along her back and over her cheeks, dripping like tears down her legs.

The stranger laid on another swat that reverberated through the trees. With a pitiful cry Charlie writhed and twisted in Scott's grip. But her struggles were useless; he held her wrists firmly and she was no match for his strength.

She'd always loved being carried piggyback from some cleverly orchestrated accident, feeling tiny and protected. But this was different. And the forced intimacy was a further humiliation. Now it only made her hyper-aware of the spectacle she was making of herself. Her small breasts were pressed into Scott's muscled back and the thin wet T-shirt offered so little cover she might as well be naked. Her legs flailed impotently in the air, but she couldn't bring herself to wrap them around Scott's waist; that would only add to the lascivious display. She was probably deafening him with her cries, but she was in too much distress to care.

She caught a glimpse of the sunburnt Swedish man to her left. He stood with his arms crossed, watching impassively as another hard whack wrenched a howl from her. Her bottom must be the same bright red as the man's face and shoulders. It certainly felt as burnt.

Tears of pain and regret blurred her vision as she babbled frantic pleas and promises, apologising again and again. 'I can't take it back!' she sobbed in desperation.

'No,' her punisher agreed, 'but you can take your punishment for it.'

'And learn from it,' she heard someone add. The professor? The Swedish girl? She had no idea.

Each wail of pain was met with grim silence as the group witnessed her disgrace. Their unspoken approval heightened the sense of shame and by the end of the punishment, Charlie was feeling truly sorry for what she'd done.

Scott eased her down gently and she sank to her knees on the grass. She felt terrible. Abandoned. Alone in a world of people she had wronged. She could never make it up to them. Bereft, she put her head down in the grass and sobbed with heartfelt remorse.

'There, there,' Scott said, the kindness returning to his

voice. 'You've paid the price. It's all over now.' He crouched down beside her and gathered her in his arms.

Charlie clung to him, soaking his shirt with her tears and choking out guilty apologies between sobs. He held her for a long time and when her tears at last subsided she realised that everyone else had gone.

Feeling dazed and oddly euphoric, she blinked up at Scott, sniffling. He helped her to her feet and passed the skimpy hotpants to her.

'Thank you,' she whispered shyly, turning away to draw them up over her throbbing burning bottom.

'Come on,' he said, 'I'll take you back to the Visitor Centre.'

She took his hand and allowed him to lead her a few feet before stumbling in the grass. 'Oh!' she cried, crumpling to her knees. 'My ankle!'

Preventive Measures

Carly Watson scribbled furiously, trying to keep up with Mr Balfour's recitation of fourth declension nouns.

'... *senatus* ... *senatum* ... *senatui* ... *senatu* ... And the plural: *senatus* ... *senatuum* ... *senatibus* ...'

The third declension had been a nightmare. All those irregularities. It was the year 2054; why did they still have to study Latin, of all things?

St Bartholomew's School for Girls was unusually old fashioned. Its Governors believed in the traditional methods of education and, as such, the girls had none of the modern gadgets that made life so much simpler and easier for their peers in other schools. Within the walls of St Bartholomew's was a school that did not seem to have changed much in the past century.

'There are no adjectives which follow the fourth declension,' said Mr Balfour, 'only nouns.'

Carly breathed a sigh of relief. She was already losing track of all the different forms of words she'd learnt. Sometimes she would stare at a word for a whole minute, unable to recall if it was a noun or a verb.

'Adjectives follow exclusively the first, second and third declensions. Now, if we –'

A sudden knock at the door interrupted him and he frowned at his pupils as if they were to blame.

'Come in.'

The door swung open to admit Jane Rossiter, a prefect. 'I'm sorry to interrupt, Mr Balfour, but I'm to give you this.' She handed him a note.

Mr Balfour took the folded slip of paper and dismissed Jane with a curt nod. He read the note silently and looked up.

'Carly Watson,' he said.

Carly had been reading over her notes. She jumped, startled. 'Yes, sir?'

Mr Balfour gazed at her sternly. 'You're to report to the Headmaster's office.'

She blanched. 'I . . . But I . . .'

'Now, young lady.'

Trembling, Carly got to her feet and crossed the room on shaky legs to take the note from the Latin master. Mr Balfour closed the door behind her and she was alone in the corridor. She looked at the note, but all it said was that she was to report to Mr Fortescue. Carly had no idea what it was about, but it couldn't be good. With a nervous gulp, she set off for the Headmaster's office.

There were two girls waiting outside his office, perched on the antique settle. Carly knew them both. The one nearest the door was a tall brunette named Pamela Whiteley. She had a resigned expression on her face. Next to her sat Jocelyn Drake, captain of the girls' lacrosse team. The slender redhead was wearing her gym kit. Both girls looked as nervous as Carly. She took her place beside Jocelyn.

'What did you do?' Carly whispered.

Jocelyn shrugged. 'I've no idea. I was called away from practice with no explanation. I expect I'll find out.'

'What about you?' Carly whispered to Pamela.

'Oh. I don't know either,' she replied, not sounding entirely convinced.

'I can't imagine what he wants me for,' Carly said. 'I was just –'

Suddenly the door opened and Mr Fortescue peered out. 'Ah. Miss Whiteley,' he said, addressing Pamela. 'Come in, please.'

Pamela followed him into the office and the door swung shut behind her. Jocelyn edged into the empty space and leant close to the door. She listened for a few moments, then shook her head. 'Can't make it out,' she told Carly.

Carly was about to get up and stand by the door to listen herself, but the silence was broken by an awful *swoosh-crack!*

From within, Pamela cried out.

Carly and Jocelyn looked at each other in horror.

The sound was repeated and again Pamela yelped.

Frozen with fear, the girls held their breath for the third stroke and wilted with relief when there wasn't a fourth.

After a few moments, Pamela emerged, sniffling and rubbing her backside. She scurried past the waiting girls without a word.

Mr Fortescue was at the door again. 'Drake,' he said sharply. 'You're next.'

The office swallowed Jocelyn the way it had Pamela, and Carly held her breath in the long silence that followed. She could hear the murmur of voices, but she couldn't make out what was being said. Finally, the sound of the cane penetrated the thick oak door and she winced in sympathy with each stroke, imagining poor Jocelyn bending over in her gym kit, touching her toes. What had she done? Was she lying about not knowing?

Pamela had got three strokes. Jocelyn got five.

When the door opened again Carly's stomach seemed to plummet into her feet. She felt ill as she watched a tearful Jocelyn hurry past her, clutching her bottom. Carly could swear the angry red cane wheals shone through the tight white cotton of her gym shorts. She shook her head to rid herself of the image.

'Watson,' said Mr Fortescue without preamble, 'your turn.'

At least the suspense was about to end, she told herself. Not that it was much comfort.

Mr Fortescue stood beside his desk and directed Carly to stand in front of him. 'You are aware of school policy on cheating, are you not?'

'Yes, sir,' she said, bewildered, 'but I haven't cheated on anything, sir, honest!'

The Headmaster's lips curled slightly in what seemed a mockery of a smile. 'No,' he said. 'But you will.'

Carly stared at him, uncomprehending.

'That is, you *would* have,' he corrected.

'Sir, I – I don't understand. I've never cheated in my life.'

Mr Fortescue nodded. 'I know it's hard to accept, Watson. But it seems that some of the parents were beginning to find St Bartholomew's too old-fashioned. They asked for some modernisation. Therefore, the Governors have instituted a new discipline policy. It has proven effective in other schools and I'm sure it will prove just as effective here.'

He seemed to be waiting for Carly to ask what it was. When she didn't, he continued.

'The Pre-Misbehaviour Programme catches misbehaviour *before* it occurs. And we know that, without intervention, you would have cheated on Friday's Latin exam.'

Carly gasped.

'Yes, Watson,' he said, nodding. 'Fourth declension nouns *are* difficult, aren't they? And you're barely keeping your head above water in Mr Balfour's class. Abigail Holland sits just to your right. And she can be careless about not covering her work.'

As he spoke, Carly knew he was right. The thought had crossed her mind on the last exam. And today, trying to keep straight the twelve forms of *senatus*, she couldn't help but consider it again. As a last resort, but nonetheless . . .

Mr Fortescue turned to his desk and picked up the evil-looking length of rattan. With a sigh he gestured to the armchair in the centre of the room. 'Cheating is a serious offence, Watson. And I can't award you fewer than six strokes.'

Carly thought she would faint.

'Raise your skirt, lower your knickers and bend over.'

'But I wouldn't have cheated, sir,' she offered feebly. 'It just crossed my mind, but I wouldn't really have done it.'

The Headmaster shook his head. 'That's what every girl says. But it isn't true. The Programme doesn't concern itself with what you may have *considered* doing; it only acts on what you *will* do. Now that you know your future you

119

can choose to change it. But only because you *know* it's what you will do. Now, assume the position, please.'

Her head was spinning with the paradox, but she didn't dare disobey. Not after hearing what had happened to Pamela and Jocelyn. And she was to get *six* strokes! With shaking hands, she raised her pleated tartan skirt. She hooked her thumbs in the waistband of her white cotton knickers and tugged them down until they pooled at her ankles. Then she bent over the back of the chair, her hands on the leather seat. It was slick and warm, no doubt from the previous girls' hands and tears.

Mr Fortescue adjusted her skirt and shirttail so that they were high up over her back. Then he rested the cane against her bottom. The rattan was also warm. 'I expect you to stay in position. If you move it will earn you an extra stroke.'

She trembled.

Then she felt the air stir behind her as he drew back his arm and delivered the first terrible stinging stroke.

Carly yelped and squirmed in place as the sting intensified and became a hot throbbing blur of agony.

The next stroke seemed to cut her in two and she cried out, resisting the urge to reach back and protect her burning flesh. She forced herself to stay in position, however.

The third was even worse and she howled with pain, writhing over the chair. She was only halfway there.

Number four caught her low, just beneath the cheeks. Tears flooded her eyes and she seemed to wilt over the chair, helpless against the onslaught of the savage implement.

Another stroke and she was sobbing and gasping for air. Her bottom felt as though it was being sliced apart, but there was only one more stroke.

Mr Fortescue didn't make her wait long. He gave her the final stroke and Carly howled. Then she abandoned herself to helpless crying. It was over.

'You may get up, Watson, and adjust your uniform.'

Stiffly, she obeyed, sniffling and wiping her nose on her sleeve like a little girl. She inched her knickers up her legs, uttering a little hiss of pain as they made contact with her burning backside.

'Very well,' said Mr Fortescue. 'You may return to class. And I trust I will not need to see you back here again.'

'N-no, sir,' she whimpered, her head down.

She left his office in the same disgrace as Pamela and Jocelyn. And there were two more girls waiting outside now. They had heard her punishment. Carly hurried past before they could speak to her.

Carly Watson attacked the Latin with renewed vigour, determined not to be bested by dead Romans. They'd already got her caned. And for something she hadn't done . . . yet. Well, she would have done, though. The caning was meant to stop her doing it. It was bizarre, this new discipline policy. It made St Bartholomew's seem almost as modern as the outside world.

Several girls were summoned to Mr Fortescue's office in that first week. Finally, when the gossip mill had made the rounds, an announcement was made in assembly about the Pre-Misbehaviour Programme.

Carly translated the sentences in the book, concentrating hard. She was so focused on the task that she didn't even hear the knock at the door. It was Jane Rossiter again. The girl's voice made her jump. Then Mr Balfour was looking at the note she had handed him and glancing in Carly's direction.

No, Carly thought, the dread making her light-headed. *No, I'm not going to cheat now. It's a mistake.*

Mr Balfour read aloud the name on the paper and it took Carly a moment to register that it wasn't hers.

Beside her Abigail Holland went pale and rose shakily to her feet.

(*This story was inspired by the film* Minority Report, *which takes place in a futuristic society. The public is kept safe by a special division called Precrime, which apprehends criminals before they commit crimes. I couldn't help but find it an irresistible idea for a school CP story.*)

121

Escape to Alcatraz

Is there anything worse than sightseeing with your parents? Their presence is a constant reminder of my childhood, which they haven't seemed to notice is over. I'm eighteen, not eight. I don't need to be told to come away from the railing, especially not in front of the cute English boy in ripped jeans who's been watching me all afternoon. The older man he's with has the same features – clearly his father. The boy and I share a weary eye-rolling glance about the burden of chaperones.

With my mom it's the same old nagging. When are you going to college? When are you going to meet a nice boy (emphasis on 'nice')? What are you going to do with your life? Jesus.

My dad is only slightly more tolerable, with his droning history professor voice, quizzing me on names and dates about the island prison. Bor-*ing*. If I do decide to go to college I definitely won't be following in his footsteps.

I really couldn't care less about the tour of the Rock. Or the view of San Francisco from the ferry. I mean, it's a cool city and all, but like, I've seen it in a million movies. I'm only interested in one kind of scenery: the male kind.

And there are some cute guys on the tour. There's the English boy. And another one whose accent I can't place. Hungarian? Oh, and the guy who raised and lowered the gate to let us stampede onto the ferry. Though he's too clean-cut for me, really.

But best of all were the three prison guards. Well, they're not really guards. Just tour guides in uniforms. They looked convincing enough. And they were *hot*. Aaron, Jack and Michael. I made sure to read their name badges.

I sucked in my breath when I saw the handcuffs dangling from Jack's belt. He's the youngest, probably in his mid-twenties. Blond, boyish and sorta cute. Totally fuckable. I made sure to squeeze past him at one point – *really* close – and brush against his crotch. He couldn't take his eyes off me after that. My mom was scandalised.

Then we were in D Block – solitary confinement. The prisoners called it Sunset Strip, to go with the other corridors between cellblocks: Broadway, Park Avenue, Michigan Avenue... Well, there was some old guy, an ex-prisoner, who used to pull a button off his prison outfit and throw it in the air and hunt around in the dark for it. I looked straight at Jack and with a flick of my red hair said I could think of much more interesting ways to amuse myself, all alone in the dark. He actually blushed!

Aaron flashed me a warning glance that went straight to my cunt. He was clearly the one in charge. Fortyish. Tall, lean and wiry with jet-black hair shot through with grey. Wicked goatee. His stern look inspired even raunchier thoughts and it was all I could do not to ask him to demonstrate how the handcuffs worked.

It was chilly in the prison, but I had dressed to impress in a white ballet wraparound top. No bra, of course; I don't really need them. The top showed off my belly and the little gold ring in my navel. And the cold air showed off the peaks of my nipples.

I waited until Aaron and Jack were behind me and then I bent over to tie my shoe. My tight jeans sit so low on my hips they nearly come off when I do that, but it's worth it. If the view of my hot pink thong above the waistline wasn't enough, they got to see the cleft of my cheeks too. And I know I've got a nice ass. They weren't complaining.

The third one, Michael, was describing how the cells locked when I did it and I heard his voice catch in his throat. Just for a second. But it was a meaningful second. He didn't seem like the easily ruffled type. He's probably not much older than Jack, but the glasses add distinction.

The rest of the tour was totally boring, but I managed to have fun anyway. I always do. Especially when it's at the expense of my uptight parents. I'm a merciless tease and I enjoyed getting the three guys worked up. Perhaps they'd all jerk off in the bathroom later. Thinking about me. I'd certainly be thinking about *them*.

But now that we're back on the ferry, my parents have to go and ruin the mood.

'Why do you always have to embarrass us, Sara?'

'Oh, come on, Mom, like you were never my age.'

'I had too much self-respect to flaunt myself like that in front of strangers,' she says with a sniff.

I roll my eyes. 'What*ever*.'

Now it's my dad's turn. I try to tune him out, watching the little drama unfolding on the ferry gangway. A child has dropped something in the water and from his screams you'd think the world was coming to an end. Boo-hoo-hoo.

My dad is still pontificating and I decide I've had enough. If they don't give me some room to breathe I'm gonna start screaming myself. The ferry's just about to leave and I suddenly have a brilliant idea. Ours was the last tour of the day. And this is the last ferry to the mainland.

'I have to go to the bathroom,' I announce. For my dad's benefit I add, 'Female trouble.' He looks away and my mom sighs dramatically.

Then I make my escape. I slip past the cluster of stragglers on the gangway, back onto the island. I stand at the end of the line, as though I'm just having a last look at the prison. Then I inch away from the crowd until I reach the dockside buildings. It's ridiculously easy. No one even notices; they're too focused on the bawling child. The evening sky throws convenient shadows and I duck behind a dark clump of bushes and crouch down to wait. The kid's father finally manages to rescue the toy and the ungrateful brat snatches it away. I smother a laugh.

Within moments the ferry sets off across the black velvet bay, taking my parents with it. There is a moment's surge of childish fright, but the sense of freedom soon replaces it. I'm alone! They'll be panicking very soon, searching the bathroom and peering overboard to see if I've jumped.

I have no idea what will happen when they discover I'm gone, but they'll probably have to turn the ferry around and come back for me. That will be a-whole-nother lecture and a major guilt trip, but at least for now I have the precious gift of some time to myself. The entire island is mine.

I smile and begin winding my way up the switchback path towards the dark hulk of the prison. It looks even more foreboding under the deepening sky. It's cold and blustery and I'm starting to shiver in my skimpy outfit. No problem. I'll be inside soon. Maybe I'll explore some of the areas they didn't take us to on the tour.

'Hey, you!'

I jump like I've been shot, my heart pounding wildly. I can't tell where the voice came from. And the shadows make it impossible to see very far. There's the sound of running boots and I don't know which way to turn. Terrified, I run towards the ruins of the warden's house as the voices shout to each other over the wind.

'Where is she?'

'Over here!'

'Get her!'

'Stop or I'll shoot!'

With a little cry I skid to a halt, covering my head and closing my eyes. I'm in deep shit now. The boots slow to a walk, crunching on the gravel, and I cower as they draw nearer.

'Get your hands where I can see them!'

Imagining a policeman's gun trained on me, I raise my trembling hands, spreading my fingers to show I'm un-armed. Me and my stupid ideas.

'I'm sorry,' I start to say. 'I missed the ferry and I just –'

'Quiet! Down on your knees, hands behind your neck.'

Tears well in my eyes. I've never been arrested before. My voice cracks. 'I'm sorry . . .'

'She doesn't follow orders very well, does she?'

'No, she doesn't. But then she wouldn't be trying to escape if she could follow orders.'

'Wouldn't have been sent here in the first place.'

What the hell are they talking about? I wince as I kneel on the hard ground, blinking back the tears and wondering how much trouble I'm in. And how I can get out of it.

There is a metallic clink and the cold feel of steel around my right wrist. A rough hand repositions my arm behind my back and secures my left wrist beside it.

'On your feet, girl.'

I stumble up awkwardly, still formulating excuses, when I find myself face to face with Aaron. My mouth falls open and I see Jack and Michael off to my left.

Before I can speak, Aaron turns me towards the prison and plants his hand firmly in my lower back. 'March,' he says gruffly.

A surge of heat floods my groin as I take in the situation. It warms to an insistent little throb as they lead me back to the cellhouse. I had my fun earlier. Now it's their turn to play.

I jump at the clang of metal as Jack unlocks one of the Broadway cells – C Block, I think. He slides the door open and I peer inside at the hard wooden bed on the left. The rooms are only five by nine feet, like a cage in some ancient zoo. On the tour, everyone had filed into them for the geeky experience of being Al Capone for a few seconds. Now the thought of being locked in fills me with perverse excitement.

'What's your name?' Michael demands.

'Sara.'

He laughs scornfully. 'Your surname, girl. Or weren't you paying attention when we explained the rules? Prisoners are addressed by their surnames only.'

Blushing, I whisper, 'Delaney.'

Jack is leaning against the bars of the open cell with a cocky smile, his arms crossed over his chest. 'I don't think she was listening to a word we said earlier.'

Behind me, Aaron unlocks my left wrist and leads me towards the cell. 'Obviously,' he agrees. 'Or she'd know that unauthorised absence means disciplinary action.'

His words make me light-headed and I can barely stand. I'm expecting him to shove me inside and slam the door, locking me in. But he stops just outside the door and looks back at Jack. 'Give me your cuffs,' he orders.

Jack obeys, relinquishing them without question while I wonder what Aaron has in mind. He locks the second pair around my left wrist. Then he pushes me backwards roughly, against the cold bars.

'Arms up, Delaney,' he says sharply, like a drill sergeant. 'Over your head.'

'Look, I –'

His eyes flash and he draws himself up. 'You are required to obey all orders without delay or argument. It's very simple. If you break the rules, you will be punished.'

It's a direct quote from the prison rules they'd read on the tour. His words make my pussy ache with the dirty thrill of powerlessness. I do as he says, melting under his authority. I'm astonished at my compliance.

The handcuffs clatter noisily as Aaron locks them around the bars. The horizontal crossbar traps my arms high above my head, stretching and displaying me.

The three jailers stand back, surveying their prisoner with satisfaction.

Michael turns to his superior and murmurs something. I only catch the phrase 'taught a lesson'. It makes me squirm.

'Oh yes, she'll be punished,' Aaron says with the sombre demeanour of a hanging judge. 'But if you like you can play with her first.'

I look at him, wide-eyed and pleading. But he's in total control. Immune to girlie tricks.

I can't help but notice the bulge in Jack's uniform trousers and he catches me looking. He shifts his feet and I grin. I'm thankful my own arousal isn't as obvious.

Michael watches the exchange and he slips the police truncheon from his belt. A symbol of power, meant for subduing prisoners. He smacks it gently against his palm, staring me down. I lower my eyes to the floor. Placing the end of the truncheon underneath my chin, he makes me raise my head. I flush deeply and do my best to look contrite.

Now that Michael has cowed me, Jack steps forward. With boyish eagerness, he cups my breasts, squeezing gently. I can't suppress a little moan as my body responds. Then he reaches around behind me, his fingers feeling along my spine for the ties that hold my top together.

I whimper. 'No . . .'

Suddenly Michael strikes the bars with the truncheon, startling me into silence with a resounding CLANG! He glances over his shoulder at Aaron and smiles, enjoying this sanctioned sadism.

Jack unties the knot and peels the flimsy shirt open, unwrapping me slowly like a gift. My nipples pucker at the exposure and he lets the flaps of my top hang at my sides, framing my small pert breasts.

Jack cups his hand over my right breast and slides his finger languidly back and forth across the hard bud of my nipple, sending electric currents of sensation through my body. I draw in a sharp breath and he seems to like my response.

'Good girl,' he says.

Michael murmurs agreement and reaches out to tweak my left nipple. I twist away with a little yip as Jack does to the same thing to my right. My cunt pulses in response and I strain against the handcuffs. I'm not going anywhere.

Michael places the truncheon in my lower back and I gasp at the touch of the cold polished wood. He pushes firmly, urging me to arch my back. I comply, blushing furiously at the way it thrusts my tits out for them.

Relishing my helplessness, both men lower their mouths to my chest. Behind them I see Aaron watching and I shut my eyes against the humiliation of being used so shamelessly in front of him. Both tongues probe and flutter against my nipples, stimulating me almost beyond endurance.

Then Michael raises his head, replacing his mouth with cruel fingers that twist and pinch, making me cry out softly. 'There are lots of ways to punish a naughty girl. Especially in her naughty places.' He slips his hand down between my legs and gives my pussy a sharp swat through my jeans. I jump.

'But if you'd like us to stop, all you have to do is say, "Please, sir, I'm ready for my punishment now".'

I turn scarlet, horrified at the prospect. I moan with shame and then Jack's teeth close gently on my nipple. I'm grateful for the handcuffs; I wouldn't be able to stand up on my own. When I sag against the bars I feel the truncheon press against my back again.

My body jerks in response to every little nip and flick of Jack's tongue. I maintain the lewd position while Michael plays the truncheon over my body, making me quiver. Suddenly, he thrusts it between my legs. The position forces me on tiptoe and I bite my lip as he grinds it against my dampening crotch. I clamp my thighs around it, overwhelmed by the sensations.

Jack has my tits to himself now and he watches my face as he rolls the nipples between his fingers, increasing the pressure until I wince and then relaxing his grip. A sharp tweak. Then a kiss. My head is spinning.

Michael removes the truncheon and as his fingers smack my crotch again I know I won't be able to take much more of their torture. I'm terrified by the threat of punishment, but I'm also thrilled to the core. I have no choice. My face burning, I force myself to say it. My voice is barely audible.

'I'm ready for my punishment.'

'What?' Michael asks, mockingly cupping his hand to his ear. 'I didn't hear that, Delaney.'

Hanging my head in misery, I say what he wants to hear. 'Please, sir, I'm ready for my punishment.'

Jack gives my nipples a final pinch and he and Michael turn to their leader.

With a half-smile Aaron unhooks a jingling keyring from his belt and releases me from the handcuffs. I sink to my knees on the floor, rubbing my wrists petulantly.

'We've never had a female inmate before,' he says, standing over me imperiously. 'But I doubt whether a spell in solitary would teach you any kind of memorable lesson. Of course, there's always the Dungeon . . .'

I glance nervously along the corridor, remembering the tour. The Dungeon was what the prisoners called the cellblock in the basement. It dated from the island's days as a military prison in the nineteenth century. The cells were still used in the 1930s for unmanageable prisoners.

Aaron watches the play of emotions across my face for a few moments before offering me a thin smile. 'No, I think perhaps something more . . . humbling.'

He pulls me to my feet and my heart flutters as he guides me through the door into the tiny cell. Jack and Michael watch like hungry wolves, taking up positions just outside the cell.

'Take your jeans down.'

I blink in surprise.

He repeats his command, clipping the words with a military precision that makes my cunt twitch.

When I hesitate he shakes his head slowly, like I'm a naughty child. He looks behind me and starts to say Michael's name.

'No!' I beg, afraid of what Michael will do. 'No, I'll do it!'

My hands are shaking too much to manage the zipper, but the jeans are stretchy, so I simply pull them down.

Jack makes an appreciative noise and I regret the hot pink thong at once. I turn sideways, but there's no way to shield myself from their gaze. I'm a pet in a cage.

Aaron sits on the edge of the bed and beckons me to his right side. And I realise what he has in mind. A hot flush covers my entire body and I clasp my hands beseechingly, like a silent movie heroine.

He lowers his voice. 'Come here, Delaney. Over my knee.'

My own knees threaten to buckle and I do as he says, turning my back to the open door and the two guards outside it, watching.

Aaron guides me over his lap and I stare ahead at the peeling paint on the wall at the back of the cell. A tiny ancient sink juts from the wall and the cell is so cramped I could reach out and touch it if I wanted.

I flinch when I feel his hand on my bottom. Just a pat, but it makes me jump. He gives each cheek a firm squeeze and I feel his hand lift away. I've never been spanked before in my life and I have no idea what to expect. I hold my breath.

With a resounding slap he brings his palm down on my right cheek. I arch my back with a yelp. He smacks my left cheek almost immediately and I writhe on his lap, clutching the edge of the bed. His hand imparts a wicked sting, covering each cheek completely.

'You've been a very bad girl,' he says, spanking me hard and fast. 'Flirting and teasing us all day. You ought to be ashamed, making such a spectacle of yourself.'

Behind me I hear Michael call me a cockteaser. The derogatory terms only make me hotter. Yes, I *am* a shameless little slut, tease, whore. And right now all I can think about is how wet the gusset of my thong is. My captors must be able to smell me.

The spanking increases in tempo and intensity and I can't help kicking and wriggling. My jeans have slipped down my legs and they're tangled around my ankles. I kick both legs up at a particularly hard slap and Aaron swats my thigh.

'Keep your legs down,' he snarls.

But I can't. Every time his hand connects with the tender flesh of my bottom, my feet leave the ground. He rests his hand on my cheeks, a warning. Meekly, I lower my feet to the floor. There's a purposeful step behind me and someone's boot comes down on my jeans, pinning my legs.

'That's better,' Aaron says, running his fingers over the reddened flesh. I wriggle under his touch, noticing for the first time the distinct hardness under my rib cage.

His fingers slip down along the crack of my bottom, tracing the outline of my thong. He presses his knuckles into the gusset and I gasp, pressing back. My pussy is so swollen it hurts. When he starts to peel the thong down, I resist, suddenly self-conscious about the other two seeing my arousal. He ignores my protest.

'She's dripping wet, the little whore.' Michael's comment is mortifying, but I can't hide myself from them.

The spanking continues with renewed vigour and I yelp and struggle, making far more of a spectacle of myself now than I did on the tour. And all I can think about is the exquisite humiliation of being completely at the mercy of three men with the power to do whatever they want with me.

At last Aaron lets me up and I stumble to my feet, hobbled by the jeans twisted around my ankles. My hands drift to cover my shaved pussy, but Michael uncoils himself from his station by the cell door and slaps them away. His predatory eyes gleam behind the glasses. Every little show of force excites him more and I feel myself dampen in response. I'm tempted to make a run for it just so he'll chase me, tackle me and haul me back with added brutality.

'Strip,' he says, his voice low and menacing.

He doesn't need to tell me that resistance will earn me more punishment. My bottom is already burning and I don't think I can take any more. I obediently disentangle my shoes from my jeans and slip them off. I take my time folding the jeans and positioning them carefully on top of the shoes. When I can't stall any longer I flick my eyes back up to Michael. His cock looks ready to burst out of his pants.

'The mattress,' I hear Aaron say from behind me. 'Bring it out here.'

I look over my shoulder to see Jack stripping the cell. He pulls the thin mattress off the bed and drags it out into the corridor.

I stare at it, my shirt hanging open and my thong around my knees. I can't help wondering how many hardened criminals have passed sleepless nights on this very mattress. The wind howls around the barren island and sharks patrol the freezing water of the bay. The sense of isolation is overwhelming and it only enhances my vulnerability.

Michael crosses his arms expectantly and I scurry to obey the unspoken command. I shrug out of my top and add it to the pile of clothes. I hesitate at the thong. Even though it's not covering anything, it's my last shred of dignity. I stand before him nervously.

'Everything,' he prompts without a trace of pity.

I tremble all over as I bend down to slip the thong off. The little scrap of material is positively soaked. Embarrassed, I wad it into a ball.

Before I can hide it under the rest of the clothes, Michael holds out his hand. My cheeks blazing, I surrender it to him. He inspects it, then tucks it into his pocket, his eyes shining.

'Who's first?' Jack asks, breaking the edgy silence.

I bite my lip in anticipation. The commanding officer usually gets first crack at the spoils of war, but I sense Aaron is more into discipline than sex. And Michael's a sadist, so I'm sure he has something special in mind.

'Why don't you go first, kid?' Michael says to Jack, taking me by the arm and pushing me towards the mattress. 'I want her ass.'

A little cry catches in my throat at this revelation and I stare at him in horror. But first I belong to Jack. Trembling with fear and desire, I sink to my knees on the mattress. Jack already has his pants down and I gasp at the size of his cock. Not that I'm that experienced, but I've never even imagined anything that size before. He glances at the others with a hint of self-consciousness.

'Go on,' Michael urges.

It's all the encouragement he needs. His cock stiffens in response and swells even more. He pushes me down on my back and I wince at the feel of the rough mattress on my tender backside. I press my legs together, my thighs slick with my juices.

Jack takes me by the ankles and raises my legs and bottom as he guides his cock towards my hungry sex. I put my arms above my head to grip the top edge of the mattress, bracing myself.

He eases the head in and I tense, waiting for him to plunge the rest in. I'm expecting it to hurt; I *want* it to hurt. But now that he's got me where he wants me, he's suddenly gone all shy. Frustrated, I thrust my hips up against him, urging him to take me. When he hesitates I look him straight in the eye and say, 'Typical boy. All talk and no action.'

133

The soft laughter behind me has to be Michael's. *He* knows what I want.

'Not so tough now, are you?' I taunt. 'You won't last five seconds.'

His boyish features darken with sexy menace and I feel the head of his cock twitch inside me. I open my mouth to egg him on further, but there's no need. He plunges himself in up to the hilt, making me cry out. He pulls me up by the ankles with each thrust, driving me onto his cock with excruciating force.

I howl at every thrust, digging my fingers into the mattress just to hold on. I had never realised there were so many nerve endings in my pussy. Every single one is alive and screaming with pain and pleasure as he fucks me harder and rougher than I've ever dreamed possible. My sweaty thighs shake with the effort and he releases my ankles, going even deeper as I wrap my legs around his muscular torso. I won't be able to walk when he's finished with me.

Jack slows his rhythm, savouring each slow languid stroke and my accompanying gasp as his pelvis slams into mine. He slides nearly all the way out and waits for me to open my eyes and look up at him before driving his cock in again, making me wince and hiss through my teeth.

On my right I hear the sound of a zip and Jack looks up with a grin. I start to turn my head, but he impales me again and rolls us both onto our sides. He hooks his left leg over my right, spreading me open for Michael, whose purposeful fingers are smearing something cold and wet on the puckered rosebud of my anus. I tense with sudden fear and offer a feeble struggle, but Aaron's voice cuts the air.

'Do you need to be handcuffed again, Delaney?'

My sex pulses at the threat and I try to relax as I feel Michael's finger probing the opening. He slides it inside and swirls it around. I can't help clenching around his finger and his whispered approval turns my face scarlet. He withdraws and I feel his cock demanding entrance. Jack is still inside me and I stare into his face with wide fearful eyes as Michael pushes himself inside. Slowly. Forcefully.

134

When I yelp he twines a hand in my hair, pulling my head back to growl in my ear.

'This is what you've been begging for all day, isn't it?'

I shudder as he draws himself out, only to drive it back in, hard.

'Isn't it?'

'Yes,' I manage to choke out.

He gives my hair a sharp tug. 'Yes what?'

Jack rams me from the front and I whimper. 'Yes, sir.'

They take turns thrusting in and out, commenting all the time on my helplessness. Every inch of my skin seems to vibrate with intensity. Then they change the rhythm and I quiver as the two cocks meet inside, separated only by a thin wall.

The humiliation is made complete by Aaron's looming presence. I have never felt so alive. I've escaped to a world where there are no rules to weigh me down, no parents and no moral code to oppress me. Only the freedom of pure debauchery.

I cry out with wild abandon as both cocks pummel me mercilessly, filling me up and making me desperate to come.

Suddenly, Jack tenses and his breathing quickens. He grips my arms tightly as he empties himself into me in hot little spurts.

Michael isn't far behind and I cling to Jack as I feel the jets of Michael's sperm in my deflowered ass.

As both men lie panting and spent on either side of me, my own sex throbs, hungry for release. I slip my hand down between my legs, desperate to join them in the afterglow.

Michael is quick to grab my wrist and stop me. I want to cry in frustration. But my eyes are drawn to Aaron, who looks down at me severely. I melt under his black gaze, knowing I've broken a tacit rule. I give a little whimper as first Jack, then Michael, withdraw, leaving me empty. I know I'm about to be punished again.

'On your knees,' Aaron says softly, unbuckling his belt.

I do as I'm told, an obedient little submissive now. The mattress is soaked with our mingled juices and sweat and my legs are sticky with come. It's all I can do to keep my hands away from my clit. One touch is all it would take.

He pulls his belt sharply through the loops. I jump at the flapping sound it makes, but I keep my eyes on his boots.

'Elbows down,' he instructs. 'Bottom up.'

I obey instantly, pressing my forehead into the damp mattress. I'll be a good girl for him and take my whipping. I'll take anything they want to give me. I'm theirs.

The belt lashes down against my bottom and I wince, but I don't cry out. The sensation washes over me, stimulating me further. Another stroke and I gasp as though I've been penetrated again. I experience each slap of the wide leather belt as pleasure. It reverberates through my body and for a moment I think I might climax from the whipping alone. But I'm beginning to appreciate the agony and ecstasy of delayed satisfaction and I know this is more a preparation for Aaron than for me. I'll get my turn after him. If I'm good.

He stops and orders me up on my knees. When he presents his cock to me I swallow it gratefully, like a treat. My tongue traces enthusiastic circles around the shaft, flicking the tiny ridge underneath the head. He strokes my hair as he would a pet. I cup his balls in my hand, pulling them forward and tightening my grip. It doesn't take him long. Within seconds he erupts in my mouth, flooding the back of my throat.

When the spasms cease I look up at him, feeling genuine pride at having pleased him. I offer him my wrists, a pleading look of submission in my eyes. His harsh features soften and he gives me an indulgent smile. He locks the handcuffs into place and pulls me to my feet, leading me into the cell.

Someone has replaced the mattress and Aaron guides me onto it. I stretch my cuffed hands out over my head and close my eyes as he parts my willing legs. He slowly draws his fingers up the inside of my thigh and I squirm as I anticipate the touch that will send me over the edge. At last his fingers reach my sex, teasing me gently before caressing the swollen bud of my clit. That's all it takes. I throw my head back with a soundless cry as the wave breaks over me, sweeping me under. Shattered, I curl into a ball and surrender to the blissful little aftershocks that make me gasp and moan.

The chirping of a cell phone penetrates the haze and Aaron's voice answers it.

'Yes, she's here,' he says. 'She's safe.' There's a pause and then he adds, 'No, it's all right. We've got an extra bunk here. Why don't you come back for her in the morning?'

From somewhere miles away I hear the cell door clang shut. The key turns in the lock and I close my eyes.

'Lights out, Delaney,' someone says. I have no idea who.

The Dinner Party

I arrive at the house just as the evening light is fading. The
crisp autumn air chills my bare arms and I stand hesitating
on the steps. I can hear nothing inside.

A wide six-panelled door dominates the façade, a
gleaming black portal between classical white pillars. All
the sash windows are shuttered from within. I feel exposed
by the semicircular fanlight above the door, the only
source of light. It is as though a cold eye is watching me.
Inspecting me.

My hand rests uneasily on the brass knocker. It seems
too heavy to lift. As if urging me on, or perhaps mocking
me, a brisk wind sends a flurry of leaves scuttling down the
street. It sounds like laughter. I turn my head to watch
their flickering papery shapes as they are swallowed by the
shadows of the oak trees lining the street. For a moment
the darkness beckons. My stomach flutters and I tremble,
like a bird poised on the edge of flight.

I make myself turn back to the house. Its stately
proportions and imposing symmetry enhance my apprehension. I feel isolated, like a soldier out of step with the
rest of the squad.

My nervous fingers close around the brass ring and send
it against the striking plate – once, twice. I wince at the
boldness of the sound. It feels as though I am demanding
entry rather than requesting.

I wait, shivering in my blue silk gown and hugging my
thin frame in the icy spill of light. A wisp of hair teases my
neck. I tuck it back into the loose chignon I've tied.

The door swings open and a maid gestures for me to enter. She is older than me, perhaps forty, and her face betrays no expression. Her sombre black dress and white pinafore are immaculate, as orderly as the house itself. She ushers me into the entrance hall without a word, then closes and locks the door behind me.

The hall is a study in balance and proportion. A door to my left mirrors one to my right and their matching pediments make me think of pincers. A sweeping staircase rises out of sight beyond a pair of Doric columns. The intricate carving of the white plaster ceiling and cornices seems like a giant wedding cake.

From deep inside the house come the sounds of a dinner party. The low hum of voices, laughter, the clink of glasses. The lively strains of some Baroque music – Vivaldi, perhaps. My mouth waters at the aroma of rich food – heavy and decadent. I can also smell coffee, so the meal has presumably just ended.

Despite its size, the hall is warm and I follow the maid as she leads me through a door at the far end. Although the majestic marble fireplace is clearly meant to be the focal point, my eyes are drawn immediately to the only item of furniture inside – a low wooden bench placed in the centre of the room.

It is perhaps six feet long and three feet high. At one end is what I at first take to be the headboard of a bed. Three holes are cut into it – one large and two small either side. For a moment I am puzzled. Then my stomach twists and I know it for what it is: a pillory. At the other end is a smaller board with two holes. A wide leather strap encircles the bench at its midpoint.

I glance nervously at the maid, but her face remains impassive. She unbuckles the strap and lifts each of the two hinged boards in turn. Then, her hands folded, she regards me with solemn expectation.

An unpleasant weightlessness overcomes me as I lift my right foot to approach. My step falters and for a moment I am afraid I will faint. The maid does not offer to help. I draw in a low shuddering breath as I manage the few steps from the doorway to the centre of the room. To the bench.

I can almost feel the colour drain from my face and throat as I stand before the austere wooden apparatus, my arms crossed protectively over my chest. I sink slowly to my knees on the bench. I wipe my clammy palms on my gown before placing them on the wood and edging towards the pillory.

Slowly I straighten my legs until I am lying on my stomach. I could be presenting myself on a masseur's table. Except that I'm not.

One at a time I find the grooves for my ankles and my heart lurches as the board snaps into place over them, trapping my legs. A pin slides into a metal catch and then the maid's dress rustles as she moves to the head of the bench.

I place each slender wrist in its waiting groove and the maid guides my neck into position with cool efficient fingers. Like a nurse impervious to a patient's terror over the approach of a needle, she ignores my frightened whimper as she locks the board in place. Her polished black shoes vanish from my line of sight.

My breathing grows shallow as I hear the creak of leather and feel her loop the strap around my waist, slipping it through the buckle and drawing it tight it with a brisk tug that forces the air from my lungs.

A burst of raucous laughter from the dinner party reminds me that I am not alone. I can still hear the music, the lively strings as inappropriate to my situation as balloons at a funeral.

The maid lifts my dress and tucks the skirt up over my back. The starchy material of her pinafore rasps against my stocking tops and then her fingers slide into the waistband of my knickers. I moan slightly as she tugs the delicate silk down my legs, exposing my bottom.

From the corner of my left eye I watch her leave. She closes the door and I hear her shoes clacking smartly across the marble floor, their cadence diminishing.

The pillory is snug against my neck; I can only turn my head the barest fraction in either direction. I can just make out the fireplace to my right, the closed door on my left. In the distance the music swells to a bright finale and after a pause a mournful cello takes over. Still the chatter and laughter continue.

I stare down at the lavish arabesque motif of the Persian carpet beneath me. Its intertwining vines and flowers occupy my entire field of vision as I wait, my skin chilled despite the flickering warmth of the fire in the hearth. A tendril of memory teases me. Something about imperfections.

With my eyes I trace the path of each loop and swirl, counting the delicate blossoms, focusing on their shapes and colours to distract myself from the sudden lull in the party. I imagine the maid informing the revellers that the preparations have been completed.

One pale vine curls in an arc, sprouting five golden flowers.

Their voices reach me again, this time low and purposeful.

The tremulous cello lingers on the air like a fading dream.

Golden flowers give on to red, then blue, tangling and untangling.

I hear the voices growing louder.

The strings answer with the urgency of arrested passion.

Beneath me, a maze of vibrant colour.

Behind me, the opening of another door.

And far away, still, the deep and moody cello.

I lose my place in the pattern as the room begins to fill with people, all chatting amongst themselves as though I'm not even here. A man with a grating voice is relating an anecdote which makes several people laugh at each stage. I suspect it's a story he tells at every social gathering.

To my right I see a pair of graceful stockinged legs, the feet in red stiletto heels. A man walks close behind her, following her liquid steps as she takes up a position near my head. She stands with her toes slightly turned out, her well-muscled calves flexed. A dancer.

A group of men clusters to my left. Their cultured accents and the silly nicknames they call one another suggest they are old school friends. One of them stumbles and a bit of honey-coloured liquid splashes the carpet. His companions laugh uproariously, deriding him as a young blonde maid crouches to mop up the spill. She doesn't look at me.

The voices surround me and I feel strangely disembodied, like a ghost they cannot see. I cast around as much as I am able to, but I can't find the maid who brought me here and restrained me.

A peculiar slicing noise silences the party and I go cold, my anxiety increasing. I tense the muscles in my legs, straining upwards against the board. But it is securely locked.

A shadow comes to rest behind me and to the left. Is it a man or a woman? Something cuts the air like a sword and then cracks like a pistol. A timeless silence engulfs me and then my bottom registers what has happened. Pain flares across my cheeks and I gasp for air, too breathless to cry out.

The room buzzes with hungry fascination, the voices lowered to conspiratorial whispers. I writhe in my wooden prison, unable to move more than an inch in any direction.

The shock begins to subside, but not the pain. For a moment I wonder if it will keep intensifying. Then a second stroke tears my mind away from the first. I yelp and strain against the pillory, my eyes watering with the burning pain.

One of the men hisses theatrically and comments on the accuracy of the stroke. He sounds as if he knows what he's talking about.

The lady with the red shoes moves a few paces to the right and then returns to her companion. She murmurs something – assent or approval – to him.

I am hyper-aware of the details of the room as I seek to distract myself from what I know is coming. I take a deep breath and hold it, waiting for the impact. When it doesn't come I'm forced to exhale, only to feel the cane slash down across my cheeks the moment I do.

Gasping and whimpering, I struggle in vain to focus on the flowers, the dancer's feet, anything but the searing pain flaring across my helpless bottom.

A log in the fireplace pops noisily. A lady nearby gives a birdlike little shriek and the guests around her laugh. She scolds them as the cane slashes down again and my own cry drowns out their mockery.

I squeeze my eyes shut and strain to hear the music again. I can just make out a high icy violin, its sustained wavering note a counterpoint to my suffering.

My eyes fill with tears and I watch them fall onto the carpet, darkening one red flower beneath me. My gaze is drawn back to the red shoes. The dancer stands at a branching in the pattern where the vine divides into three serpentine coils. I trace one of the coils back to my flower, watching its colour deepen like blood.

The men snigger cruelly, regressing to schoolyard bullies as they delight in my ordeal. My sense of self dissolves with every cruel stroke, every humiliating comment, every burst of laughter.

A hard stroke falls in the tender crease between buttock and thigh. The world goes white behind my eyes and the pain drags a guttural animal sound from my throat. A woman giggles madly and I choke down the flash of anger that threatens to surface, twisting my head from side to side. My hair tumbles free of its knot, spilling down to obscure my face with its dark waves. My dignity crumbles with it.

The cane wrenches another wild cry from me as my chastiser's unerring accuracy earns another smattering of applause. The dancer paces away for a closer look at my bottom, then returns to the exact same spot on the rug. As the punishment continues I watch her make this tiny journey again and again, as though her part in this is choreographed. I can no longer hear the music.

Suddenly my memory stirs. Imperfection. By tradition, each Oriental rug has an imperfection deliberately woven into it. A reminder to mere mortals that only God can create perfection.

Desperate for some tether to reality, I search the carpet for its imperfection. I tell myself that if I can find it, the punishment will stop. Through the curtain of hair I scan the interlacing pattern for anomalies, fully aware of the irrationality of my quest.

Laughter. Glasses clinking.

Another stroke.

I scream.

A short-lived burst of anger gives way to surrender and I drown myself in tears as I succumb to the helplessness of my situation. I hear my voice as if from far away, sobbing, pleading, promising. Anything if only it will stop.

Golden flowers and pain. Red shoes and pain. Laughter. Tears. Pain.

The cane rises and falls and I struggle to find myself in its remorseless progression. The voices have blurred into incoherence. We are all underwater, but I am the only one drowning. Through the slowing of time I finally spot the flaw in the perfect fabric – a golden swirl with three blue flowers on my right, two blue flowers on my left. I barely feel the stroke that follows my discovery.

I am lost at the edge of reality. Utterly powerless, I am reduced to the most primitive elements of pure experience. A cipher.

Tears stream down my cheeks. I barely notice when the guests begin to filter out of the room, leaving me alone with my suffering and my empty revelation. Two blue flowers where there should be three. It seems to define my being, my existence distilled to this single irrelevant fact. The door behind me closes and their voices continue beyond it. Their tone is of fulfilment, like pack animals sated by a fresh kill.

The maid returns. With businesslike detachment she unlatches the pillory and releases me from the bench. For several moments I lie still, oddly bereft by the offer of freedom. Then, slowly, I stagger to my feet. My knickers pool round my ankles and my skirt falls back into place, the silk cool against my bottom. I cannot bear the thought of pulling my knickers up over my scorching flesh. I step gingerly out of them, leaving them behind.

The maid leads me to the door and I look back at the scrap of blue silk lying discarded beside the bench.

Someone will tidy them away, but for now they are proof that I was here, that I exist. My face is wet with tears, but there is no one to notice.

We cross the entrance hall again. I move slowly, stiffly, as though in a dream. She opens the door for me and I step through it, out of one world and into another. A world of rules and reason and fairness. A world of predictable sensations and knowable truths. The door clicks shut behind me. It has swallowed my experience, my pain.

When I reach the street I glance back at the house. The cold moonlight illuminates its lines and angles, its relentlessly symmetrical windows like eyes that do not see me. With a heavy heart I begin my uncertain journey home.

Ginger Tart

It was exquisite – the perfect blend of sugar and spice. The burn of the crystallised ginger made Haley's mouth tingle and she closed her eyes, savouring the sensation. She had to restrain herself from stealing any more. There would be plenty for her later. No one would miss it. Nor would anyone miss the wine.

Haley adjusted her cap. The hateful little white doily always ruined her carefully tousled pixie cut. She checked herself, making sure her uniform was in order. Mr Bathurst was always pestering her about her apron being crooked or her top button being undone. As if anyone would notice. To the elite who dined at Asquith Hall she was nothing but a pair of hands that set fancy meals in front of them and took the empty plates away when they were done.

Her apron was definitely straight, but she wondered if he'd notice that she'd shortened her skirt yet another inch. Probably. The man could spot an irregularity from the next county. His pernickety nature was the thing Haley hated most about her job. Mr Bathurst prowled the hotel like a fussy Victorian butler, looking for things to criticise and people to scold.

Haley was too young to be hiding her assets under such an unflattering uniform. If her boss was so concerned about attracting gentlemen to Asquith Hall, he should realise the opportunity girls like Haley presented. A flash of leg, a glimpse of cleavage and they'd be loyal patrons.

What man didn't fantasise about a sexy French maid? Well, besides Mr Bathurst. Really, it was a crime that someone so good-looking should be so strait-laced.

Authority figures had always been her biggest turn-on, but Mr Bathurst seemed blind to the possibilities. He was quick enough to reprimand her for every little mistake, but he was immune to her playful insinuations. Such a waste.

She sighed and stole a peek out into the dining hall. It was almost time to serve the soup. It was a small affair this afternoon – a birthday celebration for Sir Peter Something-or-other. Marissa had told her that he was a friend of Lord Asquith's. It explained why Mr Bathurst was at his punctilious best. The Man Himself was here.

Lord Asquith's portrait hung above the fireplace in the oak-panelled hotel lobby. He was dressed for the hunt, standing beside a magnificent white horse. His dark hair was combed back and there were flecks of silver at his temples. He held a riding crop by his side, as though he was tapping it against his thigh. Lord Asquith had been invading Haley's fantasies since the day she saw it. She could evoke his image with photographic clarity: his imposing stature, his aristocratic nose, his compelling black eyes.

But it was the riding crop that fascinated her most of all. Her bottom would tingle with unfulfilled need every time she passed the portrait. And when she confided her feelings to her boyfriend, Matt, he incorporated the peer into the kinky threesome fantasies he whispered to her in the mornings as he fondled her awake.

Haley had only met Lord Asquith once, six months before. And it had been disastrous. He had held a huge New Year's party for his friends in the Great Hall. And he had generously let the hotel staff use one of the smaller rooms for their own party.

Haley was there with Matt, who was almost as eager as she was to see him in the flesh. They were both rather tipsy and Matt wanted Haley to sneak off to one of the hotel rooms with him.

'You're insane!' she giggled. 'Do you want me to lose my job?'

147

'Come on, no one'll see.'

Haley scanned the room and, sure enough, there was Mr Bathurst, standing near the bar. 'Uh-uh. Bathurst's got ESP. He'll know.'

Matt looked thoughtful for a moment. Then he grinned devilishly. 'So offer him some favours in exchange for looking the other way. As long as I get to watch.'

Haley nearly choked on her champagne. Matt was a voyeur of the highest order, but he still sometimes surprised her.

'You're right,' Matt continued, scrutinising her boss. 'He *would* make a good Mr Darcy.'

Haley shook her head sadly. 'He may be gorgeous, but I'm no Elizabeth Bennet. He's completely un-seduceable.'

Matt shrugged. 'Too bad. It's his loss. We'll just have to take our chances.' He took Haley's arm and made as if to drag her off.

'Stop it, Matt! It's not worth the risk.' She pulled away.

Matt affected an exaggerated pout, looking so boyish and adorable that she was tempted.

'Very well,' he said. 'But your prudery has a price.'

'Oh yeah?'

He arched an eyebrow. 'Two prices, in fact.'

'What's the first?'

'We crash the fancy party.'

A naughty grin spread across Haley's face. 'Oh, yes,' she purred.

The Great Hall was as festive as Haley had ever seen it, but the party was nowhere near as raucous as the staff's one. Garlands hung from the portraits of staid, dour-faced old men. Balloons with trailing streamers bumped against the great hammer-beams above them. But the guests were polite and restrained. Dressed in tasteful finery, they glided through the party with patrician grace. There would definitely be no photocopying of bottoms here.

'Real class,' Haley said admiringly.

'Yeah.'

She scanned the room for Lord Asquith, but she couldn't see him anywhere.

148

Matt cleared his throat. 'Now for the second price.'

'Which is?'

'Your knickers. Give them to me.'

She squirmed. 'OK. Just let me go to the loo and –'

He caught her by the arm. 'No. Right here.'

Her eyes widened and her cheeks flooded with warmth. 'Everyone will see!'

'Yes, I expect they will.'

Astonished at his boldness, Haley's body nonetheless responded to the idea. But there was no way she could do it *here*. Not in front of the wealthy and titled guests of Lord Asquith.

'No,' she said firmly. 'Forget it.'

'I suppose I'll have to take them off myself, then.'

His hand crept up under the hem of her short red dress and Haley shrieked in surprise, making everyone nearby turn to look at them. She dissolved into gales of embarrassed laughter. The onlookers turned away with disdain, no doubt lamenting the lack of discipline in schools today.

'They should bring back the birch,' muttered one prim dowager.

'Come on,' Matt said, leading her deeper into the room.

Nervously, Haley allowed herself to be led, wondering if he would really go through with it. The thought thrilled her and she imagined herself after a few more glasses of champagne, stripping off and dancing on the tabletops.

Matt pinned her against the Jacobean panelling and slipped his hand under her skirt again, cupping her cheeks and making her moan. He drew his hands around her thighs and gently rubbed his knuckles up and down the damp gusset of her panties. Haley shivered. Then he slid his hand under the elastic and peeled the flimsy red lace down below her skirt. French knickers. Matt's favourite. With a whisper, they slipped down her legs and she stepped out of them.

Matt held out his hand expectantly.

Haley was emboldened by the exhibitionistic thrill of being bare underneath her dress. It brought out the mischief-maker in her. She picked up her panties and

149

dangled them in front of Matt. Then when he reached for them she pulled them away, hiding her hand behind her back.

'Oh no,' she said with a teasing smile. 'You'll have to catch me first.' And she raced for the nearest door, her high heels clicking on the waxed oak boards.

When she reached the door she glanced back over her shoulder. She didn't see Matt anywhere. He must have gone out through one of the main doors at the other end, intending to cut her off.

The funhouse thrill of being chased excited Haley even more. She didn't know where the door led, but she didn't stop to worry about it. The room she found herself in was sophisticated and elegant, with dark antique furniture and heavy velvet curtains. A faded Persian rug sprawled beneath her feet and a fire crackled in the hearth. She paled as she realised where she was: she'd stumbled into one of the family's private rooms.

Terrified of being caught, she whirled round to run for the door and crashed headlong into someone. Champagne splashed all over the man's dinner jacket and Haley babbled an apology, frantically brushing at his lapels as though she could wipe away the champagne like so much dust.

'Oh my God, I'm so sorry! I didn't mean . . .' Haley froze. It was Lord Asquith.

He didn't speak. But his quiet bearing intimidated her more than any rebuke. Champagne dripped from the base of his now-empty glass onto the rug. His jacket was probably ruined. But his expression was inscrutable. The bottomless black eyes betrayed no emotion. They simply regarded her, unblinking.

Spellbound, Haley couldn't look away. The silence stretched between them like a hangman's noose. Asquith held her with his penetrating gaze until her own eyes felt starved for moisture. Finally, she blinked, breaking the spell and the silence.

'I'm so sorry,' she repeated, shaking her head. 'I got lost and – I wasn't watching where I was going.' She winced at her inane words; he was well aware of that. But she had to say *something*. The silence was unbearable.

He wasn't looking at her, though. He was looking at something on the floor between them. He placed his glass on a nearby table and bent down to retrieve the scrap of material. Haley turned scarlet as he held her knickers up inquiringly, stretching them between his fingers like a scientist examining some new discovery. His eyes met hers again and still she could read nothing in his face.

Without a word he calmly used them to blot at his jacket. Haley could only stare at him in blank-faced astonishment. When he was finished he tucked her wet knickers into his pocket. He eyed her impassively for a moment and then continued on his way, leaving her alone in the room.

When he had gone Haley realised she was trembling. It was only when she found Matt again that she was able to shake off the moment.

'Aha, there you are!' he said, beaming like a kid with a secret to tell. 'You'll never guess who I just saw.'

Haley turned to him, ashen-faced. 'Lord Asquith.'

'That's right.'

'No. My knickers . . .'

'What about them?'

'They're . . . in his pocket.'

Matt looked doubtful. 'Are you taking the piss?'

Haley shook her head, bewildered. She hardly believed it herself.

Matt thought about it and then burst into laughter. 'Brilliant! Though you should have charged him a tenner at least. Those were expensive.'

Haley blushed and slugged him hard in the shoulder. She felt exposed and vulnerable. But the thought that Lord Asquith had her panties in his pocket was delicious. A sweet violation.

'Are you nervous?' Marissa asked with disbelief.

Haley jumped. 'Of course not,' she said hurriedly. 'What makes you think I'm nervous?'

'Well, your hands don't usually shake like that.'

Wiping her clammy unsteady palms on her apron, Haley fabricated an excuse. 'Oh, I just . . . I didn't have breakfast. My hands get shaky when I don't eat.'

Marissa bought it. 'Well, try not to spill wine on the guests,' she offered with a sympathetic smile. 'Mr Bathurst will go postal.'

'Don't worry.'

The truth was that Haley was extremely nervous. And not just because she would see Lord Asquith again. She and Matt were planning to host their own little party the next night and it was up to Haley to procure the refreshments.

The intimate gathering only required two waitresses and Haley tried to focus on her duties and avoid eye contact with the guests. Normally that wouldn't have been a problem. But she could feel Lord Asquith's eyes on her, boring into her as though he could read every thought in her dirty little mind.

While Marissa was clearing away after the first course, Haley lingered in the kitchen long enough to shove two bottles of wine into her rucksack. Then she heard Mr Bathurst coming and she scampered back out to join her co-worker.

Another course. Another bottle. And another near-interruption by Mr Bathurst. This was not as easy as Matt had said it would be.

The staff were meant to keep a record of how many bottles they opened for a party. It was some accountant's job to see that the figures matched. Sir Peter and his friends were putting it away like lads at a stag night and Haley was sure no one would question whether they'd drunk ten bottles or twenty.

'Haley? Are you sure you're OK?' Marissa asked. 'You're white as a sheet.'

'Yeah, I'm fine. It's just hot in here.' She mopped imaginary sweat off her face and hurried back out to the guests, doing her best to avoid Lord Asquith.

At last, it was time to serve the pudding. There was enough for everyone to have seconds. But they weren't as gluttonous with the ginger as they'd been with the wine. Reverting to well-trained public schoolboys, they ate the portions they were given and soon began to take their leave.

In the kitchen, Haley eyed the leftover ginger covetously. 'Marissa, do you mind letting me stay and clean up by myself? I could really use the extra money.'

'Sure, no problem.'

Marissa was a sweet girl, but hopelessly gullible.

When the guests had left, Marissa slipped away as well, leaving Haley on her own. Mr Bathurst was nowhere to be seen and Haley heaved a huge sigh of relief. Finally!

She wrapped the rest of the crystallised ginger in cling film. Then she stuffed it into the side pocket of her rucksack, along with another bottle of wine for good measure. Now that the hard part was over, it was time to clean up.

There was one open bottle of wine with about a glass left in it. She sniffed it. The wine smelled sweet and flowery. She was no connoisseur, but she could tell it was good stuff. Unable to resist, she held the bottle to her lips and treated herself to a taste. It was heavenly. She let the flavour dance on her tongue for nearly a minute before having another gulp.

'Just what do you think you're doing, young lady?'

Jolted, Haley whirled to face her accuser, spilling wine all down her front. 'Mr Bathurst!' she gasped, wiping pathetically at her apron. 'I . . . didn't realise you were still here.'

'Obviously.' His sharp eyes swept the kitchen, taking in the empty ginger dish, the cling film and the bottle she'd been swigging from. His gaze came to rest on the bulging rucksack on the floor. The neck of a wine bottle jutted from it obscenely.

Haley began to tremble.

'A connoisseur of good wine, I see.' His tone made it clear he recognised the bottle.

She was busted; there was no point in lying. 'It's the first – the *only* time, Mr Bathurst, honest. I just thought no one would miss a couple of bottles.'

'A couple of bottles? Young lady, do you have any idea how much "a couple of bottles" of Château Ducru-Beaucaillou costs?'

Haley lowered her head. 'No.'

'About £70 a bottle.'

Her mouth fell open.

'So how many bottles have we got here?'

With a shudder, she sank to her knees and reached inside the rucksack as though she expected the contents to bite her. One by one she took the bottles out, setting them carefully on the stone flags. One. Two. Three. Four.

Mr Bathurst watched her, his arms crossed imperiously across his chest. 'I trust you were planning to reimburse Lord Asquith?'

She opened her mouth and closed it again. What was she supposed to say?

'I'll take that as a no,' Mr Bathurst said. 'But you're going to pay for it one way or the other. Do you have that much money?'

Haley felt ill. 'No,' she whispered. She was really for it this time.

He walked the length of the kitchen, deep in thought.

'I'll work it off, Mr Bathurst,' Haley said in desperation.

'I don't think that quite meets the bill, young lady. Not for theft.'

She lowered her head. Theft. It was such an unfriendly word.

'You will stay here while I fetch Lord Asquith. We'll see how he wants to settle the matter.'

Horrified, Haley couldn't get up from the floor. She stared at the wine, marvelling that it could be so expensive. Bloody Matt. It was all his fault.

When she heard the second set of footsteps she felt as though the warders had come to escort her to the gallows. She remained where she was, kneeling like a penitent. Perhaps Lord Asquith would take pity on her in her wretched state.

A pair of knife-pleated black trousers stopped directly in front of her.

From behind, she heard Mr Bathurst's voice. 'Come on, girl. On your feet.'

Haley stumbled to her feet, unable to look up. She stared disconsolately at the floor.

'And so we meet again,' came the baritone voice of Lord Asquith.

'You know this girl, your Lordship?' Mr Bathurst asked, surprised.

Asquith chuckled. 'Our paths have crossed before.'

Haley cringed. She prayed he wouldn't tell Mr Bathurst the circumstances.

'How poetic,' he said in a sporting tone. 'This time you're the one covered in wine.'

She glanced down. The bright red stain on her apron might as well have been blood.

Asquith contemplated the row of bottles on the floor. Then he nudged the rucksack with his polished shoe. 'What else have you got in there, my girl?'

Again she couldn't read him. It was unnerving. His cut-glass accent made her squirm as authority always did. But no schoolteacher had ever stolen her knickers.

'Um, just some ginger, sir,' she mumbled, still too afraid to meet his eyes.

'Just?'

She felt tears prick her eyes. Why were they torturing her?

'Look at me when I'm speaking to you, please.' His gentlemanly phrasing only enhanced his authority.

Haley obeyed, fingering the edges of her wine-drenched apron.

'What is your name?'

Swallowing audibly, she raised her head. He was dressed less formally than last time, but he was just as striking. His black eyes seemed to look right through her. 'Haley Devlin, sir.'

'Haley,' he repeated. 'Tell me something, Haley. Are you wearing knickers this time?'

She blushed furiously and darted a glance at Mr Bathurst, but he merely raised his eyebrows.

'Well?'

'Of course, sir,' she said, realising the ridiculousness of her statement as she said it.

He chuckled at that. 'Of course.'

She burned with shame, but it was a delicious sort of shame. He was toying with her.

'Show me.'

Here it was. The gauntlet. There was only one way to reclaim some of her dignity. With a coquettish smile she raised her skirt to display the black French knickers she was wearing. Just like the ones he had confiscated at the party.

Lord Asquith nodded his appreciation. 'Do they meet with your approval, Mr Bathurst?'

He inspected them with the same cold appraising eye that scrutinised her cap and apron and always found fault.

'Acceptable,' he said. 'Just.'

His indifference astonished her. Then again, she *had* been shamelessly flirtatious with him when he'd first hired her. He knew she was a promiscuous little tart. He probably even knew the sort of games she and Matt got up to.

'So we come to the issue of atonement,' said Asquith calmly.

Haley gulped.

'Oh, you expected to walk away scot-free, did you, my girl?'

She shook her head.

'I'm sorry, I didn't hear that.'

Her cheeks burned. 'No, sir.' She glanced at the open door and then back at Lord Asquith. 'What – what are you going to do?' she asked in a quavering voice.

'I'm not sure yet,' Asquith said. 'What do you think, Mr Bathurst?'

'Personally, I think she needs a damned good thrashing.'

Haley thought she would faint. She squeezed her legs together in a vain attempt to still the throbbing between them.

Lord Asquith was nodding. 'Yes, that might do her

good, mightn't it? Right, my girl. Remove your uniform, please.'

She blinked. 'S-Sir?'

He smiled pleasantly and looked at Mr Bathurst. 'I'm certain she heard me.'

'Yes, she must have done,' Mr Bathurst responded, mirroring his smile.

Asquith raised his eyebrows expectantly. 'Haley? Are you going to remove your uniform or must I do it?'

Baffled, Haley glanced from one to the other. Both men were watching her expectantly. Sternly. She had no choice but to submit.

Her hands shook with uncertainty and anticipation as she untied her apron and slipped it off. Mr Bathurst held out his hand and she surrendered it. He folded it meticulously, placing it on the counter like a blood-stained exhibit in a murder trial.

Unbuttoning her uniform blouse was more difficult. Her nervous fingers could barely manage the buttons and the more she fumbled, the more awkward the moment became. At last she got it off and handed it to Mr Bathurst as well. It joined her apron and she reached back to unzip her skirt.

'Just a moment, Haley,' Mr Bathurst said, narrowing his eyes. 'Have you shortened that skirt of yours?'

She bit her lip to keep from giggling. Suddenly she was back at school, caught by the headmaster for altering her uniform.

'Yes,' she said, grinning impishly. 'I thought the customers might like it.' She tried to meet his expression with cocky impertinence, but their scrutiny was too much to endure and she looked down at the floor again.

Lord Asquith sighed. 'Well, well,' was all he said.

She found the zip and stepped out of her skirt. Standing in the kitchen in her black bra and knickers, she felt exposed and aroused.

'Your underwear too,' Asquith said.

Haley glanced at the open door. 'But – someone might come in, sir,' she said plaintively.

Asquith didn't respond. His silence was a command.

The fear of getting caught was half the thrill, Haley reminded herself. She unhooked her bra, baring her pert breasts. The hard buds of her nipples advertised her excitement. She hesitated, then shyly slid her knickers down, looking over at the door once more before stepping out of them.

She gathered enough courage to draw herself up and hold them brazenly out to Lord Asquith. He took them from her, the corners of his eyes crinkling as he offered her the slightest of smiles. He held them to his nose and sniffed deeply.

Mortified, Haley buried her face in her hands. Asquith seemed determined to quash every shred of confidence she managed to muster.

There was sound and movement behind her, but she didn't dare look out from behind her hands. Mr Bathurst was opening drawers and rummaging through them. She heard the clink and clatter of knives and other cooking utensils.

'I think this will do,' Mr Bathurst said.

Asquith voiced his agreement.

Haley stubbornly resisted the urge to look.

'Right, my girl,' Asquith said in a maddeningly amiable voice. 'Up you get.'

She peeled her hands away from her face and saw him patting the large butcher's block in the centre of the kitchen. Mr Bathurst stood beside it. He was holding a long wooden spoon, smacking it lightly against his palm.

Filled with exhilarated trepidation, Haley climbed up onto the butcher's block. The wood was cool beneath her naked bottom and thighs. She could feel the scarred surface beneath her, the work of many knives.

'On your back,' Mr Bathurst ordered.

Her fear forced her to make light of the situation. 'If you're planning a virgin sacrifice, I should warn you . . .'

'Do we need to gag you?' Asquith asked.

Her eyes widened. 'No, sir,' she whispered.

He smiled then, a divinely wicked grin that turned her knees to water.

She lay back, crossing her arms over her breasts, her legs hanging over the edge of the block. She stared up at the array of pots and pans twirling lazily above her. The harsh lights of the kitchen made them glint with a clinical chill. She could hardly breathe.

'Legs up,' said Mr Bathurst.

Haley gasped. What were they going to do to her? She looked at him pleadingly.

Asquith tutted with disapproval. 'She isn't being very obedient. Perhaps we should restrain her.'

Heat engulfed her like a wave, threatening to drown her. There was something strangely liberating in the casual way they were discussing her. She had no say in what happened to her. The helplessness was intoxicating.

Mr Bathurst glanced around the kitchen. 'I doubt there's any rope in here.'

Asquith was looking off to Haley's left. 'What about . . .'

He moved out of her line of sight and returned with the roll of cling film. Haley bit back a giggle. All they needed to do now was truss her up like a turkey and stuff her full of . . .

'Legs up, girl!' Mr Bathurst commanded, giving her a sharp swat on the thigh with the wooden spoon.

She yipped and raised her legs up, an obedient little maid, if a rather wayward one. She was seeing her boss in a whole new light.

Asquith held the cling film up to her right leg. He wrapped it around her ankle several times, spooling it out to reach the rack where the pans hung above her. He wound the plastic around the rack and tied it off. Haley tugged at it, surprised at how strong it was.

He repeated the procedure with her left leg, pulling it to the side so that her legs were splayed. They would be able to see absolutely everything. She prayed they couldn't see how wet she was.

Asquith didn't stop there. He pulled her arms up over and behind her head. Then he wrapped her wrists together and secured them to the legs of the block. The position thrust her breasts up like an offering. Finally, he passed a wide strip of cling film over her waist, around and underneath the surface of the block, pinning her tightly to it. She tried to struggle in her bonds, but the plastic was much stronger than it looked.

'Jolly good stuff, this,' Asquith said with a chuckle.

'Just the thing,' Mr Bathurst agreed, tapping the wooden spoon against Haley's upraised backside.

She flinched, dreading the first smack. She'd been spanked before, but only as a prelude to sex. This promised to be far more intense.

'This is what happens to naughty maids who steal from their masters,' he said sternly.

Haley had fantasised about Mr Bathurst before. In her mind he rebuked her for her cheekiness and punished her in childish ways. It was safe as a fantasy. Because then she was in control. Now she was completely at his mercy.

The spoon connected sharply with her bottom, delivering a potent sting. She yelped. Another stroke. Another sharp report of wood against flesh. Another cry of pain. She pictured the precise little red circles it must be leaving on her pale skin and she writhed on the butcher's block, unable to escape the stinging blows.

'Oh, please, sir,' she whimpered between strokes. 'Oww! I'm sorry, really – I'm so – oww! – sorry!'

They ignored her.

Lord Asquith walked round the butcher's block, watching calmly as Mr Bathurst spanked her. He stopped directly behind her, placing his hands on her shoulders.

He held her down firmly while she tried to wriggle away from the wooden spoon. Then his hands crept slowly down her front until they were cupping her breasts.

Through the pain, Haley moaned and shivered at his touch.

His attentive thumbs brushed back and forth over her nipples, making them stiffen. He pinched them between thumb and forefinger.

Then the wooden spoon directed Haley's attention back to her burning backside. She howled with pain as Mr Bathurst increased the force and tempo, scolding her for her indolence, her impertinence, her indiscipline. She had forgotten all about the stark view she was presenting to him. She struggled against the cling film, causing the rack to shake. Above her the pots and pans clanged and clattered together in raucous accompaniment to her cries.

Asquith increased the pressure on her nipples, rolling them between his fingers. They stiffened fully, responding to his touch with aching compliance.

Gasping and panting for breath, Haley couldn't focus on either the spanking or the fondling. The sensations began to blend into one.

Asquith commented favourably on her responsiveness, but Haley was in orbit. She was so intent on finding the balance between the pleasure of his touch and the pain of the spanking that his voice was only a fuzzy echo in the back of her mind.

She closed her eyes and drifted deeper into submission. She felt Asquith's warm breath on her throat and she arched invitingly, as though presenting herself for a vampire's kiss. His lips travelled down her neck, lingering above her left breast, making her yearn for his contact. His tongue found the hard bud of her nipple, circling it and teasing it. Haley gasped and the sound seemed to fill the cavernous kitchen. She realised that the spanking had stopped. Not daring to open her eyes, she waited for Mr Bathurst's touch as well.

And when his hand came to rest between her legs she arched her back as much as her position would allow, straining to meet his fingers.

Asquith's teeth closed softly on her nipple with just enough force to make her whimper. She knew her boss would be feeling the dew the action produced.

Mr Bathurst's fingers probed and stroked her sleek wetness, making her writhe and squirm. The fire of the spanking had subsided to a warm pulsating glow. She felt herself climbing and her breathing quickened and grew shallow.

Asquith twisted a hand in her hair, pulling her head back to expose her throat even more. His lips and teeth

161

caressed the vulnerable flesh there and she shuddered as gooseflesh rose on the back of her neck.

Mr Bathurst trailed his fingers over her sex, teasing her and making her grind her hips obscenely to get what she wanted. She was so close. He had to know it. Why didn't he finish her off? She wanted both of them. They could take turns with her. One could hold her down while the other . . .

'I think she's enjoying this far too much,' said Mr Bathurst.

The hand between her legs stopped and she groaned with frustration. Mr Bathurst patted her tender bottom, making her wince.

'Indeed,' Asquith said. 'Bad girls aren't meant to enjoy their punishment.'

Why not? Haley wanted to whine.

'Mr Bathurst, would you do the honours?' Lord Asquith was holding a long chef's knife out to him.

'Certainly, your Lordship.'

Haley's eyes widened with terror. Mr Bathurst placed the knife between her breasts and pressed the tip of the cold blade against her skin. She forced herself to stay absolutely still as he drew it sensuously down along the length of her body, stopping at her navel. Then he slid the blade underneath the cling film and sliced through it, releasing her. He repeated the operation with her legs and her arms, though he left her wrists wrapped together.

Asquith stood her up and turned her around to face the block. 'Now, bend right over,' he said.

She obeyed, her legs weak from the bondage and the unfulfilled throbbing need. Surely now they meant to have their way with her. She stretched across the block, presenting herself.

'There is a punishment Victorian governesses used to find most effective on naughty girls. I think it's especially appropriate for you, Haley.'

She had no idea what he was talking about.

Mr Bathurst was somewhere behind her and to the left. She thought she heard the refrigerator door open and close, but she paid it no mind. Haley closed her eyes and waited. She was their plaything, their slave. They could do anything they wanted.

Her reverie was interrupted by the intrusion of something cold and slippery between her glowing cheeks, too high to reach her sex. At first she thought the hand had lost its way and she adjusted herself to assist.

'Be still,' Asquith said sharply.

The oily finger pressed gently against the little puckered rosebud and Haley cried out.

'No! No, please!'

'Hush. Do you want your bottom smacked again?'

Awash with shame, she shook her head frantically. She lowered her head to the butcher's block, mortified at the intrusion. The finger slipped inside her, greasing the passage not even Matt had explored. She was a virgin there. It was a bizarre sensation, but not entirely unpleasant. Still, she wished his hands would roam lower, to where she desperately needed attention.

Gradually, she became aware of a peculiar sound behind her. Some sort of scraping. For a moment she was afraid someone was at the door, but the invading finger was still moving inside her. Surely he would have stopped if someone came in. No, they were definitely alone.

But she couldn't puzzle out the scraping sound. Like the rasp of a knife against . . . something.

Without warning, the finger withdrew. Haley heaved a sigh of relief and relaxed against the block. There was a clink as the knife was laid aside. Then Lord Asquith was in front of her. He took her cling-wrapped wrists in his hands, stretching her out across the block until she stood on tiptoe.

'Since you're so fond of ginger,' he said, the corners of his mouth turning up ominously.

Then Mr Bathurst was behind her and she flushed deeply. Now it was his turn. But the cold probe didn't feel like a finger and all at once it became clear. With an embarrassed cry she tried to pull away, but Asquith held her wrists firmly.

Mr Bathurst spread her cheeks apart with the fingers of one hand while inserting the ginger root with the other. It had a slightly coarse texture, but it didn't hurt. She made herself relax, surrendering to the penetration.

Suddenly she became aware of a distinct warmth. The ginger began to tingle and she squirmed, waiting for the unfamiliar sensation to pass. But it didn't pass. The warmth developed into a sharp piquant burning, like the effect of hot peppers on the tongue.

As the feeling built, Haley found herself writhing against the butcher's block, trying in vain to escape it.

'Oh, please,' she begged. 'It burns!'

One of her tormentors chuckled, but said nothing. It was clear they knew exactly the effect it would have.

Whimpering as the fire intensified even more, Haley struggled against Asquith, trying to pull away. She danced from foot to foot, inadvertently clenching her cheeks and intensifying the sting.

'Now, now,' he chided. 'None of that, my girl. You're going to take your medicine.'

Mr Bathurst was tearing off a long sheet of cling film, presumably to restrain her kicking feet. But instead, he wound it high around her legs and waist, pulling it tightly up between her cheeks like a transparent thong. It pressed the ginger further inside, holding it securely in place. Haley wailed in misery and wondered if it was possible to die of embarrassment.

The burning showed no sign of dissipating. The men exchanged a look and traded places. Mr Bathurst took firm hold of her wrists.

She closed her eyes, feeling faint.

Lord Asquith caressed her over the cling film, making her jump. The plastic retained the heat from her desire as well as the ginger, making the pressure of his touch even more agonising. The ginger continued to burn with each movement of Asquith's skilful fingers, and she whimpered with pain even as he pleasured her.

Then she was climbing again, quickly and steadily. Sensations shot through her like jolts of electricity and she uttered little gasps and sighs as she struggled both to escape and encourage them. Each time she tensed her muscles she felt the ginger burn.

At last she felt the rising swell of ecstasy and it overtook her with singular intensity as she arched her back, pressing herself into his fingers with breathless abandon. Her eyes squeezed shut, she imploded as the surges of her climax battered her from within.

It lasted so long it was almost unbearable, but soon the throbbing began to subside and she collapsed over the block, panting and shaking and unable to straighten her legs. Mr Bathurst released her hands and she crumpled to her knees, trembling and spent.

It was a long time before she found the strength to stand. She hissed as her movement reawakened the spicy sting of the ginger. With a shaky hand she reached for the cling film at her waist, ready to unwind it and free herself.

Mr Bathurst smacked her hand smartly. 'And just what do you think you're doing, young lady?'

She stared at him, bewildered. 'I . . . I just . . .'

He was holding her uniform. 'Get dressed.'

Bewildered, Haley knew she must obey. But when she reached for her knickers, Lord Asquith plucked them away. 'I'll keep these,' he said, tucking them into his pocket.

Haley blushed and finished dressing, wincing at the unremitting burn. Relaxing her cheeks was impossible.

Mr Bathurst went to the cupboard and got her a fresh apron. 'Here. You can't very well wear yours.'

When she was dressed she stood before them for inspection. Did they intend to send her home with the ginger still inside? Oh, Matt would love that.

Mr Bathurst smiled. 'Mrs Marjoribanks's party is in the Wellington Room. They're expecting tea.'

The Improvement Session

I smoothed my clammy hands down over my skirt, trying not to think about why I was here. The room was unpleasantly institutional. There were no pictures on the sickly yellow walls, not even one of those soulless corporate still lifes you get in chain hotel rooms. There were no magazines or newspapers to read. Even citizens' advice leaflets might have provided some distraction. There was nothing to do but fret.

I shifted on the hard wooden bench. I felt too hot, too cold, too apprehensive. Too restless to sit still, too paralysed with dread to move. How had they found out? I'd replaced the money as soon as I'd been able to and I was so sure no one had seen me. But two weeks later I'd come home to find the letter sitting on my little hessian doormat. I knew from the return address that it wasn't good news.

Dear Miss Parrish,

I regret to inform you that you have been selected for Improvement under the Young Employees Act 2014. As you will be aware, selection for Improvement is based upon reports submitted by employers concerning conduct in the workplace. You are therefore required to attend Mountjoy Discipline Centre at 10.00 am on Saturday 17th March.

Please note that the Improvement procedures may in the short term impair your ability to drive a vehicle. For this reason you should not drive to the Discipline Centre

*and return transport to your residence will be provided
after the Improvement session.*

   Yours sincerely,
   Winston Graham
   Improvement Registrar

The bland official note didn't say what to expect. It read like a nag letter from the dentist, patronising and unavoidable.

We all knew about the Young Employees Act. Since corporal punishment was abolished in schools, the hang 'em and flog 'em brigade had been clamouring for a return of birching for adult hooligans. If childhood was to be sacrosanct, they argued, then citizens should pay for their crimes once they were old enough to appreciate the consequences of their actions.

Terrified of being late, I'd got to the Centre half an hour ahead of time and the unsympathetic receptionist had suggested I go for a walk until it was time for my appointment. I'd circled the building twice in the chilly wind before she would finally admit me. A retinal scan confirmed my identity and she ushered me into the narrow waiting room. I had to surrender my handbag and watch and she told me my personal items could be reclaimed after the session.

I couldn't stop replaying the events that had got me sent here. I hadn't really stolen the money. I'd even thought of asking Mr Northcote for a loan, but he'd have given me one of his lectures about being prudent and frugal. The petty cash held three times what I needed and I was sure he wouldn't miss it if I paid it back quickly. Which I did. But he must have noticed and known it was me. He dissembled well. He never said a word about it – not even after I got the letter. It was business as usual for that awful two-week period. If I hadn't known he was watching and gloating I might have believed he didn't notice my preoccupation. The waiting was a punishment in itself.

The door swung open and I jumped as though electrocuted. But there was nothing to fear. Yet. It was only another girl, looking as nervous as me. She offered me a fleeting smile and perched on the edge of the bench opposite me. She had long legs, long dark hair and a faraway expression, as though she couldn't quite believe she was here. The silence was oppressive, but I couldn't think of anything to say. Eventually she spoke.

'You here for Improvement too?'

I nodded, knowing and yet not knowing what it meant. I started to say it was my first time, but that sounded too much like certainty that there would be other times, so I kept quiet.

'I'm Alex,' she said after another ponderous silence. 'Alex Lawrence.'

I tried to relax a little and forced a smile. 'Natalie Parrish.'

There was so much I wanted to ask, but I was afraid of the answers. Had she been here before? Did she know what was going to happen? How bad would it be?

The mean little room had two doors. One led in; one led out. My eyes flicked occasionally to the exit door, but I didn't speculate about what was beyond it. I didn't dare.

Before long we were joined by others. Felicia Lighthart, a tall blonde who looked dressed for a day in court. Liz Kenton, whose sporadic chatter only heightened the anxiety. And Hilary Gosling, a pale little thing with ginger hair and a hunted expression who didn't speak beyond telling us her name.

We alternated between silence and banal comments that led nowhere. Traffic. The weather. No one spoke of the one thing that crowded everyone's thoughts. There was no clock in the room, so I had no concept of time. I had no idea if I'd been there ten minutes or an hour.

Suddenly the door banged open to admit a willowy girl with a shock of bright red hair. She sat cross-legged on the bench next to me, a study in defiance as she met our eyes with a challenging stare. I suspected the little rebel had been here before and was trying to impress us with her bravery while really pissing herself with fear.

A key turned and the other door swung silently open to reveal a man in a white coat who introduced himself as Dr

Maxwell. He had a rich velvety voice which seemed at odds with his impersonal demeanour. He adjusted his glasses and read our names off a clipboard, each one sounding like an accusation. Like dutiful schoolgirls we answered as each name was called. The rebel was Bryony Catesby.

'You were late, Catesby,' he said. 'Nine minutes.' His brow furrowed as his pen scratched at the clipboard.

Bryony looked at the floor, but didn't speak.

'Right,' he said brusquely. 'This way, please.' He held the door open and we filed out of the room. Fluorescent tubes buzzed overhead as he marched us down the antiseptic corridor like lambs in a slaughterhouse.

We turned a corner and he gestured us through a door marked PREPARATION. Inside he handed each of us a plain white shift. No underwear. There was no privacy to change. Dr Maxwell simply leaned back against the wall and eyed us sternly while he waited.

Bryony stripped off immediately, as though to prove she wasn't bothered. One by one we followed suit, some brazen, others turning away shyly to undress. Our keeper seemed not to care, though his eyes noted everything.

Felicia undressed with quiet outrage, folding her designer suit with violent little movements before slipping it into the pigeonhole she'd been assigned. I suspected she was a legal secretary or a trainee solicitor, but if she felt her rights were being violated, she didn't speak up.

I hugged my shoulders, chilled by the impersonal treatment as Dr Maxwell took our blood pressure. In any other context, the numbers would have been alarming. Then he measured our heights and made notes on the sizes of our wrists and ankles. He even measured the circumferences of our thighs. I exchanged a worried look with Alex, whose deep brown eyes were welling with tears. The routineness only enhanced the degradation. None of us wanted to face the Improvement session, but neither could we endure being poked and prodded any longer. At least the 'preparation' had stopped Liz's nervous chatter.

The doctor finally recapped his pen, signalling an end to the humiliating ordeal. Alex's hand sought mine and gave

169

me a sisterly squeeze. I squeezed back, wishing I could offer comfort or reassurance. Solidarity would have to do. He led us back down the corridor and into what looked like a lecture theatre. Now my heart really began to pound.

Thirty or more people sat before a raised platform on which stood a large construction of wood and metal. A padded bench ran the length of the device, angled downwards at the front. It was covered with the sanitised paper used in doctors' offices – soilable, disposable. Behind the bench was a motorised arrangement of gears, pistons and wheels. Six rectangular leather attachments, each a foot square, were suspended on articulated arms from a complicated mechanism above. One for each of us.

Dr Maxwell strode to the dais and addressed the watchers in a strong clear voice. 'Good morning, ladies and gentlemen. We've invited you here today to show you the most important advance in Improvement technology since the passing of the Young Employees Act: the XR-703.'

He indicated the contraption behind him with a sweep of his arm, like a Victorian magician about to perform some dazzling feat. But there were no oohs and ahs from this crowd; only the scratching of pens on paper and the occasional creak of a seat as someone shifted position.

'As you know, the Act itself was based on experiments into motivational techniques carried out at the University of Ipswich in the early 2000s. It was found that learning outcomes for all but top-performing student volunteers could be improved if they were subject to corporal correction for poor performance.'

The six of us exchanged nervous glances at the words 'corporal correction'. Hilary's hands drifted to cover her bottom and I turned scarlet at the thought of all these people watching. I had known that Improvement involved some form of physical punishment, but I'd had no idea it would be like this. I stared at the device, trying to imagine it in action.

The doctor continued to speak, warming to his theme as we huddled closer together.

'The Young Employees Act put these principles into action for people between the ages of eighteen and twenty-five. And, as you know, it has been a great success. Productivity in the workplace has soared, and youth crime has plummeted. But there have been criticisms. There have been occasional claims of favouritism or of undue severity on the part of Improvement Administrators. In addition, the limited supply of trained Administrators has meant that the Programme could be applied effectively only to the worst offenders. In practice only the worst-performing 15% or so were likely to be Improved. Some randomisation was introduced, so that employees further up the scale did not feel altogether immune, but it is well known that it is certainty of punishment rather than severity that is the real deterrent.'

I glanced at Alex, who was mesmerised by the lecture, her lips parted, her eyes wide with disbelief. From behind us Felicia murmured something and someone else gasped. I closed my eyes, not wanting to know what had been said or how much authority the words had.

Dr Maxwell continued, oblivious to our suffering. 'Each Young Employee is graded on a weekly basis under various performance criteria that include punctuality, application and attention to detail. A weighted scheme is then used to assign selection probabilities. Under current weightings an employee in the lowest 10% can expect to be called for Improvement about once per year –' he smiled again as he added '– although very few employees remain in the lowest 10% after their first visit.'

This brought a chuckle from the audience and I couldn't help but look over at Bryony. She tried to hide the mixture of anger and shame in her eyes, but her bravura had run its course. She was one of us now.

Dr Maxwell turned from the machine and gestured towards us. 'Here we have a group of young employees who are scheduled for Improvement. Some of them are here for general poor performance, and others for specific offences. But that need not concern us. The machine has been programmed to take account of that.' He turned

171

towards us and his smile lost any pretence of warmth. 'Step up here, if you would, please,' he said. As if we had a choice.

We shuffled forward, glancing about self-consciously. Even Bryony was looking discomfited. If she had been sent for Improvement before, it must not have been like this. We stood like shell-shocked refugees, staring at our feet and shifting nervously. Behind us was the machine. In front of us were the people who would witness our disgrace.

'I have to pee,' I heard Liz whisper urgently.

'The XR-703 will allow us to extend the benefits of Improvement much further up the scale. Once the machines have been fully deployed, we will have the capacity to offer annual Improvement visits to 50% of the young workforce. Imagine the benefits that that will bring! Of course in reality we will continue to use a weighted scale, but now perhaps the worst-behaved employees will receive monthly Improvements and only those in the top 25% will be spared entirely. We will finally be able to use the Ipswich research to its full potential.' He spread his hands in a magnanimous gesture and his listeners nodded with approval.

There was a short question and answer period where various refinements were proposed and discussed, but none of us were listening. It was bad enough to be 'selected' like lab rats to run a maze, but the objectification was utterly mortifying.

I stared into the middle distance, trying to dissociate myself from the situation. Surely we'd already been punished enough. First the wait, then the indignity of the assessment and now this unbearable suspense. I was already cured of any desire to 'borrow' money again.

Suddenly, Alex squeezed my hand, jolting me back into the moment. Dr Maxwell was making adjustments to the machine, referring to the measurements on his clipboard to raise or lower the leather paddles to the appropriate height. When he was finished he consulted his notes and called Felicia's name. She looked helplessly at the rest of us and then made her way slowly to the machine as a funereal silence swallowed the auditorium.

The doctor pointed to the end of the bench nearest us. He guided Felicia into position and my legs felt made of water as I was finally able to visualise what was about to happen to us.

Her face was a picture of abject misery as she stared out at the emotionless audience. She bent forward over the bench, wincing as the protective paper crackled beneath her. The noise was jarring in the stillness. Dr Maxwell buckled a leather strap around the backs of her thighs, just above the knees. He placed a second around her ankles, anchoring her feet to the floor. She lowered her head as he instructed her to extend her arms. When he was satisfied with her position he strapped her wrists to a ringbolt in the floor in front of her. Finally, he ran a wide strap across her waist, securing her with her bottom well up.

Hilary was next, chewing her lip as she stretched herself across the bench and allowed herself to be strapped down to the left of Felicia.

'Alex Lawrence.'

Like an aristocrat summoned to the guillotine, Alex released my hand and walked with dignity to her place next to Hilary. I could see the tremor in her gait, but her determination gave me courage. And shortly thereafter, I took my place beside her.

The angled bench forced my bottom up high and I moaned self-consciously as the various straps were buckled into place. I strained against the leather, testing it, but I was thoroughly restrained. None of us were going anywhere.

Next came Bryony, no trace of the proud warrior in sight. She meekly took her position next to me. I looked up to see Liz standing by herself at the edge of the platform. She looked forsaken and my heart went out to her. I suspected she was the weakest of all of us. But she didn't have to wait long before she was summoned and then secured on the end to Bryony's left.

Dr Maxwell crossed in front of us and I watched his brown leather shoes as he returned to the side where

Felicia had been positioned. I heard a gasp from there, but couldn't see beyond Alex. Then there were footsteps and Hilary gave a short little cry. Alex stiffened as Dr Maxwell paused in front of her. Then he stepped in front of me and lifted the hem of my shift, as he'd done to the others. I blushed as he tucked it up over my back. He continued down the line until we were all bare from the waist down. Prepared.

'Now then, ladies and gentlemen,' he said, turning to face his audience again. 'As you are about to see, the machine is incapable of mercy, of lenience. It will apply the punishment it has been programmed to administer. No more, no less. It can also be programmed for differing levels of severity. For instance, this is Catesby's second Improvement session and she reported late today. Her punishment will be adjusted for that.'

There was a sharp intake of breath beside me and I didn't dare turn to look at Bryony. I kept my head down and watched her fingers clenching and unclenching in helpless anxiety. Our collective dread was palpable.

'While a human disciplinarian might be moved by tears or pitiful entreaties, the machine has no such weakness.'

This prompted a few murmurs of approval.

But then the gears behind us began to whir and my eyes flew open. There was a loud crack and a squeal, but I didn't feel anything. Baffled, I looked around wildly before realising that I hadn't been hit. Another crack and another squeal, this time from Alex. I gritted my teeth and waited for my turn, but the next smack came from further down on my left. Not Bryony. Liz.

I tensed, waiting, only to hear another thwack and another cry. Maybe the machine had been programmed to spare some of us. Alex yelped again and my heart leapt with cowardly relief. But it was only temporary; the next one was for me.

I jerked forward as the leather connected smartly with my exposed bottom on an upward swing, covering both cheeks fully. I cried out in pain and astonishment. I squirmed and struggled against the straps, but I was firmly pinned. Beside me Bryony yelped and then yelped louder as the leather struck her twice in quick succession. I felt betrayed by my own desperation, ashamed that I'd wished everyone else to suffer so that I might be spared. I listened, every muscle taut, as the leather paddles wound back on their springs and were released at intervals with no discernible pattern, eliciting cries and shrieks from the others one by one. The uncertainty over where they would strike next meant that I was constantly anticipating, constantly on edge.

Another stroke found me and I howled in chorus with Bryony, whose bright red hair was an unpleasant reminder of how red my bottom must be. While the rest of us only received one stroke in sequence, Bryony always got two. Listening to the smacks and the accompanying cries of pain was distressing enough, especially when it was the girls either side of me. But the waiting was truly awful.

Far down on the right I could hear Hilary's breathless whimpers spiralling into ragged cries as she pleaded with Dr Maxwell to let her go. I forgave her the 'me' not 'us' as the leather lashed my tender cheeks again, reminding me of my own earlier weakness. Beyond her, Felicia's yelps maintained a note of outrage, as though she was drawing strength from her anger. Bryony's ostentatious display had been just false bravado; now she cried out with total abandon at each pair of strokes. Poor Liz was sobbing like a child and I wondered if she was managing to keep control of her bladder under the circumstances. I couldn't even imagine the incremental humiliation of losing control.

I turned my head to look at Alex. She was just to my right, her cheek inches from mine, so close we could have kissed. Her fearful eyes locked on mine and she flinched soundlessly as her body jerked in response to another stroke.

Hilary again. Bryony, twice. Then me. The pain was terrible, unrelenting. The implement lashed me again and again. It must have been programmed to vary the point of impact slightly with each stroke. My whole bottom was blazing with pain and it wasn't long before tears were streaming down my face.

Dr Maxwell stood on the right, near Felicia, presiding over our suffering with scientific detachment. His distance from us – both emotional and physical – only enhanced the sense of helplessness. I felt tiny and insignificant. Being left to the mercy of a remorseless machine was dehumanising. It was far worse than being dealt with personally by a human being.

Dr Maxwell was saying something, but I couldn't make out a single word. I wasn't sure I wanted to hear it anyway. The only sounds I registered were the relentless crack of the leather paddles and the accompanying yelps and howls. I feared the worst for Liz, though I didn't dare crane my neck round to look. I could no longer distinguish Felicia's cries from Hilary's. Bryony was long past any delusion that she could win against a system like this. Alex's fragile resolve had crumbled and her long hair hung down, obscuring her face as her body heaved with mute wretched sobs.

I stared straight ahead at the audience, frightened and compelled by the fascination on their faces. Another stroke. I yelped, wept. They leaned forward, their eyes scanning the miserable row of us.

Finally, when it seemed like it would never end, the whirring of the machine tapered off. The only sounds were our pathetic sniffles and choking sobs. My bottom pulsed with intense terrible heat and I had never felt sorrier in my life. I was determined never to be sent here again, determined to be a model employee from now on. I wouldn't steal so much as a pencil from the supplies cupboard again. Mr Northcote wouldn't recognise the new me.

Released from our bonds, we walked stiffly back to the room where our clothes sat neatly folded in their pigeon-holes, their tidiness seeming to mock the indignity we'd just suffered.

But it was deserved, I reminded myself.

Dr Maxwell addressed us in a slightly less abrupt tone now that it was over. 'There remains one last requirement. You must each write a brief summary of what you have learnt from the session and the ways in which your behaviour will improve as a result. The Registrar will take this into account in assessing future performance reports.'

We stood around a tall table of the kind you find in banks while he gave each of us an official form. Hilary started at once, scrawling what looked like a lengthy confession of everything she'd ever done wrong. Felicia wrote one neat sentence and I could see the words *confidentiality* and *clients* as I peered sidelong at what she had written. I didn't know what to write. It seemed such a schoolgirlish imposition – 'How I Was Punished for Being a Bad Girl' by Natalie Parrish.

Finally, I just put pen to paper and let it flow. *I am most dreadfully sorry for my dishonesty. I promise that I will never take money from the petty cash again.*

When we'd all finished, Dr Maxwell took our summaries and told us we could get dressed. No one said a word as we did, hissing and wincing with pain as we eased our knickers up over our sore bottoms. We avoided looking at one another until the receptionist came to escort us out again. Alex met my eyes one last time and the ghost of a smile crossed her features. I mirrored her expression, but she turned away before I could say goodbye.

Two days later, I arrived home to find a letter on my doormat. I felt the colour drain from my face as I tore it open.

Dear Miss Parrish,

I have just finished reviewing the Improvement Under-takings given by Candidates at the Cautionary Improve-ment session on 17th March. I was most disturbed to read your confession of theft. I am afraid that I must require you to attend the Discipline Centre once again at 1.00 pm on Saturday 31st March.

I have referred this matter to the Youth Court, which will determine the level of Correction to be administered. However, you should be aware that this is a considerably more serious matter than your original referral, which according to my records was for general disrespect to your office manager. It is usual for the level of Correction to be upgraded from Cautionary to Salutary for a second visit, but after reviewing your records I have concluded that you would benefit from a further upgrade. I shall therefore be recommending you for Exemplary Correction.

Yours sincerely,
Winston Graham
Improvement Registrar

Kissing the Gunner's Daughter

'Reporting for duty, sir,' Emily said, touching the brim of her cocked hat.

Sebastian gaped at her.

She stood stiffly to attention, keeping her eyes front as her twin brother circled her, scrutinising her. The Royal Navy uniform was a perfect fit. The bumfreezer jacket and buff waistcoat hid her feminine curves well. Below the stiff turnback collar, her dainty neck was disguised by the black stock and white shirt-frill. Not even the tight white breeches betrayed her true sex.

Her dark hair was pulled back away from her face and tied with a velvet ribbon. But the bicorn hat would draw the eye away from her delicate facial features. And Emily knew that life at sea would harden her. She could never pass for a grown man, of course. But in Sebastian's uniform she looked every inch a midshipman in His Majesty's navy. A young gentleman in training to become an officer.

Sebastian Vane had no stomach for adventure, despite their father's ambition that he command a King's ship one day. Conversely, Emily deeply resented the thought of being sent to finishing school while her brother fought glorious battles against the French. At eighteen, she was a burden on their father, as she had no intention of marrying. She refused to condemn herself to a life of domestic duty, and she skilfully alienated every potential suitor her father chose for her.

'Will I pass?' she asked, pitching her voice a little lower.

Unable to speak, Sebastian simply nodded his head in admiration. 'I think you just might.'

'Thank you.' Emily turned to regard herself in the cheval mirror. She and her brother might be satisfied with her appearance, but it was Lieutenant Trevelyan she must convince.

She was nervous, but she did her best to conceal it from Sebastian, lest he change his mind. The twins had traded places before and no one had known the difference. But this time there was no going back.

Lieutenant Trevelyan was the son of a post captain who had known the Vane family for years. The twins' father, a prominent Member of Parliament, had prevailed upon the captain to get Sebastian a midshipman's place aboard HMS *Nemesis*. He thought some time in the navy was just what the lad needed.

The redoubtable young lieutenant had dined with the Vanes many times and Emily always pleaded with him to share his stories about life at sea. Trevelyan naturally assumed she wanted to hear about brave victories and he indulged her with accounts of capturing French and Spanish prize ships.

She listened politely; however, her interests were a little less romantic. And when Trevelyan happened onto the topic of naval discipline her heart gave a little leap. She found it remarkable that the men subject to such harsh punishments did not resent it. But Trevelyan assured her that it was necessary for maintaining order on board a ship. The men would sneer at a captain who was lax in his discipline and think him soft. The cat-o'-nine-tails wasn't used indiscriminately, but it was used often. However, that was a punishment only for common seamen. Midshipmen were treated differently.

Sebastian dreaded any talk about his impending naval career, but Emily couldn't get enough. She loved hearing about the midshipmen most of all.

The 'young gentlemen' were not put to the lash. Instead they were punished with a rattan cane. Trevelyan told them once about a young gentleman who had failed to batten the hatch to the powder magazine properly. This was a serious oversight and Trevelyan ordered him below deck and sent for the bosun. The lad was bent over a cannon and caned severely across the seat of his breeches, which offered scant protection. The position was known as 'kissing the gunner's daughter'. The image had been indelibly imprinted in Emily's mind.

'He was most attentive to his duties after that,' Trevelyan said with a meaningful glance at Sebastian.

The boy looked forlornly at his untouched dinner.

Emily pressed her thighs together.

Another evening Emily had the lieutenant to herself in the library. As usual, she insisted on stories and he obliged. She had to rein in her fascination as she teased out the details and nuances that intrigued her, grateful that her brother had gone to bed.

Occasionally an even more severe punishment than caning was ordered. Then the miscreant's hands would be tied together underneath the barrel of the cannon and he would be flogged on the bare bottom with the boy's cat, a smaller cat-o'-nine-tails made of whipcord. Trevelyan explained that the miscreant was required to make his own cat, which the first lieutenant inspected personally.

His authoritarian voice made Emily squirm with secret delight as she pictured herself in the place of the unfortunate who had displeased him. And late at night, alone in her bed, Emily replayed her fantasies while her fingers strayed inside her nightdress. It was the stern face of Lieutenant Trevelyan she saw when her body writhed and bucked in guilty pleasure.

Her punishment fantasies centred around Trevelyan disciplining her as a boy. But sometimes her struggles caused her to reveal her feminine charms to him. He never broke stride; with a rakish grin he told her he'd known she was a young woman all along. Then he took her to his cabin and had his wicked way with her.

But this was no longer merely fantasy. What would he do if he did discover her true sex? A man who impersonated an officer would be hanged from the yardarm. But there was nothing in the Articles of War about punishments for ladies. The lieutenant would have to devise his own.

Emily gazed at the midshipman in the mirror. She cut a dashing figure in the uniform and looked quite a handsome lad, if a little soft. That would not earn her any lenience from Trevelyan, though. It was that very softness he was charged with reforming.

Closing her eyes, Emily forgot her brother's presence as she indulged her favourite fantasy.

In her mind she faced Lieutenant Trevelyan nervously as he delivered a scathing reprimand about her misconduct. He stood before her, an imposing figure in his long frock coat and fore-and-aft hat. Though she knew it was the boatswain who administered punishments, Emily liked to imagine the lieutenant caning her himself. Perhaps her misbehaviour would be such that only an officer was qualified to address it.

'The Navy, Mr Vane, is founded on discipline.'

Emily flinched as he showed her the cane and tapped the cannon with it.

'You know the position, boy.'

Trembling, Emily bent over the cannon. Trevelyan slowly unfastened her breeches and peeled them down, exposing the quivering pale flesh of her bottom. She knew that the other midshipmen would hear the cuts of the cane up on deck, but she would not give them the satisfaction of hearing her cry out.

She held her breath as Trevelyan raised the cane . . .

'Emily?'

At the sound of her brother's voice she shook herself out of her reverie, flushing deeply. 'Sorry,' she murmured. 'I was just thinking of the lieutenant.'

Sebastian made a face. He couldn't understand her lust for adventure at all. The prospect of going to sea with Trevelyan terrified him. But their father would not be persuaded against it. It would make a man of him.

Suddenly Sebastian bit his lip. 'I don't know, Em,' he said. 'Someone is bound to find out.'

Emily met her brother's eye with confidence. 'Why should they? I'll be careful.'

'I couldn't bear the disgrace if we were discovered. Father would die.'

'You mustn't worry.'

A light breeze stirred the curtains, bringing with it the sound of an approaching carriage.

The twins froze, listening. Sure enough, the horses' hooves stopped just outside.

'He's here,' Sebastian whispered, apprehensive.

A delicious shudder ran through Emily, tickling her like tiny feet scurrying over her skin. 'Come, Sebastian. We don't have much time.'

She snatched her chemise and corset from the bed and helped Sebastian into them. He gasped as she pulled the laces of the corset tight. Emily smiled. There was some satisfaction to be had in inflicting the torments of feminine undergarments on a male. Tomorrow he'd have to fasten the stays himself.

The twins had been rehearsing for weeks, and Sebastian's slight frame wore his sister's clothes well. His transformation was even more striking than Emily's. He was lost inside the heavy brocade gown and bonnet.

'Take a look,' she said, gesturing at the mirror.

Sebastian crossed the room in three awkward boyish strides.

'You haven't been practising,' Emily lamented. 'You must remember to walk as I showed you. Take small steps. Everyone waits for a lady.'

He nodded, swallowing nervously.

'Now show me your curtsey.'

He managed a clumsy plié.

'I expect it will have to do,' she said with a sigh. 'But you must work on it.'

Sebastian nodded. 'And you must remember to stand with your feet apart. Let your elbows go. Don't be graceful.' He examined her hands doubtfully. 'And get these dirty as soon as possible. They're far too ladylike.'

Emily's stomach fluttered in a sudden frisson of fear. There were so many ways she could slip up. Then what would she do? Throw herself on the mercy of the captain?

'It's best if you don't come down,' she said. 'I've been brooding all week about Father sending you to sea, so he won't be expecting to see me. Just stay up here – as me – and mope in my room. Refuse to go down tomorrow as well. Stay here sulking and practise being me.'

Sebastian laughed. 'We're both mad, you realise. Absolutely mad.'

'Ah, yes, but it's the adventure of a lifetime! Just imagine if I should pass the examination for lieutenant!'

'You could be a captain one day.'

'Or an admiral!'

'And what shall I do?' Sebastian mused. 'Make up with one of your spurned suitors and marry?' He batted his eyes coquettishly and they dissolved into laughter. But a sombre mood soon descended. This was the last time they would see each other for a long time.

'Just mind you don't find yourself on the wrong side of the lieutenant,' Sebastian warned, his face pale. 'He won't brook any weakness.'

Emily blushed and looked down at her shoes. The candlelight shone on the gleaming buckles. Her strange obsession with discipline was the one thing she'd been unable to confide in her brother. Rather than confessing that the prospect thrilled her, she feigned nonchalance. 'Oh, he doesn't frighten me,' she said with a plucky grin.

Suddenly, they heard their father, calling for Sebastian.

Sebastian straightened Emily's hat and dusted down her coat. After one last look he handed her his books and sextant. 'Good luck, Em,' he said. 'I shall miss you.'

'And I shall miss you.' Tears threatened to well in her eyes and she blinked them back. It wouldn't do for a future captain of Nelson's navy to be seen weeping like a girl.

'Will you write to me?' Sebastian asked.

Emily drew herself up proudly. 'Of course.' She took his hand and kissed it, giving a little bow. 'My sweet sister.'

Then with a final glance in the mirror, she hurried off to meet her fate.

* * *

Emily had studied the books with diligence – Norie's *Epitome of Navigation* and Clarke's *Complete Handbook of Seamanship*. She was familiar with much that a midshipman was meant to know, in theory, at least. But she was completely unprepared for the bewildering reality of it all. She marvelled at the array of rigging towering above her. Everywhere there was frantic activity that would seem like chaos to an outsider. Orders were bellowed from one end of the ship to the other. Men scrambled up and down the ratlines without so much as a downward glance. She watched as the hands aloft loosed the headsails and topsails and got the ship under way.

She could barely contain her excitement as the *Nemesis* left land behind and headed out into the ocean. But the unceasing corkscrew roll of the frigate soon took its toll on some of the new midshipmen, who staggered about with ashen faces while the seasoned crew looked smug. Emily was glad she was not alone in that particular misery. And most of the lads seemed to be suffering worse than she was.

In the days that followed, Emily often caught sight of Lieutenant Trevelyan, but he paid her no mind. She watched him whenever she could, straining to hear his voice. He issued orders with a natural authority that made her legs weak. Men touched their forelocks to him and scurried off to do his bidding. The dampness between her legs could easily make her forget she was supposed to be a boy.

Trevelyan stood on the quarterdeck with his feet well apart and his hands clasped behind his back. Emily was still learning to balance on the pitching ship, but the lieutenant stood as solid as the mainmast. She longed for an excuse to approach him, to speak to him, if only to impart some trivial bit of information and await his orders.

'You, boy!'

She jumped.

It was Wagstaffe, the oldest inhabitant of the midshipmen's berth. At twenty-five, his chances of making lieutenant were slipping away, and it did not improve his temper.

It took a few moments for Emily to realise he was addressing *her*.

'The master wants to know why you aren't at lessons with the rest of us.'

'I couldn't find my way, sir,' she mumbled, lowering her head. She regretted her show of submission instantly. Sebastian had instructed her to make eye contact.

'Lost, are you, snotty?' he sneered.

Emily had never before been spoken to in such a manner and she had no idea how she was meant to respond. That was one thing Clarke's *Seamanship* couldn't tell her. But she screwed up her pluck, raised her head and pushed past him. 'Beg pardon, sir,' she said gruffly.

Behind her she heard him laugh. Her face burned. She was annoyed with herself. Any show of weakness would make her a victim among her shipmates. She had to be more assertive.

When she eventually found the others and took a seat the sailing master glowered at her. Then he called on her to tell him the equation relating the leeway to the trim of the sails. He let her flounder with tangents and cotangents for nearly a minute before silencing her disgustedly. Blake, a younger midshipman, was only too happy to supply the correct answer, smiling loftily at the unfortunate Mr Vane.

She glared back at him and was immensely pleased with herself when Blake looked away, abashed.

But her triumph was short-lived. The next day the master berated her for miscalculating the ship's latitude. Most of the others got it wrong too, but she was already in his bad books from the day before. Emily loathed the tedious lessons. Navigation was going to be her downfall, she was certain. And the endless hours of inactivity dampened her spirits. When would they get to fight?

The morning's lesson was finally over and Emily was relieved to be left alone to study. She peered out over the waves, squinting through the eyepiece of her sextant. She found the sun in the half-silvered mirror and slid the index arm round carefully until the image was superimposed on the horizon. Clamping the sextant, she read the angle off the scale. Simple enough. It was the calculations that defeated her. Sebastian had warned her that her mathematical skills would need improving, but sines and cosines were not her strong point. She had been so impetuous about the enterprise that she simply hadn't given trigonometry much thought.

'So what's our latitude, Mr Vane?'

She jumped at the familiar voice, nearly dropping her sextant. 'I haven't done the calculations yet, sir,' she said.

Trevelyan gestured for her to continue, but he made no move to leave. 'Very well, then. Carry on.'

Emily grew even more nervous. She'd never get it right with him standing over her.

She tried to shoot the sun the second time, but her fingers trembled so much that she couldn't hold the instrument still. The sun was a jumpy golden gash in the mirrors, but she clamped it anyway and looked at the angle. Then she realised she'd forgotten the angle of the first sight. She'd have to take it again and risk his disapproval. Then there were the calculations and corrections, which she had yet to be successful with. She suspected her position line would be off by several degrees.

Trevelyan stood immobile, but Emily could sense his growing impatience. She began to panic. 'Sir, forgive me, I . . . I'm still learning the calculations.'

He frowned. 'My boy, you should have learnt those before setting foot on board. You were meant to be studying these many weeks past.' His voice was strict and unsparing. He had been charged with the duty of making a man of this delicate boy. No one knew better than Emily that he took his responsibilities very seriously.

'Yes, sir,' Emily said, crestfallen. She had no excuse to offer him.

'The sailing master thinks you lack application.' He held out his hand for the sextant and for a moment she feared he would tell her she had no place on board, that they would set her down in the next English port. But instead he put the eyepiece to his eye and took the sight himself.

He read out the angle and Emily noted it. He took the second angle and looked at her enquiringly.

'Now, Mr Vane, how do we combine the two sightings?'

That much she could do. 60° minus the second angle should be equal to the first. But what came next? The index error? She searched her mind, but came up blank.

Frightened as she was, she thrilled at his nearness as he stood looking down on her. She fixed on the impeccable cut of his uniform. She could see the ropes twisting round the anchors on every single gilt button.

He had asked her a question. Oh, yes. The sightings. Emily searched her mind for an answer. She wanted desperately to please him, to prove herself worthy. But she was completely lost. True, she had neglected her studies; but her desire was also clouding her ability to concentrate.

His ice-blue eyes glittered. 'Perhaps I should have young Blake assist you.'

The comment rankled. She had been feeling so much better after staring Blake down the day before. Now he was eroding what little confidence she'd acquired. Bristling, Emily held her tongue.

'Come on, Mr Vane. Any of the master's mates could have done these calculations by now.'

'Then perhaps the master's mates should do it, sir,' she blurted out. 'Surely an officer has more important things to do than play with numbers.'

She regretted it the instant she said it. Trevelyan's face hardened and she realised the enormity of her mistake.

She swallowed. 'I'm sorry, sir. I . . . forgot myself.'

Trevelyan was eyeing her severely.

Her cheeks burned. 'Sir, I . . .' What could she say?

'That will be quite enough from you,' he said softly.

Her head lowered, she stared fixedly at a coil of rope at her feet. She felt light-headed and if she'd been wearing a corset she might have swooned. Emily had to remind herself that she was no longer a lady. When the silence became unbearable she raised her head to face him.

'Report to the gun deck at eight bells in the afternoon watch.'

Blanching, Emily struggled to keep her voice steady. 'Aye aye, sir,' she said, touching her hat with unsteady fingers.

The lieutenant turned and walked away down the deck.

She recalled Trevelyan saying once that he liked to be present when he had ordered punishment. He said it reinforced the formality. She was frightened, but also exhilarated. The shadow of a smile touched her lips at the thought of him seeing her caned. There was the familiar tingling heat between her legs and she had to glance down to make sure there was nothing outwardly visible. The wetness felt conspicuous in her tight breeches. She tugged gently at her waistband, moaning a little at the pressure of the seam against her crotch.

The forenoon watch had barely begun; she had several hours yet to wait. She looked around to see if anyone might have been within earshot, but she was alone. Perhaps no one else had heard the exchange. Then they wouldn't know to listen for the telltale swish of the bosun's rattan. She could hope.

She busied herself as best she could, trying not to think about what was coming. But every time the ship's bell rang out her pulse quickened. In her head she heard the lieutenant's pronouncement over and over again. She couldn't concentrate on anything but her impending punishment.

At ten minutes before eight bells, the new officer of the watch came on deck. It was time. Emily didn't want Trevelyan to get to the gundeck before her.

She forced herself to hold her head up, in disgrace but not dishonour. Her heart banged behind her ribs and her legs wavered like a drunken sailor's as she made her way below deck.

The gundeck normally bustled with activity and noise. Now it was deserted. Trevelyan must have given orders. Emily was thankful for that. While witnesses might strengthen her resolve to take the punishment bravely, she didn't know how she would face them afterwards. She stood beside one of the twelve-pounders, caressing its cold body. It was so much larger than she had imagined back home. Very soon she would be bent over it, suffering under the cane.

The air was warm and heavy and Emily felt the back of her neck begin to prickle. For a moment she regretted taking Sebastian's place here, but she shook off the thought disgustedly. She had wanted adventure. She had *demanded* it. Now that she faced her fantasies at last, she had no choice but to follow through.

She lifted her head proudly. She was a King's officer. If she flinched at the prospect of a caning, how could she ever face the French in battle? Or look in the mirror?

In the distance she heard the ship's bell herald the end of the watch. Then the sound of boots on the ladder. This was it. She took several deep breaths to calm herself. No one would know how much she secretly wanted this.

Lieutenant Trevelyan appeared with Harmwell, the bosun. Emily flinched when she saw the stout malacca cane he carried. She lowered her head, hoping they would take it for penitence and not fear.

Trevelyan's stern voice boomed in the confined space. 'Mr Vane seems to think navigation is beneath him. But I think we have the means to teach him some humility. Haven't we, Mr Vane?'

'Yes, sir' was the only answer to that. Emily thought she would melt.

'Twelve good hard strokes, I think, Mr Harmwell.'

'Aye aye, sir.'

Trevelyan nodded solemnly towards the cannon and Emily steeled herself as she turned towards it. She removed her hat and laid it aside. Then she placed her hands on the cannon. With her legs together she bent forward at the waist, sideways over the gun. She knew she must bear the indignity.

'Not like that, lad,' came Harmwell's gruff voice. 'Along the gun. One leg either side.'

She choked back a gasp. She hadn't pictured it like that! The idea of wrapping her legs around the barrel seemed indecent. It was the way a gentleman rode a horse. But she obeyed, straddling the cold metal and stretching herself out along its length, presenting her bottom for the cane.

At that moment she wished she could see Trevelyan's

190

face. What expression did he wear? Stern indifference? Sadistic pleasure? She didn't dare turn round to see.

Emily flinched as she felt the malacca touch her bottom, measuring the first stroke. She tensed in anticipation, waiting. An age passed before Trevelyan gave the command for the punishment to begin.

The cane drew back and she heard a low deep whistle as it cut through the air. It sliced into her bottom with a loud *thwack!* She was unprepared for the force of the stroke and she yelped, more out of surprise than pain.

'One,' Harmwell counted.

The sting began to bloom in a line across her bottom and she fought the urge to reach back and clutch the burning flesh. Her breeches offered no protection at all. The position pulled them deep into the cleft of her bottom, separating her cheeks. A perfect target.

Emily gritted her teeth for the next stroke and managed to stay silent as it painted a second burning stripe across her posterior.

'Two.'

The third stroke forced a sharp intake of breath and she clung to the cannon as tightly as she could. Her arms trembled with the effort and her hands were clammy against the metal. In her fantasies Trevelyan had usually tied her wrists together. That would be a mercy now. The possibility of disgracing herself by leaping out of position was a challenge she hadn't counted on. Sweat trickled down her face and she panted, waiting for the next stroke.

Again the bosun's rattan met her tender bottom. She hissed through her teeth, determined to stifle her cries. Trevelyan was watching; she could not bear his reproach.

'Four.'

Harmwell's dutiful counting was strangely humbling. It was clear he got no pleasure from this; he was simply obeying orders. It was inexplicably erotic. The lieutenant's power over her was absolute.

As the caning continued Emily found herself floating, as though watching from outside herself. She could take this; perhaps she was toughening up. Trevelyan was doing what he had promised her father he would do: making a man of her. There was something poetic about that.

A particularly hard stroke forced another cry from her and she cursed herself for her weakness. She heard the bosun counting the strokes, but the numbers meant nothing to her. Intense as the pain was, Emily felt invigorated. It was the ultimate challenge. The proving ground. This was what she'd wanted. Her beloved lieutenant was having her flogged for insubordination and he was overseeing the punishment personally. Had he been waiting for the opportunity as well, to do his duty by the fainthearted boy?

Harmwell counted ten and Emily breathed deeply, pacing herself for the final two strokes. She could imagine the spectacle she made – her bottom turned well up, her tight breeches inviting the sting of the cane. Trevelyan had no idea he was watching a *girl's* bottom and the secret knowledge gave Emily a lewd little thrill. She squeezed her thighs against the cannon, stimulating herself as the penultimate stroke fell.

'Eleven,' counted Harmwell.

Emily held her breath for the last stroke, but the lieutenant interrupted.

'The final stroke,' he said, 'is always the hardest. Make this one count, Mr Harmwell.'

'Aye aye, sir.'

She sensed the cane drawing back and she gritted her teeth, squeezing her eyes shut tightly.

The last stroke slashed through the air and into her bottom, its impact echoing in her head like a musket shot. She was lost in a strange haze of pain spiced with pleasure. It was not unlike being drunk. Her body was tingling and the throbbing in her sex was almost unbearable. She longed to rub herself against the cold metal of the cannon, to tighten her legs round it until the pleasure exploded within her. But she would have to wait. She would take care of it later that night, in her hammock in the midshipmen's berth.

The bosun gave a little cough and Emily shook her head to clear it.

'You may stand up, Mr Vane,' said the lieutenant.

She slid to her feet and stood up shakily. Then she raised her eyes to look Trevelyan in the face. It was important to regain her dignity.

'Have you revised your opinion of navigation, Mr Vane?' the lieutenant asked.

'Yes, sir. I most certainly have, sir.'

He eyed her sternly for a few moments before addressing the bosun. 'Leave us, Mr Harmwell.'

'Aye aye, sir.'

They were alone. The silence quickly became oppressive. A bead of sweat rolled down her face and she dared not rub it away.

At last he spoke. 'Well, Mr Vane?'

Was it her imagination or had he emphasised the 'Mr'?

'S-sir?'

'Look at me when you're spoken to, lad.'

Emily tried not to blush, but it was impossible. Warmth flooded her face as she raised her eyes.

The lieutenant looked as austere as ever, yet there was a strange light in his eyes. 'Did that satisfy your curiosity?'

She swallowed. 'My – curiosity, sir?'

'Yes, your curiosity. Or have you forgotten our conversations in your father's library?'

Horrified, Emily lowered her head. She didn't know what to say.

The silence was broken by a harsh bark of laughter and she looked up, startled.

'You took that as well as any boy,' said Trevelyan, smiling broadly. 'I had my suspicions from the first, but your insubordination gave you away. Your brother would never have dared.'

Emily turned scarlet. 'I don't know what to say, sir.'

'You might thank me.'

'Thank you, sir.'

He nodded in acknowledgment. 'And now I should like to examine Mr Harmwell's handiwork.'

She blinked. 'Sir?'

Trevelyan gestured at the cannon. 'We'll have your breeches down, Emily.'

Amazed that she could possibly flush any deeper, she hesitated.

The lieutenant's expression grew severe again and he drew himself up. 'That was an order, Mr Vane.'

She gulped. 'Aye aye, sir.'

Then she turned away and her hands fluttered to her waist to unfasten her breeches. She looked nervously down the length of the gundeck.

'We're alone,' Trevelyan reassured her. 'Continue.'

It was so strange, baring herself like this before a man. She moved as though in a dream state, undoing the buttons at her knees. Her breeches pooled round her ankles. She'd done this often enough in her fantasies, but the reality was embarrassing, excruciating.

'Back in position,' Trevelyan ordered.

Emily did as she was told and her breeches slid down over her shoes. With her bottom on display and her bare thighs wrapped lewdly around the gun the position was positively obscene. She moaned in exquisite shame as she lowered her forehead to the cannon. The barrel seemed warmer now and its hard surface pressed into her exposed sex.

She gave a little cry of surprise when she felt Trevelyan's hand against her bottom. His fingers traced the marks left by the cane and she shuddered at his touch.

'A commendable job,' he pronounced. 'Our Mr Harmwell has a strong arm.'

'Yes, sir,' Emily gulped.

The lieutenant continued to examine the marks – slowly, thoroughly. He cupped her cheeks in his hands and squeezed firmly, making her gasp. The blood pounded in her head and again she felt faint. Then his fingers did the unthinkable. They slipped down along her crease and in between her legs.

Instinctively, Emily cried out and reached behind to shield herself, rising up out of her position.

'Oh, no,' chided the lieutenant, smacking her smartly on her tender backside. 'Stay where you are.'

194

Mortified, she obeyed.

'Perhaps you need restraining,' he suggested.

Her ears burned at those words. Out of the corner of her eye she saw him reach for a coil of rope. Her breathing grew shallow as he crouched beside her and tied her wrists beneath the barrel, so that she embraced the cannon. Then he resumed his examination.

His skilful hands explored her sex, probing and fondling the slick folds. Emily stiffened and made a little whimper. But she didn't protest; she didn't dare risk breaking the spell.

The ropes let her imagine that this was just another part of her punishment. She pulled at them to reassure herself that she was truly at his mercy.

His fingers described careful little circles over and around the bud of her sex and she gasped at his expert stimulation. She hadn't known such ecstasy was possible. Her mouth opened in a soundless moan as the attentive fingers slipped inside her. The pain in her bottom had subsided to a dull pulse that mirrored the throbbing in her sex. She writhed wantonly as his fingers worked in and out of her, making her body jerk with pleasure.

Emily imagined that she was being caned again, this time bound naked to the grating up on deck. The entire crew stood watching as the lieutenant painted stripes across her disobedient bottom, counting dispassionately while she yelped and writhed in delirious torment.

When he withdrew his fingers, she squeezed her legs tightly around the gun, protesting with a petulant whimper.

But he wasn't finished with her. Again his fingers slid inside where she was warm and hungry. And this time his other hand caressed her as well, spreading her open and tweaking her little nub, hard. His attentions elicited gasps of alternating pleasure and pain and Emily threw her head back, arching against him, urging his fingers deeper inside her.

She was climbing fast, straining violently at the ropes, drowning in the liberation of total surrender. All at once

195

the climax overtook her and the blood pounding in her ears sounded like the firing of the ship's guns.

For a long time neither of them said a word. Emily hung limply over the cannon, exhausted and panting. Trevelyan untied her hands. She stood on unsteady legs as she put her breeches back on and replaced her cocked hat.

'I hope you don't think that's the end of the matter,' he said gravely.

Misunderstanding, Emily's eyes widened. 'Oh, sir, you wouldn't tell the captain . . .'

Trevelyan gave her a conspiratorial smile. 'Probably not. I expect we can come to some arrangement. We can discuss it tonight. Report to my cabin at two bells in the first watch.'

Emily flushed. She felt her sex moistening again at the prospect. 'Aye aye, sir.'

'Navigation is important, Mr Vane,' he said. 'But action at close quarters is the true test of any officer.'

Bursting

Julie had to go. Desperately. She hadn't reckoned on so much traffic on the way back from the airport and she'd thought she could survive till she got home. It was usually a half-hour drive, but today everything was conspiring against her. First she got stuck behind a tractor for several miles. Then there was a patch of roadworks. And now this bloody bus trundling along at a snail's pace. She sounded her horn in irritation, knowing it wouldn't do any good. Overtaking wasn't even an option; she couldn't see around the bus.

She squeezed her legs together, trying to sit as still as possible. Her jeans felt unbearably tight. The slightest movement was agony and threatened to make her lose control.

She'd already passed the one dodgy petrol station where she might have used the loo, but she'd been less desperate then. She wasn't going to double-back now and there was no point in leaving the main road for a pub; she might as well gut it out until she made it home.

It had been an awful visit with Melanie. Though the girls had been inseparable throughout school, they'd lost touch for several years after university. And while the emails exchanged through Friends Reunited made it seem like no time had passed, the reality had been unbearable.

A weekend in the south of France had sounded like paradise to Julie. Unfortunately, Melanie's paradise included two shrieking babies and a gormless husband who thought fart jokes were the pinnacle of wit. Julie's polite smile became increasingly strained as she counted the minutes until she could leave. She'd used the headache excuse early on but by the end of the visit no faking was necessary. She'd even lied about the flight time to get away earlier, preferring to kill the final three hours at the airport.

Her haste to leave had clouded her judgment and she'd had two vodka tonics in the airport bar to obliterate her memories of the awful visit. Then she'd had a cup of tea on the plane to sober up for the drive. She'd needed to relieve herself when the plane landed, but her suitcase was – amazingly – already on the carousel. The queue for the ladies' stretched out the door, so she'd ignored the urge in her eagerness to be home again. Now she was really suffering.

Briefly she considered pulling over to pee in the bushes, but she didn't fancy braving the nettles or ruining her heels in the wet grass. It was only another few miles.

The bus lumbered to a stop and Julie watched helplessly as an elderly man shuffled to the door and climbed the steps with excruciating care. She couldn't take it any more. She threw the car into reverse and backed up enough to see around the bulk of the vehicle. The road was clear ahead and she stamped the pedal, squealing her tyres as she overtook. An oncoming car appeared over the ridge and blared its horn at her, but she made it into her own lane, finally achieving some speed.

Her bladder ached as she watched the speedometer climb to 80, then 90. She was on the home stretch. It wouldn't be long now.

She glared at a speed camera warning sign as she sailed past – a crude likeness of an ancient box Brownie that was supposed to encourage you to slow down. But the boxes seldom had cameras in them. She'd certainly never been flashed by one on this familiar road. Not that it would deter her now anyway.

Almost there, almost there, she told herself, swerving to avoid the suicidal pheasant that emerged from the hedgerow. She skidded a little on the wet road and had to brake hard to regain control of the car. Her handbag slid off the passenger seat, spilling its contents noisily onto the floor.

Julie cursed and leaned across to retrieve things, wincing at the discomfort in her bladder as she bent down. The car wavered on its course as she felt around under the seat for her phone. She had just rescued it, and was raising her head to look up at the road again, when she saw the fence rushing towards her.

She cried out and hit the brakes, but not before the nose of the car crunched into the wooden slats and she lurched to a painful stop in the gravel of a farm track. Almost immediately she saw the flashing lights of a police car in her rearview mirror.

'Nooo!' she cried, a long plaintive wail of dismay. 'Not fair!'

For a moment she was tempted to do a runner – just floor the accelerator and race home, run inside and relieve herself. The cop might chase her inside the house, but she could shout her explanation through the closed bathroom door and present herself contritely to him afterwards.

But she was also aware of the alcohol in her system. If she made him chase her home he would assume the worst. She wasn't drunk, but there was no way she'd pass a breath test. Besides, he could easily take her down before she made it inside the house. That old goat Mr Beddowes across the road would love to see her arrested outside her own front door.

With a groan of misery, she shut the engine off. The car shuddered unpleasantly before going silent and Julie tried not to think about all the liquid sloshing around inside her.

The police car eased to a stop behind her. Squirming in her seat, her heart pounding, Julie watched the officer stroll up to her car with all the casual confidence of official-dom. He radiated control. He was about forty, and his posture and crew cut suggested ex-army. Clean-cut and no-nonsense. Impossible to bargain with.

She pushed the button to open the window and was surprised when it didn't respond. Of course. The engine was off. With a shaky hand she tried to turn the key, but the ignition didn't respond either. Brilliant. It didn't matter, though, as the policeman was already opening her door.

'In a hurry?' he asked coolly.

Though she loathed his sarcasm, Julie forced a meek smile and a nervous laugh. 'As a matter of fact, yes.' She looked up towards the gate. She'd only nosed into it, cracked the boards but not destroyed it. 'I just ... I swerved to avoid a pheasant and went off the road.'

'Where were going you in such a hurry?'

'It's a little embarrassing, but ... well, I'm pretty desperate for the loo.'

'Oh?'

Did he expect her to elaborate? What more was there to tell?

'Yes. I'm just back from a week in France and I thought I could wait till I got home.'

He raised his eyebrows with imperious mockery. 'I see. You held it the entire time you were in France, did you?'

Julie shook her head, flustered. 'No, I mean I'm on my way back from the airport. The queue was too long when I got off the plane.'

His expression didn't change and she gestured wildly at her suitcase behind her as if she needed to prove that she'd been to France. But he was looking at her hand and she realised she was still holding onto her phone. Had a death grip on it, in fact.

'My handbag fell,' she explained hastily, indicating the clutter on the floor of the passenger seat. 'I wasn't using the phone. I was just picking things up when I saw the fence and it was too late.'

'I thought you said you swerved to avoid a pheasant.'

Cold sweat began to prickle on her forehead and she suddenly understood how interrogators got people to confess. She was volunteering irrelevant information that only made her look guiltier. Surely an innocent person wouldn't behave this way.

'I did, but then –'

'Do you know how fast you were going?' he asked steadily.

She winced as her bladder reminded her of her predicament. 'I have no idea, but I know it was too fast. I'm really sorry. It was just an accident. I'll leave a note for the farmer and pay for the damage.'

He was unmoved. 'You were weaving about on the road too. Before avoiding this alleged pheasant.' His insinuating tone implied a myriad of potential crimes she might be guilty of. Finally, he asked the question she'd been dreading. 'Have you been drinking?'

'No! Well, a tiny bit. At the airport before I left. But that was hours ago. I swear I'm not drunk!' She cringed at her words. Only the guilty insisted like that. 'Look, there *was* a pheasant. But I only went off the road when I was trying to pick things up off the floor. When my bag fell.'

Though it was the truth, she knew how implausible her story sounded as she babbled it to him. Her composure was crumbling fast in the face of his pitiless authority. Wildly she imagined asking him if he thought she had a corpse in the boot, but she thought better of it.

'Please,' she said at last. 'I'm really in pain. I have to go.'

She was halfway to trying the engine again when he placed his hand on her arm.

'Just a minute, miss. Would you step out of the car, please?'

Julie gave him a pleading look, but she knew she had no choice. She turned slowly in her seat and set her feet on the ground, one at a time. She heaved herself out with a little gasp and looked up just in time to see the bus she'd overtaken. It rumbled past smugly. In the back seat a little boy stuck his tongue out at her.

'Please, officer . . .'

'What's your name?'

His question caught her off guard. 'Julie Pembroke,' she said.

'Very well, Miss Pembroke. Come with me, please.'

She followed him as he led her round the back of her car. When they reached the other side he leaned back against the passenger door and crossed his arms over his chest.

'Right, Miss Pembroke. Show me how desperate you are.'

She blinked. 'What?'

'You did say it was urgent. You can do it here,' he said, nodding down at the ground.

She could only stare at him in wide-eyed horror.

'Come along, Miss Pembroke,' he said testily. 'I haven't got all day.'

'But I – I can't,' she said at last.

'I thought you were in pain.'

Her cheeks blazed. 'I am, but . . . But I can't go in front of you.'

'I see. It's so pressing it's worth risking the lives of everyone else on the road, yet suddenly you've lost the urge, is that it?'

'No! I mean yes, I have to go, but . . . I just –'

'Then go.'

'Look, I can't do it here. Can't we at least go to my house? Or a pub?'

'Right here, Miss Pembroke. Right now.'

Tears stung her eyes and she gave a loud sniffle, hoping to elicit some sympathy.

'If you want me to give you a break you'll have to show me how urgent it was.'

'But I . . .' Her protest petered out. He was going to stand there waiting, all day if he had to, until she did it. *If you want me to give you a break* . . . Did that mean he'd let her off then? She didn't dare ask.

Her car shielded her from the road. Passing motorists would see only the two vehicles. Slowly, helplessly, Julie sank to her knees in front of him.

With shaking hands she fumbled at the top button of her jeans, finally manoeuvring the zip down. She had to rise a little to get her jeans over her hips. Why hadn't she worn a skirt? It might have allowed her a little modesty. Instead, she had to push her jeans all the way down to her ankles in order to spread her legs wide enough to see where she was aiming. It was a precarious position: balancing awkwardly on her high heels, her bare bottom and exposed

202

sex hovering above the gravel roadside. Men had it so much easier.

There was a crunch of gravel as her captor shifted position, reminding her that she was not alone. He loomed over her, waiting.

Julie hesitated at her panties. They were nothing special – just simple white cotton – but they were her last vestige of dignity. Taking them down would be the point of no return; her debasement would be complete.

She looked up at him one last time. He sighed and glanced at his watch.

Overwhelmed with shame, she hooked her thumbs in the waistband of her girlish knickers and slid them down to her knees, then to her ankles. She had never known such a feeling of vulnerability before. She tried not to imagine the picture she presented.

Julie covered her burning face with her hands and waited for the act that would bring her torment to an end – physically at least. She anticipated a gushing stream of warm piss, the ecstasy of relief so long delayed. But her bladder wouldn't let go.

She whimpered softly, trying to block the situation from her mind so she could relax enough to get on with it. Her legs quivered with the effort of squatting. Taking a deep breath, she told herself that relief was finally here, she could finally let go. She pictured waterfalls, the running tap, but it was obvious that nothing was going to help. The position was uncomfortable and the mortifying presence of the watcher made the act impossible. The aching only intensified while the prospect of relief retreated with every passing second.

'I can't,' she moaned through her hands. Her toes were going numb from the pressure on her feet and she thought her knees would give with the effort of crouching if she had to stay there much longer.

The policeman was silent for an agonising period and she finally peeled her hands away from her face, peering out at him like a child hiding from a scary movie.

'Get up, Miss Pembroke,' the officer said testily. 'You've

wasted enough of my time.' It was clear he thought she was lying – about everything. She was just another lawbreaker willing to make up any pathetic story to get out of trouble.

She yanked her panties and jeans back into place, wincing at the persistent discomfort in her bladder. Resigned to her fate, she got to her feet, staring glumly at the road, still feeling the urge but knowing that it wasn't going to happen without privacy.

He took her by the arm and led her to the police car. Then he opened the back door and guided her inside. She sat uncomfortably while he closed the door and walked round to the front of the car to climb in behind the wheel. There was a squawk from the police radio, followed by a burst of unintelligible dialogue.

Julie sat slumped in the back seat while he riffled through papers and finally produced a form. So this was it – she was under arrest. But wouldn't he do that at the station? He hadn't so much as asked her to walk a straight line; he had no proof she was drunk. And forcing her to squat on the roadside – surely that wasn't by-the-book procedure either.

'Um, listen,' she ventured at last, her desperation making her bolder. 'Am I under arrest or what?'

He regarded her with an expression of bored disdain. 'All in due time, Miss Pembroke. I have many things to check before I can book you. You've brought it on yourself.'

His unshakeable calm was maddening. 'Then isn't there at least some way of hurrying it up?' she blurted out. 'I really have to go.'

He glanced at the form, then back at her, deep in thought. He made a great show of setting the paper down on the seat beside him. 'If it's that important to you, there might be a quicker way of dealing with you.'

Horrified and grateful in equal measures, Julie was in too much distress to care what he had in mind. Anything to avoid a ticket, arrest, being kept here any longer with her cramping bladder. She nodded frantically.

'Very well,' he said, his lips curling in a half-smile. He got out of the car and opened her door for her.

204

When she stood up again she felt her insides twist and she nearly asked if she could have another go at peeing. She was pretty sure she could manage it now. But she didn't want to jeopardise the chance he was giving her.

The policeman patted the fender. 'Over the bonnet of the car.'

'What?'

'You heard me, Miss Pembroke.'

Before Julie could process the instruction, he swiftly unbuckled his heavy police belt and pulled it flapping through the loops.

'The alternative is corporal punishment,' he continued, eyeing her sternly. 'You're a little old for it, but I believe I'll be able to teach you a lesson.' Seeing her hesitation he added, 'Last chance. You can submit to the thrashing you richly deserve. Or I can get on with the process of booking you. We *might* get back to the station in an hour or so.'

There wasn't a trace of pity in his ice-blue eyes as he doubled the belt and Julie knew she hadn't misunderstood him. She quickly scanned the road in either direction, as though someone might have overheard.

Reluctantly, she edged forward. She stopped in front of him, her face burning. Then she stretched herself over the car. She was grateful for the small mercy of not having to look him in the face, but the position put added pressure on her bladder. Wincing, she pressed her forehead into the warm metal of his car as she waited.

If she'd thought her jeans would offer some protection, she was wrong. His belt met the tight denim with a sharp report. She yelped and leapt up, clutching her bottom.

'Back in position,' he growled. 'I haven't even started.'

Julie lowered herself back over the car, her cheeks blazing with pain.

The next stroke dragged a guttural moan from her and she kicked one leg up as the strap licked across her bottom.

Julie heard the approaching roar of an engine and she forced her head down as far as she could, knowing that the passing driver could see exactly what was happening to her. She heard the leather whisk through the air behind her again and she cringed in anticipation. The leather flashed across her cheeks just as the car passed, making her yelp and writhe.

Again and again the policeman's heavy belt painted wide fiery stripes over her bottom, eliciting cries of pain and outrage from her. Her bladder ached more than ever and she was certain the urgency intensified the pain of the whipping. The two torments fed off each other and she sobbed in misery, trying to shut out the sound of yet another car coming from behind them. She'd never known so much traffic on this road.

And then it happened. He delivered a particularly hard stroke to the undercurve of her buttocks. The force of the blow made her struggle and kick and she felt a tiny trickle escape. With a cry of despair she gritted her teeth and tried to pinch off the flow, squeezing her legs together violently. Despite her writhing, his steady rhythm didn't falter. The pain of the whipping was too intense; she couldn't concentrate on anything else.

Her muscles relaxed and she wilted over the car as the trickle became a stream and she felt the warm liquid seep into her panties and finally into the denim of her jeans. The belt stopped its assault.

'Well, well,' he said and pulled her up and away from the car, standing her before him.

Mortified, Julie hid her face in her hands with a little sob as the warmth spread from the gusset of her panties down her right leg, soaking her jeans. She could picture the dark stain as it advanced, unstoppable and unmistakable. The relief of letting go at last was matched by the awful indignity of her situation. She had pissed herself once when she was a very little girl. And that was exactly how she felt now. Very little.

The cop watched the wet patch continue to spread from her crotch down her legs. He pulled her hands away from her face and down to her sides. She turned her head away in shame. She didn't think the gushing stream would ever stop. There was no sound. The hot piss ran silently between her legs, drenching her.

Finally the flow began to lessen and Julie sighed at the near-orgasmic relief of being empty again. But her relief was short-lived.

'Take your jeans off.'

Julie hesitated, weighing the humiliation of baring herself (again) against the shame of keeping the pee-stained things on. She kicked off her heels and peeled the wet denim down her legs with a disgusted wince. The air was cool against her damp legs and bottom and she dropped the jeans in the dust at the policeman's feet, moving her hands to cover her wet panties.

He lifted her chin and made her look at him. 'A naughty little girl who wets her knickers deserves a good sound smacking – over my knee.'

She didn't think it was possible to blush any more, but her face blazed again as he led her to the rear of the car and seated himself on the bumper. He pulled her gently across his lap. Julie squeezed her eyes shut tightly as he adjusted her position and placed his hand in the small of her back.

Without further discussion he brought his hand down on her right cheek with a resounding slap, reawakening the sting in her bottom. She bit back a little cry, not wanting to give him the satisfaction of seeing her disgraced any further.

She couldn't restrain a whimper as he struck the left cheek even harder. The thin wet fabric clung to her bottom and she knew it would only enhance the image of her punished cheeks, glowing bright red through the soaked cotton. Julie kicked and struggled, but he held her firmly in place as he peppered her bottom with sharp swats that rang out like pistol shots in the crisp air. However, the pain was nothing compared to the sheer humiliation of being upended over a man's knee and spanked like a child.

He delivered a fast volley of smacks and Julie thrust both hands behind, fingers splayed across her punished cheeks in an effort to shield her burning skin.

The policeman merely tutted and pinned her wrists against her back before continuing with a series of even harder slaps. Utterly helpless, Julie had no choice but to accept her punishment.

Now that she was no longer distracted by her desperate need to pee, she could focus on what she'd done. She'd been very reckless, it was true. And if she was honest with herself, she shouldn't have been driving at all. She deserved this and she was very lucky to be given this childish punishment as an alternative to jail.

Sensing her submission, the policeman slowed his cadence.

'Six more,' he pronounced. 'Just to remind you.'

Julie braced herself, determined to take it with dignity. If there was any traffic, she didn't notice. But nor would she have cared.

His heavy hand cupped her right cheek before lifting and returning to deliver an astonishing blow. Julie gasped, but did not cry out.

'One,' he counted.

The second stroke covered her left cheek with equal fire and this time she whimpered a little.

'Two.'

Though she tried to be brave, the next one made her cry out, kicking her legs frantically. She slipped off his lap and crouched beside the tyre, clutching her bottom and gasping at the pain.

'Three,' he said. 'Get up, Miss Pembroke. You've three more to go.'

Meekly, she got to her feet and stretched across his lap again, offering her bottom for another smack.

'Four.'

His relentless counting made it seem like a judicial sentence being carried out. He paused between swats, just long enough to allow the initial burn of the previous one to fade before laying on the next. Julie was crying by the time he gave her the fifth stroke and she moaned, telling herself it was almost over.

'Five.'

The last swat was the hardest of all, but Julie was so lost to the world of tears that she didn't even hear him count.

Her bottom throbbed with pain and yet she felt calm. Purged. In more ways than one. She clung to the policeman, soaking his trousers with her tears. Even though he was the one who had inflicted the punishment, it was his comfort she needed.

It was some time before she was able to get up again. She stood shakily, rubbing her sore bottom and looking at the ground. 'Thank you,' she murmured at last.

He nodded curtly as he slipped his belt back through the loops. 'I trust you'll remember this next time you're in a hurry,' he said with impeccable professionalism, as though he'd merely issued her a ticket.

'I will, officer.'

'Now come along. I'll drive you home.'

She trudged back to her car to retrieve her things and he put her suitcase in the boot underneath where she'd just been spanked and strapped. She threw her wet jeans in beside it, preferring not to put them back on. Wincing with pain, she lowered herself gingerly into the back seat. And she tried hard not to imagine the sight she'd present to nosy Mr Beddowes when she was brought home in a police car, wearing only her wet knickers and sporting a very red bottom.

Just Another Story

If there's one hard and fast rule of writing, it's *Write what you know*.

But Josephine had been writing what she *didn't* know all her life. What was the point of writing something if you already knew it? That was the beauty of fiction. It was all about fantasy. Escapism.

On the page she could be anything or anyone. She could live anywhere, in any time, experience anything, everything. She had total control over her characters and could give herself all the best lines. The men she lusted after in reality were hers to manipulate in fantasy. They became strict disciplinarians who would punish her thinly veiled protagonists for any infraction. All her dirtiest dreams came true on the page. Reality was a pale substitute.

'Yes, but how do you know you're getting it right if you've never actually experienced it?'

It was an editor's job to ask such questions, but Josephine sensed there was more to it than that. Clive had a natural insouciance that made him impossible to read. Was that little half-smile meant to be cynical? Or suggestive?

'That's just rhetoric,' she said with a dismissive wave. 'It's something pretentious writers say. As though being able to tell stories is some sacred calling and you profane it unless you spend hours plodding through tedious facts.'

Clive leaned back in his chair, his blue eyes glittering. 'Who says field research has to be boring?'

She blushed, gazing into the depths of her gin and tonic as though reading tea leaves. It was always slightly strange, chatting casually over drinks with this man who read all her naughty fantasies with a purely critical eye. He would suggest having a character slippered instead of caned, or advise that she'd overused the phrase 'good sound spanking'. All with the same professional detachment he used to point out an awkward piece of syntax. And all without the slightest hint of embarrassment.

His voice flawlessly navigated the special language of her desires, giving real authority to words that made her squirm. He always seemed to home in on choice phrases when he reviewed her stories with her. Naughty girl. Smack your bottom. Over my knee, young lady. And she always thought she sensed an emphasis on the word 'corrections'.

'I'd like to discuss some corrections with you, Josephine,' he'd say in that low silky voice. There were a hundred expressions that took on new meaning when you had one thing dominating your thoughts. Was his schoolmasterly tone deliberate?

'Field research,' she mused, teasing the slice of lime with her fingertip. 'Hey, Google's your friend when it comes to details. I only have to type "Victorian parlour maid" and *voila* – a thousand websites offer to help.'

His slightly amused expression deepened into slyness. 'Yes, it's easy enough to describe the cut of the gentleman's suit as he puts a careless maid across his knee to warm her bottom.'

Her stockings hissed as she crossed her legs under the table.

'And you picture it very well indeed. But I can't help but wonder whether the actual experience might enhance your imagination.' As he finished his drink and set the glass down, his hand strayed to the stack of books beside him. Author copies of her latest novel, *Knickers Down*. He slipped his thumb between the pages of the top copy and the paper purred and fluttered as he drew his thumb up the book's edge, stroking it like a pet. Then he turned his piercing eyes back to her. 'It couldn't hurt, could it?'

There was no mistaking his innuendo now. Their business lunch had taken a decidedly non-business turn. Or *all* business, depending on how you looked at it.

'Oh, I'm sure it wouldn't hurt at all,' she said, meeting his eyes with a challenge of her own. 'But it's not a requirement of writing. Should crime writers commit murder for the sake of authenticity? Besides, everyone knows that the best authors are the ones who break the rules.' She stopped playing with her slice of lime and sucked its juice off her finger. 'Some might even say it's a crucial part of the creative process. Breaking the rules.'

Breaking the Rules was her first novel and it had been very popular. Only the day before, Josephine had made a list of all the books she had sold, all the stories she had published. The bibliography on her website read like an enumeration of her sins. The sheer volume was startling. How many millions of words was that? If she did a search on the number of times the word 'spank' appeared in her writing . . . well, the maths was beyond her.

That wasn't even counting the works in progress on her hard drive. The ones targeted at specific markets and the ones she'd written just for herself, the self-indulgent little treats she allowed herself occasionally and which no one else ever got to see.

But the fact was that she had written all those stories about naughty schoolgirls, careless secretaries and bratty cheerleaders without ever having been spanked.

Oh, she claimed she had been. An obsessive poster on Internet forums, Josephine described the marks from her most recent spanking and reminisced about the punishments she'd received at boarding school. She'd emulated Roald Dahl and invented a sadistic prefect who'd bullied her and spanked her with a hairbrush at every opportunity. But the life she described online was as fabricated as the fantasies she penned.

Her stories were read by hundreds of people who did know what it was like, but no one ever wrote to accuse her of masquerading, of *lying*. Surely it only validated her talent as a writer if her stories were that convincing?

'Haven't you ever been curious?'

'It's a *fantasy*,' she said simply.

'Yes. And?'

'So what if it's not as good as I imagine it?'

'How will you ever know unless you try?'

'Are you offering?'

'Are you interested?'

She hesitated. 'What if I say no?'

There was a hint of danger in his smile now. 'What if you don't have a choice?'

She felt her face grow hot and she looked down at the table, where she'd been obsessively folding and re-folding her napkin.

The waiter appeared with the bill and Josephine had a few moments to regain her composure while Clive paid it. When they were alone again she said flirtatiously, 'Very well. You've read all my stories. What game shall we play?'

His dark little laugh made her cross her legs again. 'My dear girl, I'm not suggesting a *game*. What I have in mind is right and proper punishment.'

Heat flared in her face and her voice was a hoarse croak as she dared to ask, 'For what?'

'Dishonesty,' he said coolly. 'Deceit. You see, there's this writer who's got the whole world fooled into thinking she's a woman with real experience. Now, all fiction is fabrication, it's true. But it's gone a bit beyond the books and the stories, hasn't it?'

She looked down and he gently placed his hand on top of hers to stop her fussing with her napkin.

'Josephine, I asked you a question.'

Her heart began to beat a little faster at the authority in his voice, the electricity in his touch. He knew all her secrets. Not just the superficial fantasies she wrote from behind the safety of her pen name, but the deeper ones she revealed online when she wasn't being paid by the word.

She nodded helplessly.

'Sorry. I didn't hear that.' He cupped his hand to his ear in a theatrical gesture that made her feel like a child.

'Yes,' she whispered at last.

And then he said it. 'Yes what?'

Flustered, Josephine slid down in her seat, wishing she could crawl under the table and hide. This was it. Once she called him 'sir' she would be committed. It would forever alter their working relationship. The prospect was terrifying. Thrilling.

'Yes, sir.'

The cab ride only took ten minutes, but it seemed an eternity in the foreboding silence. Josephine could think of nothing to say.

Clive's flat was eclectic but elegant. The furniture looked like family antiques, bequeathed by ancestors with very different tastes. A mahogany drinks cabinet stood in the corner of the room and he went to it. An ice bucket held a bottle of Veuve Clicquot and beside it were two glasses and a bowl of darkly red fruit.

Josephine smiled with relief. Yes, a glass or three of champagne would make this much easier. Then she realised that he was only adjusting the lights on the wall behind the teasing offering. She wilted.

When he turned back to her he wore a look of stern disapproval. Gone was the playful half-smile. He slowly removed his jacket and hung it on the coat stand. He held out his hand and Josephine slipped out of her coat, passing it to him with trembling fingers. She suddenly regretted the flirty little black dress she'd worn. Her bare shoulders prickled with gooseflesh, though it was warm in the flat.

'Right, young lady,' he said. 'Shall we begin?'

How was she supposed to answer that? A wretched whimper was the best she could offer.

Two chairs faced each other across a low table. One was plush and French. The other was plain and straight-backed. Josephine's eyes were drawn immediately to the straight-backed one.

Clive eased himself into the hard wooden chair and pointed at the spot on the floor directly in front of him. She moved forward slowly, clasping her hands round her upper body as though she were naked and freezing.

'You've been a very bad girl, Josephine, and you need to be taught a firm lesson. Writing stories is one thing, but deceit is quite another. I intend to put you over my knee and give you a good sound spanking. On your bare bottom.'

His gaze was hard to meet and even harder to look away from. Josephine shifted from foot to foot throughout the reprimand. Her faced blazed hotly as his voice unravelled her defences. *Good sound spanking.* The words did things to her.

She had a sudden little-girl memory of deliberately stranding herself in her treehouse whenever a storm was forecast. Alone, she could shriek as the wind rattled the flimsy structure and rain sliced through the thin boards. It felt enough like danger that her imagination could run wild. In her mind she was the prisoner of an evil man who kept her tied to the table leg and sent ransom notes to her parents. Once she had scrawled a note on a scrap of paper (HELP IVE BEEN KIDNAPPED) and pushed it through a crack in the boards. The wind whisked it away and a distraught neighbour two doors down called the police. The officer who escorted Josephine out of the treehouse shook his finger at her and told her that she deserved a good sound spanking for her little prank. Those exact words. After that her fantasy kidnapper punished every escape attempt with his rough heavy hand.

'That's right, my girl,' Clive was saying now, and his voice was that of both policeman and kidnapper. 'I'm going to teach you a lesson you won't forget for a very long time. Do you understand?'

She could barely form the words. 'Yes, sir.'

He nodded curtly. 'Then come here. Over my knee, young lady.'

Josephine whimpered softly as she lowered herself, trembling, into the position she had imagined countless times but never experienced. Over the knee. It was a position that existed in no other context, for no other purpose. It was the ultimate presentation of the bottom. Traditional, belittling and effective. She was humbled more than she ever could have imagined.

She pressed her hands against the floor as she stretched her legs out behind her. Her belly rested comfortably across the warm expanse of his thighs and she stared down at the floorboards. She could see his polished shoe if she lowered her head, just behind the leg of the chair.

He rested his hand on her bottom and she jumped at the touch. His soft chuckle made her writhe with embarrassment. She felt his fingers creep down to the hem of her dress and she gasped as he lifted it up. He took his time carefully arranging the skirt over her waist, smoothing it ritually into place.

She tried to imagine the view from his perspective: her legs sheathed in sheer black stockings, her black lace panties accentuating the peach cleft of her bottom, the suspender belt that would frame the target perfectly when her cheeks were bared. When. Not if. She crossed her ankles as he teased a finger underneath the scalloped lacy edge of her panties.

'Very fetching,' Clive said. 'It almost seems a shame to take these down. But you know very well that a proper spanking must be administered on the bare.'

And with that he peeled the delicate lacy knickers down to her knees, slowly exposing her round pale cheeks. She squirmed and closed her eyes, wondering how it was possible to blush any more deeply.

'And how delightfully it presents your bottom,' he said, caressing her smooth virginal skin. He teased the thin straps of her suspender belt, tracing the lines from her waist to her stocking tops. He squeezed each well presented cheek as if to test its resilience and slid his hand over the gentle curves. At last he gave her an affectionate little pat. He locked his left hand around her waist and raised his right knee, forcing her back to arch, lifting her bottom a little higher.

Josephine squeezed her thighs together, clenching her cheeks as she waited for him to begin. The preliminaries seemed to have lasted hours. Then she felt his weight shift under her and his hand connected sharply with her right cheek. She squealed at the loud smack, struggling in his

216

grasp as the stinging handprint penetrated her skin. She could feel the outline of each finger as the pain intensified. Then he did the same to her left cheek.

She kicked her legs up behind her, shielding her bottom with her shoes. He brushed her feet aside and smacked her again, eliciting a howl of pain.

Another smack, then another. And Josephine realised that she'd been right all along; some fantasies were better left unexplored. This was more painful than she'd ever imagined. Of course, she'd written about punishments that were excruciating, agonising, all those superlative descriptors. But this *hurt*. How could she ever have thought she'd like the sensation of a hand connecting ruthlessly with the tender flesh of her bottom? She heard herself begging and pleading as she struggled.

'Be still, young lady,' he admonished. 'You had best get comfortable because you're going to be here for a good long while.'

'But I – oww! No, it hurts too much! I don't like it! Oww! Please, no!'

Again that soft menacing laugh. 'Oh no, my dear. It's too late for that. This isn't about what you want; it's about what you *need*. And what you need, what you *deserve*, is a very red and sore bottom.'

He delivered several more lively smacks as he continued to scold her.

'This is punishment, Josephine. Punishment for a naughty young lady who tells lies. I intend to make a thorough job of it and I am not going to stop until I'm sure you've learnt your lesson. Do you understand me, miss?'

Smack!

'Oh! Yes, but –'

'Yes what?' *Smack!*

'Oww! Yes, sir! But I –'

'No "buts", my girl. You've had this coming for a long time and I'm going to make sure I leave a lasting impression.'

She writhed, mortified by his absolute control. He didn't neglect a single inch of her bottom and he seemed to enjoy describing it to her. How it was turning from a rosy blush to a vivid scarlet. The shame and the pain were overwhelming and after one particularly hard swat to the undercurve of her left cheek, Josephine squealed and thrust her right hand back to shield herself.

Clive caught her wrist and pinned it in the small of her back. How many times had she written that little detail?

'Naughty, naughty girl,' he said, punctuating his words with well placed smacks.

Josephine stared at the wood grain in the floorboards below her as though seeing clearly for the first time. Her imagination could never have conjured such detail.

'You'll have to eat your dinner standing up tonight, won't you, young lady?'

Oh, it was quite another thing to experience this for real. She'd had no idea. 'Please, sir,' she begged. 'I'm sorry!'

Clive was unmoved. 'You're only saying that because all your unfortunate heroines say it.'

As the spanking wore on, she could literally feel her bottom getting redder and redder under his heavy hand. She felt her knickers slip down her legs until they were tangled around her ankles. They hobbled her until she got them free of one foot, kicking so violently she made the chair rock. Clive had a remedy for that. He wrapped his right leg behind her knees, pinning her down over his left knee.

For a long time the only sounds were the distinctive and unmistakable slaps of a hand on bare flesh, accompanied by Josephine's yelps and whimpers.

She prayed no one could hear what was going on. She'd always written about hand-spankings as the mildest of disciplinary acts. Usually just a prelude to the strap or cane. But now she knew. Clive's hand was as painful as anything she could imagine. And the embarrassment only enhanced it.

At the same time, she couldn't deny her body's response. She squeezed her legs together as she began to go with the pain, to ride it like a wave.

'You're going to have some marks to show for this,' he told her.

She pictured herself admiring her bruised backside in the mirror, as she'd had so many of her characters do after being punished. The image was both horrifying and alluring.

'Are you learning your lesson, young lady?'

'Yes, sir, yes I am, I promise!' she gasped, breathless and exhausted.

His rhythm slowed and he finally stopped, caressing her sore and throbbing cheeks with a hand that must have been just as red. She lay limply across his lap, panting and a little disoriented. Pinpricks of lights were firing across her field of vision and the pulsing heat in her bottom was fading from pain into something else.

'Now then, Josephine,' he said, 'I haven't finished with you yet. There's something else you have to do.'

She moaned softly in response to his words, unable to stop herself wriggling.

'I'm going to give you six more smacks, and I want you to hold still for these. They're going to be very hard, but I think they will be good for you. After all, you don't want your first spanking to be just a few love-pats, do you? No, it needs to be the real thing.'

A cruel joke, but she had to admit that she wanted it now. Lowering her head submissively, she braced herself as he tightened his grip on her waist.

The first two smacks wrenched wild cries from her, but she managed to stay in position. Her body tensed and released as she absorbed the sting of each one. She let the pain sink in and then he was talking to her again.

'This is just the beginning, you know. There's plenty more to teach you about, so many variations on a simple theme. Positions, implements, scenarios ... There are so many ways you can be punished.'

She already knew. And the idea of experiencing every situation she'd written was daunting.

Another pair of smacks and she writhed and whimpered.

'You'll be even more prolific after you've experienced the possibilities. I can't wait to introduce you to the hairbrush, the paddle, the tawse, the cane, the birch.'

It was almost over. Josephine held her breath as he gave her the final two swats, which were devastating in their intensity. But she obeyed, accepting the pain without struggling. Drained, she hung exhausted and spent over his knee, relieved that it was over and yet strangely hungry for more.

Clive caressed her bottom and she flinched. Even the most gentle touch was excruciating.

'Now then,' he said, unlocking his leg from around hers. 'Have we developed a healthy respect for reality, young lady?'

She nodded slowly, unsure how to process the barrage of sensations.

'Is that how we answer when we've been spanked?' he prompted smilingly, as though talking to a child.

'Yes, sir,' she murmured, blushing. 'We have.'

He released her wrist and helped her to her feet. She felt drunk and she leaned on him for balance, reaching behind to touch the flaming skin of her punished bottom.

'What do we say?'

Josephine squirmed, wrapping herself in his comforting arms. 'We say thank you, sir.'

'Good girl.'

He gave her a chaste kiss on the forehead and told her to get dressed. 'Back to work with you, now,' he said. 'You have a new story to write.'

'Not so fast,' she said, looking pointedly at the champagne. 'There's something else I think you might be able to help me with.'

'Oh?'

'I've never actually written a sex scene before.'

Josephine ran the spellchecker and printed the story. She knew Clive would love it, especially since she had used their real names. She hoped he'd see it was more than just another story.

nexus

The leading publisher of fetish and adult fiction

TELL US WHAT YOU THINK!

Readers' ideas and opinions matter to us so please take a few minutes to fill in the questionnaire below.

1. Sex: Are you male ☐ female ☐ a couple ☐?

2. Age: Under 21 ☐ 21–30 ☐ 31–40 ☐ 41–50 ☐ 51–60 ☐ over 60 ☐

3. Where do you buy your Nexus books from?

☐ A chain book shop. If so, which one(s)?

_____

☐ An independent book shop. If so, which one(s)?

_____

☐ A used book shop/charity shop
☐ Online book store. If so, which one(s)?

_____

4. How did you find out about Nexus books?

☐ Browsing in a book shop
☐ A review in a magazine
☐ Online
☐ Recommendation
☐ Other _____

5. In terms of settings, which do you prefer? (Tick as many as you like.)

☐ Down to earth and as realistic as possible
☐ Historical settings. If so, which period do you prefer?

_____

☐ Fantasy settings – barbarian worlds
☐ Completely escapist/surreal fantasy

- ☐ Institutional or secret academy
- ☐ Futuristic/sci fi
- ☐ Escapist but still believable
- ☐ Any settings you dislike?

_____

- ☐ Where would you like to see an adult novel set?

_____

6. In terms of storylines, would you prefer:

- ☐ Simple stories that concentrate on adult interests?
- ☐ More plot and character-driven stories with less explicit adult activity?
- ☐ We value your ideas, so give us your opinion of this book:

_____

_____

_____

7. In terms of your adult interests, what do you like to read about? (Tick as many as you like.)

- ☐ Traditional corporal punishment (CP)
- ☐ Modern corporal punishment
- ☐ Spanking
- ☐ Restraint/bondage
- ☐ Rope bondage
- ☐ Latex/rubber
- ☐ Leather
- ☐ Female domination and male submission
- ☐ Female domination and female submission
- ☐ Male domination and female submission
- ☐ Willing captivity
- ☐ Uniforms
- ☐ Lingerie/underwear/hosiery/footwear (boots and high heels)
- ☐ Sex rituals
- ☐ Vanilla sex
- ☐ Swinging

☐ Cross-dressing/TV
☐ Enforced feminisation
☐ Others – tell us what you don't see enough of in adult fiction:

_____

_____

_____

8. Would you prefer books with a more specialised approach to your interests, i.e. a novel specifically about uniforms? If so, which subject(s) would you like to read a Nexus novel about?

_____

_____

_____

9. Would you like to read true stories in Nexus books? For instance, the true story of a submissive woman, or a male slave? Tell us which true revelations you would most like to read about:

_____

_____

_____

10. What do you like best about Nexus books?

_____

_____

11. What do you like least about Nexus books?

_____

_____

12. Which are your favourite titles?

_____

_____

13. Who are your favourite authors?

_____

_____

14. **Which covers do you prefer? Those featuring:**
    (Tick as many as you like.)
- ☐ Fetish outfits
- ☐ More nudity
- ☐ Two models
- ☐ Unusual models or settings
- ☐ Classic erotic photography
- ☐ More contemporary images and poses
- ☐ A blank/non-erotic cover
- ☐ What would your ideal cover look like?

_____

15. **Describe your ideal Nexus novel in the space provided:**

_____

_____

_____

_____

16. **Which celebrity would feature in one of your Nexus-style fantasies? We'll post the best suggestions on our website – anonymously!**

_____

THANKS FOR YOUR TIME

Now simply write the title of this book in the space below and cut out the questionnaire pages. Post to: Nexus, Marketing Dept., Virgin Books, Random House, 20 Vauxhall Bridge Road, London SW1V 2SA

Book title: _____

NEXUS NEW BOOKS

To be published in June 2009

THE GIFT OF GIRLS
Chloë Thurlow

Magdalena Wallace scores a great summer job as an intern at City accountants Roche-Marshall. But she omits to tell her boss, the mysterious Simon Roche, that she works nights as a waitress at Rebels Casino. When Magdalena learns a 'secret' system from a high-roller, she plays the tables only to lose all her university savings. Soon she is dipping into clients' money and it is not long before Simon Roche catches her in the act. As an alternative to notifying the police, he suggests she become his slave until the debt is paid. She agrees but never envisages just how far she will have to go to break even.

£7.99   ISBN 978 0 352 34520 2

If you would like more information about Nexus titles, please visit our website at www.nexus-books.co.uk, or send a large stamped addressed envelope to:
 Nexus
 Virgin Books
 Random House
 20 Vauxhall Bridge Road
 London SW1V 2SA

NEXUS BOOKLIST

Information is correct at time of printing. To avoid disappointment, check availability before ordering. Go to www.nexus-books.co.uk.

All books are priced at £6.99 unless another price is given.

NEXUS

☐ ABANDONED ALICE	Adriana Arden	ISBN 978 0 352 33969 0
☐ ALICE IN CHAINS	Adriana Arden	ISBN 978 0 352 33908 9
☐ AMERICAN BLUE	Penny Birch	ISBN 978 0 352 34169 3
☐ AQUA DOMINATION	William Doughty	ISBN 978 0 352 34020 7
☐ THE ART OF CORRECTION	Tara Black	ISBN 978 0 352 33895 2
☐ THE ART OF SURRENDER	Madeline Bastinado	ISBN 978 0 352 34013 9
☐ BARE, WHITE AND ROSY	Penny Birch	ISBN 978 0 352 34505 9
☐ BEASTLY BEHAVIOUR	Aishling Morgan	ISBN 978 0 352 34095 5
☐ BEHIND THE CURTAIN	Primula Bond	ISBN 978 0 352 34111 2
☐ BEING A GIRL	Chloë Thurlow	ISBN 978 0 352 34139 6
☐ BELINDA BARES UP	Yolanda Celbridge	ISBN 978 0 352 33926 3
☐ BIDDING TO SIN	Rosita Varón	ISBN 978 0 352 34063 4
☐ BLUSHING AT BOTH ENDS	Philip Kemp	ISBN 978 0 352 34107 5
☐ THE BOOK OF PUNISHMENT	Cat Scarlett	ISBN 978 0 352 33975 1
☐ BRUSH STROKES	Penny Birch	ISBN 978 0 352 34072 6
☐ BUTTER WOULDN'T MELT	Penny Birch	ISBN 978 0 352 34120 4
☐ CALLED TO THE WILD	Angel Blake	ISBN 978 0 352 34067 2
☐ CAPTIVES OF CHEYNER CLOSE	Adriana Arden	ISBN 978 0 352 34028 3
☐ CARNAL POSSESSION	Yvonne Strickland	ISBN 978 0 352 34062 7
☐ CITY MAID	Amelia Evangeline	ISBN 978 0 352 34096 2
☐ COLLEGE GIRLS	Cat Scarlett	ISBN 978 0 352 33942 3
☐ COMPANY OF SLAVES	Christina Shelly	ISBN 978 0 352 33887 7

- - - - - - ✂ -

Please send me the books I have ticked above.

Name ....

Address ....

....

....

.... Post code ....

Send to: **Virgin Books Cash Sales, Direct Mail Dept., the Book Service Ltd, Colchester Road, Frating, Colchester, CO7 7DW**

US customers: for prices and details of how to order books for delivery by mail, call 888-330-8477.

Please enclose a cheque or postal order, made payable to **Virgin Books Ltd**, to the value of the books you have ordered plus postage and packing costs as follows:

UK and BFPO – £1.00 for the first book, 50p for each subsequent book.

Overseas (including Republic of Ireland) – £2.00 for the first book, £1.00 for each subsequent book.

If you would prefer to pay by VISA, ACCESS/MASTERCARD, AMEX, DINERS CLUB or SWITCH, please write your card number and expiry date here:

....

Please allow up to 28 days for delivery.

Signature ....

Our privacy policy

We will not disclose information you supply us to any other parties. We will not disclose any information which identifies you personally to any person without your express consent.

From time to time we may send out information about Nexus books and special offers. Please tick here if you do *not* wish to receive Nexus information. □

- - - - - - ✂ -